W9-BMN-466

THE FEAST OF STEPHEN

Also by Rosemary Aubert

FREE REIGN

THE FEAST OF STEPHEN

AN ELLIS PORTAL MYSTERY

Rosemary Aubert

Bridge Works Publishing Company
Bridgehampton, New York

Copyright © 1999 by Rosemary Aubert

Published in the United States by Bridge Works Publishing
Company, Bridgehampton, New York. Distributed in the United
States by National Book Network, Lanham, Maryland.

First Edition

Library of Congress Cataloging-in-Publication Data

Aubert, Rosemary.
    The feast of Stephen : an Ellis Portal mystery / Rosemary
Aubert. — 1st ed.
        p.   cm.
    ISBN 1-882593-27-8 (hardcover)
    I. Title.
PR 9199.3.A9F42   1999
813'.54 — dc21   98-44000
                                                                  CIP

10 9 8 7 6 5 4 3 2

Jacket design/illustration by Les Kantourek
Book design by Eva Auchincloss

Printed in the United States of America

This book is dedicated to
my sister, Linda Proe

A special thank you to:

Geoffrey Ewing, Cheryl Conway and Barbara Phillips for sharing their knowledge and suggestions.

Jude Angiore, Sleuth of Baker Street, Warren Phillips and the Proes for their passionate promotion of my work.

Gail Hamilton, Sandra Rabinovitch and Tom Dowell for their moral support and technical assistance.

All my fellow workers at the courthouse at 361 University for their warmth, enthusiasm and patience as I worked on this Ellis Portal mystery, the previous one and the next . . .

Good King Wenceslas looked out
On the feast of Stephen
When the snow lay round about
Deep and crisp and even.
Brightly shone the moon that night,
Though the frost was cruel,
When a poor man came in sight,
Gath'ring winter fuel.

"Hither, page, and stand by me,
If thou knows't it telling,
Yonder peasant, who is he?
Where and what his dwelling?"
"Sire, he lives a good league hence,
Underneath the mountain,
Right against the forest fence,
By Saint Agnes' fountain."

"Bring me flesh, and bring me wine,
Bring me pine logs hither:
Thou and I shall see him dine,
When we bear them thither."
Page and monarch, forth they went,
Forth they went together;
Through the rude wind's wild lament,
And the bitter weather.

"Sire, the night is darker now,
And the wind grows stronger;
Fails my heart I know not how;
I can go no longer."
"Mark my footsteps, my good page,
Tread thou in them boldly;
Thou shalt find the winter's rage
Freeze thy blood less coldly."

In his master's steps he trod,
Where the snow lay dinted;
Heat was in the very sod
Which the Saint had printed.
Therefore, Christian men be sure,
Wealth or rank possessing,
Ye who now will bless the poor,
Shall yourselves find blessing.

("Good King Wenceslas", a traditional 19th-century Christmas carol)

THE FEAST OF
STEPHEN

CHAPTER ONE

I live in a country with three names. Big Lonely. Canada. Winter.

I can always smell it. It might be a July evening, the earth warm to the touch, the fragrant pine forest alive with the song of whippoorwill, the sky blazing with northern summer stars, when I turn my face to the breeze and catch the scent of snow.

And in November, the month in which my story begins, I swear I can hear winter gathering force over the North Atlantic, storming Labrador and Newfoundland, rushing Quebec and the forests of Ontario, sweeping the wide prairies, vaulting the Rockies and capturing the last stronghold of lush green, Vancouver Island.

By the third week of November during the second year I lived at the headwaters of the Don River twenty miles north of the city of Toronto, winter had fully occupied the land. Time meant nearly nothing to me, but I knew it was Friday because the mailman had come. Not a real mailman. If the abandoned government complex in which I lived had ever had a street address, it didn't have one

1

now. But by some quirk of failed government budget-cutting, the courier from the provincial capital downtown still came once a week, bringing letters and packages addressed to this outpost of the Ministry of Natural Resources on whose property and with whose blessing I lived.

The snowy wind blew in with the mail addressed to Dr. This and Dr. That, each of whom had been long gone. I might have tossed all this into the closet with the two years' worth already there, except that among the letters that would never reach their destination, I saw one that had. "Ellis Portal," the envelope said in a script dark, bold and shaky. I swallowed to quell my queasiness.

No return address, no logo, no crest of a government office identified the envelope, but it must have come from within the government or it would never have arrived via the courier. I knew all about government mail. Seven and a half years before, I had been working as a judge for the Ministry of the Attorney General of the Province of Ontario. Before I lived rent-free in this deserted experimental fish hatchery, I lived as a pauper in a tar-paper-covered packing crate further down the river. Before that I had been a criminal. My stories, consequently, are always at least partly about the dramatic downfall of unsuspecting people. This story is about that, too.

I tore open the letter. It was a blank white sheet except for a single sentence in that bold but unsteady script. *"The Lord raised up judges, which delivered them out of the hand of those that spoiled them."* Of course I recognized the quotation as from the Bible, though I couldn't have said which book or chapter or verse. I recognized, too, that like the advancing winter taking the country field by field, city by city, the quotation was clearly something more than it

2

might initially appear to be. It was a death threat. A judge gets as good at smelling threats as a naturalist at smelling snow.

I considered tossing the letter into the open fire that was my sole source not only of heat but of light. Yet, even in its primitive state, there was a certain rustic coziness to the hatchery. I had never gone into the locked laboratory that occupied a separate building of the compound, and I didn't waste much time in the deserted offices that made up another large building. Instead, I spent most of my time in the lodge that had once been the living quarters of the scientists. Judging from the number of bedrooms, once there must have been more than a dozen men and women living here in the midst of acres of forest through which ran a small, clear, clean bubbling stream. It flowed down through underground springs from the north then made its way through suburbs, parks, the city, then a concrete straitjacket of a channel, into Toronto harbor, Lake Ontario, the St. Lawrence River and then the sea.

The fire snapped and sparked into the cool air of the lodge's lounge, a high-ceilinged, wood-panelled room with a large bay window against which the snow danced. It was November 19, a little more than a month before the winter solstice. Already the nights were eating up most of the day and for the first time in my fifty-seven years, I was beginning to dread the coming of darkness, not only the darkness of the evening but also the darkness of winter and maybe even of old age, should I be lucky enough to get there.

I was pondering my melancholy fate when I caught a nearly inaudible sound above the gentle crooning of the wind. I prided myself on an extraordinary ability to pick up any hint of extraneous noise. Being a judge for ten years had greatly heightened my powers of observation. Sitting on the bench with a view commanding a courtroom full of people, most of whom had something to hide, had taught me how much truth can be gleaned simply by being watchful. I learned to judge the truthfulness of people by the earnestness of their posture, by their willingness to make eye contact, by the steadiness of their voices. Justice depended on what I noticed.

But nothing so heightened my ability to see and to hear as did living for four years as a hermit in the valley of the Don River that, though it cuts through the middle of a city of three million, can be as wild as the northern woods. I had learned, for example, that a rabbit who knows a human is nearby makes a different sound when he eats grass than a rabbit who doesn't know a human is nearby — and that the difference determines which rabbit will become my supper.

But whatever the sound I heard outside, it was so fleeting that I decided it might have been my imagination, heightened by the threatening note. I resumed my self-indulgent musings about my fear of winter closing in.

I was startled not two seconds later to hear a closer sound, a banging on the stout wooden door of the lodge. Had I been outside, I would have dived for cover, but the curtains that once graced the windows had long since been turned to better uses and whoever was out there could clearly see me.

Before I could think what to do, I heard a muffled voice shouting my street name. When I'd lived in the part of the valley that runs through downtown Toronto, I'd sometimes had to make forays into the streets, and I numbered other homeless people among my so-called intimates. It hadn't taken long before I had a nickname that was a suit-

4

able reminder both of my old life and my new. "Your Honor", was what they called me, but with a certain inflection, a sneer that was both visual and verbal. I liked that little sneer. It made me feel I belonged.

"It's me, Your Honor. Open the door and let me in. I can't stand the wind no more!"

I shoved the letter with the threatening quotation into my pocket and yanked open the door. On my borrowed threshold stood a small woman covered in white flakes, her breath frozen in an icy garland on her scarf. Her long silver hair, against which the snowflakes sparkled, tumbled on her collar.

She stepped in, shook herself. "I scratched on the window," she said, "but I guess you didn't hear me. I was tryin' not to scare you, seein' as I had to come unexpected."

"Queenie!" I answered, "Come in! How did you get up here? Come get warm! Take off all those clothes before the snow melts and soaks you." She glanced at me warily and I knew why. She was amazed at my happiness to see her. So was I. It occurred to me that my dread of the coming months of winter was as much dread of lonely isolation as of cold and darkness.

Queenie shrugged away her outermost layer of heavy woolen clothing. It was one of half a dozen layers consisting of a long fringed shawl, a thick jacket, a sweater knitted in twisted cables of Irish yarn, two lighter sweaters and the scarf that circled her throat several times.

"I seen your fire a long way off," Queenie said, removing pieces as she spoke. When she'd removed the sixth layer and was down to jeans and a T-shirt, I saw that beneath the hodgepodge was a slender woman whose wanderings on the street kept her fit, despite occasional problems with her legs.

"How did you get here?" I asked again. "Who drove you?"

"Nobody. I took a city bus north to the end of the line. Then I walked."

"But that's more than twelve or thirteen miles. You walked that far in this snow?"

Her dark eyes flashed me a look that said, "So what?" Snow was nothing to Queenie. It had taken me years on the street of knowing her before she'd revealed anything about who she was or where she'd come from, but finally she told me she was a Cree Indian, born in Moosonee, nearly one thousand miles north of her rooming house in Toronto. Moosonee is called "the end of steel", where the railroad runs out hundreds of miles north of the last reaches of any highway. It is the northernmost station of the Polar Bear Express and the Little Bear, two trains that still carry tourists and trappers toward the edge of the Arctic.

"Ain't that cold out," Queenie said. "Ain't even December. Don't get real cold until Christmas Eve."

Queenie's voice was sweet and deep with a touch of whisky slur, a legacy of her days on the bottle. She'd been on the wagon five years or more, almost as long as I, and she was at least ten years younger. But she'd had a hard life and sometimes it showed.

I drew a chair up to the fire for her. With discretion, she brushed the dust off before she sat down. "You know, Your Honor, I hate to say it, but you used to live better than this when you lived outside. Is something wrong? You sick or anything?"

In addition to having once lived in a large box, I had

6

lived also in a twenty-room house attended by a small army of "domestic assistants", so this criticism of my housekeeping stung a little. I glanced around. The lounge must once have been quite cozy with its dark panelled walls hung with photos of woodland scenes and well-executed charts showing families of fish species, all lit by a crackling fire.

But now the photos and charts were faded, the grate where the fire burned was rusted and caked with deposits of soot and ash. A layer of dust lay over the few broken chairs and the upholstered couches that once were the comfortable refuge of scientists. Old books were home to families of squeaky mice, the wood panelling was rotting, and rot dust piled up in little peaks against the base of the wall. I was glad that Queenie couldn't see the two other rooms I used: a bedroom where a nest of blankets in the corner formed my bed and a kitchen filled with the empty tin cans that served as my plates, bowls and pots. She was right. I had lived better outside. But I had the distinct feeling it wasn't *my* problems she'd come to discuss.

"You got any tea?" she asked. She wasn't being evasive. She was getting ready for a long chat. I nodded and went to the kitchen. When I came back a few minutes later with the teapot and cups that I'd long before found in a cupboard but never used, she was staring at the fire deep in thought. I knew her well enough to know that her apparent calm masked agitation.

"What is it, Queenie? What happened?"

She brushed back a strand of her thick straight hair. The fire seemed to cast a copper light along the strong plane of her jaw, softening the powerful lines of her profile. "I ain't got a lot of friends these days," she said. "Ain't never had more than a couple anyways. And they ain't exactly

7

had it easy. Still, you don't expect 'em to die on you just like that." She snapped her fingers. The sound was surprisingly loud.

"Who died?" I asked softly, "and how?"

"Melia," she said, "my best friend, Melia."

I tried to place the name. But I didn't know who she was talking about. Before I could ask, Queenie added, "I think she got poisoned."

"Poisoned — you mean she ate something bad?" In the world in which Queenie lived it was a miracle that people weren't dying of poisoning every day, eating out of garbage cans and drinking anything that had — or even seemed to have — alcohol in it. One man in her rooming house was a regular drinker of chlorine bleach.

"No. No, Your Honor, you got to listen to this." Queenie's hands suddenly reached for mine. But she stopped before she touched me and her eyes widened as she saw that my fingers were covered with a raw, red rash. I'd been bothered by it off and on for years, ever since I'd slipped on some rocks in the lower river and become infected by contact between my broken skin and the river's pollution.

She rose and walked toward a place on the wall where the panelling was crumbling. With seeming nervousness, she poked at the wood. "Melia was a wreck all the time I knew her," Queenie said. "But she was a good friend anyway. The trouble with Melia was she wasn't smart in a regular way — couldn't finish school or hold a job, always had to kinda make do anyways, if you know what I mean. Plus she had to look after her husband. He was always sayin' he was too sick to work and he could get real mean if the welfare money run out before he got the kind of food and stuff he was always sayin' he had to have. So she

8

needed extra money and she got it by begging down by the courthouse — not City Hall but the big courthouse on University Avenue. I asked her once why she picked that spot and she said people going into court either feel lucky or unlucky. If they feel unlucky, they give money to change their luck. If they feel lucky — like if they won their case or something — they give money out of being thankful. Either way, they cough up."

"Sounds like Melia wasn't so stupid," I commented.

"Right, Your Honor, not stupid, just not smart when it came to acting like ordinary people. She was a pretty raggedy looking person because she used to say that if you look bad enough it makes people feel like they're getting their money's worth when they give."

We both laughed at that, but the hollow sound of it echoed in the dark, dusty room. Queenie moved away from the wall and back into the warmth and light of the fire. Her silver fall of hair caught the glint of the flames as she leaned down and lifted her teacup off its saucer, setting the cup aside. Then she deposited a fistful of wood dust onto the saucer. She sat down and began working at the dust with the heel of her teaspoon. "Melia took care of herself," she said. "She didn't eat nothing strangers gave her or out of restaurant bins, either."

"Restaurant bins" was a genteel street term meaning garbage cans. Whenever I heard one of these euphemisms, I felt a painful combination of respect and despair.

"So that's why I know she wouldn't eat nothing bad by accident."

"But how can you know for sure she died of poisoning?" I asked.

It took Queenie a minute to answer, as if she wished to

present her case in the best possible way. I respected that. I let her think. Outside, the wind sang softly in the eaves of the lodge and the snow still danced against the panes.

"You remember that cop Matt West, the one who helped Moonstar?"

"Of course." There was no way I could forget. Matt had been a police officer working out of the Youth Bureau at the same time Moonstar, Queenie's teenaged daughter, began her long slide down that eventually cost her her life from violence and drugs. Both Moonstar and Matt had been involved in a bizarre scheme that I'd helped to unravel two years earlier. Queenie always referred to the affair as my "case". Considering the danger of Matt's work — he'd lost one of his hands on the job — I had wondered whether he were still alive.

"They give him a new job at Police Headquarters," Queenie said. "Now he's in charge of crimes committed against homeless people, even stealing. He come around to see me because I was Melia's friend and he wanted me to know what happened to her. But those cops are always investigating, no matter what they say they're doing. He asked me if Melia had any enemies. It made me laugh. Melia was the sweetest person. I told Matt that and I asked him who killed her. He acted real surprised, like the thought of her being murdered never occurred to him. But that was just an act. He said they found her dead down at the Christie Pits. You know that place?"

I knew the Christie Pits intimately. It was in a downtown neighborhood once working-class but now being gentrified by young upwardly mobile families. Twice I'd lived in houses on Crawford Street. It formed the western boundary of the Pits, a former quarry that for many decades had been a large city park. Its grassy slopes dipped deeply down from Crawford, Barton, Christie and Bloor Streets into a landscaped depression that held, among other things, a baseball diamond home to the Toronto Maple Leafs.

"Matt told me that's where they found her. He said she must have got careless because it looked like she froze to death. Only I know that's a big lie."

She shuddered. Queenie was not given to emotional display. I knew she was trying hard not to show how upset she was.

"Three reasons, Your Honor, why I know she was poisoned. First, people who freeze could be drunk, but Melia didn't drink no alcohol. And she wasn't just a reformed drunk like you and me." She smiled her sad, sweet smile. "No. Melia never drank one drink in her whole life. Second, how could a person freeze to death this time of year? It just ain't cold enough. People freeze in January, February. Not now. Even if it's snowing, it ain't freezing out."

"Queenie, it doesn't have to be that cold for a person to freeze. All it takes is a little carelessness and . . ."

"Which is number three," Queenie interrupted. "Melia was never careless. She was a real careful person. She had to make enough extra money to keep her husband. He wasn't a drunk either but he took medicine for sugar or something and she had to buy it because the government didn't cover it. And she studied herbs and that. I seen her planting lovage seeds in her room once. She said she got them from an Indian I told her about. She even made tea out of the lovage. She said I should try some for the arthritis I got in my legs. She didn't do nothing without thinking it all out first. Somebody killed her and made it look like she froze. I bet Matt West thinks so too, whether he admits it or not."

We sat there in silence for a few moments. Queenie seemed to have finished what she'd been doing with the wood dust.

"Give me your hand," she said.

"What?"

"You got that rash back. I can fix it. Take off your ring."

I wear a large heavily embossed ring that I've managed to hang on to through thick and thin. It was given to me by a friend of long ago — John Stoughton-Melville — now Justice of the Supreme Court of Canada. He gave identical rings to four lawyers on the day we were admitted to the bar more than thirty years earlier. The ring had its own stories, some of which Queenie knew.

"The promise ring," she said, as I removed it and put it on the three-legged table on which our tea things sat before the fire. The ring glowed with a rich golden sheen.

"Yes, Queenie, the promise ring. What are you going to do to my hand?"

Without answering, she took my fingers in hers. Her skin was warm with a pleasing roughness, like the roughness of wool or of soil. And she was strong. I could feel power in her fingers as she clasped mine and turned my hand palm up, and began to apply the pulverized wood dust to my skin. "My grandmother taught me this," she explained. "Us Cree didn't ever use no baby powder or nothing like that. Wood's got a special force in it. Mostly though, it just keeps your skin dry — that feel better?"

For some reason, I couldn't answer. My voice seemed stuck in my throat. It had been years since I'd enjoyed any sort of physical intimacy with a woman — not since

12

Anne, my wife. I thought I was used to being alone. I thought I preferred it. But at Queenie's touch, a painful wrenching in my chest seemed to spread to my stomach, and even my limbs.

I stood up, fumbled with a split log and gingerly balanced it on the fire. The room was filled with some unspoken emotion that seemed mutual. It was Queenie who finally broke the silence.

"Your Honor, I come here to get you back downtown to help me figure out who killed Melia. Two years ago, after you found out what happened to Moonstar and Matt, you was on the way to getting back on your feet, working for the city and all."

"That job's finished," I interrupted, turning toward her. She was sitting ramrod straight.

"Lots of people's jobs finish all the time. That ain't no excuse for living like an animal in the middle of nowhere."

I felt a sudden flash of anger. Queenie had no right to lecture me. For one thing, she didn't work either as far as I knew. Plus, I didn't appreciate gratuitous concern for my well-being. "If you came up here on some sort of charity mission, you walked a long way for nothing."

"Don't talk mad with me," Queenie said evenly, "I ain't one of the criminals you used to be the judge of and I ain't one of the kids you used to be the father of, either. I come up here for just one reason — to help me find out who killed my friend. You can do that better than anybody else."

I stood a moment longer beside the fire, trying to calm down and to understand why I was so extraordinarily upset. Queenie kept her eyes on my face but I couldn't read her expression. I sat down in a chair that creaked and shifted as I lowered myself onto it.

"What you been doing up here for two whole years?" Queenie asked softly.

"Reading, walking, thinking . . ."

"You must be all thought out by now."

"Maybe I am."

"You need to talk to people. Everybody does. And you're real good at it. That's why I need you to help me." She laughed as if at some private joke.

"What's so funny?"

"Remember those old movies where the Indians say that white people speak with forked tongues. I guess that means lying or something but that's just what I need you for."

"You need me to speak with a forked tongue?"

"Yeah. You see, Your Honor, you can talk to educated people like the lawyers and them at the courthouse. The people that used to see Melia every day and give her money. But you can also talk to the street people who knew her. You see what I'm getting at?"

"I guess so. But to what purpose? What could I hope to find out?"

Queenie interrupted. "Even if Matt West *is* supposed to look after the homeless and all, he probably thinks Melia was just some old drunk that decided to sleep outside on the wrong night. But that's not what happened and I can prove it."

"What?"

"I can prove Melia was murdered." She stood up and reached into a pocket in her jeans. "I didn't give you this right off," she said, "because I promised Melia's husband not to show it to anybody. He was afraid."

14

"Afraid of what?"

Queenie didn't answer. The paper she had pulled from her jeans pocket was dirty and ridiculously, considering my own lifestyle, I felt hesitant to touch it. But I forced back my distaste. It was not Queenie's doing that the paper was filthy. Despite her circumstances, she was meticulous. I unfolded the wrinkled sheet. With a start, I saw the same dark, bold but somehow uneven handwriting that had addressed me in the biblical quotation.

I held the paper so that firelight fell on it. I read, *"Behold, I send an angel before thee, to keep thee in the way, and to bring thee into the place which I have prepared."*

Whether she saw my hand shake or was watching my face, I don't know, but suddenly Queenie was beside me, her hand on my arm. This was the second time she'd touched me in the same hour. "You're scared of it, too," she whispered. "It's from the Bible. But what does it mean?"

"I don't know. Queenie, you need to show this to the police."

"No. They won't do nothing. Besides, I promised Melia's husband."

"If you promised him you wouldn't show anybody the note, then you already broke your promise by showing it to me."

"No," Queenie insisted. "I promised him I would show it only to somebody who would help us find out who killed Melia. That's you. You're a good detective."

"I'm not a detective at all."

"Then what *are* you?"

The question hung in the air like the sweet smell of wood smoke that mocked the shabby lodge.

"Help me. Then we won't have to argue. All you gotta

15

do is come back down to the city for a little while. I can find you a place right away. Then we go to Melia's husband and ask a few questions. If we find out anything bad or dangerous, we just go to Matt West and convince him that Melia didn't die by accident. Then he'll investigate. Is that asking too much?"

Of course it was asking too much. It had been more than seven years since I'd set foot anywhere near a courthouse. Seven years since the judicial responsibilities and a self-centered, indulgent life-style had finally broken me and burned me out spectacularly. I have never been the sort of person to do things by halves.

"Your Honor," Queenie said, rising and reaching toward the pile of clothes she'd discarded, "could you do me one favor? Could you just sleep on it? I'll leave you alone. Think about it. You can let me know tomorrow. I know you ain't got no phone but you could get somebody outside the grounds to call for you. Call tomorrow. I'll be back home by noon."

The thought of her walking back to the city startled me. "Would you like to stay the night?"

She laughed and the rich sound of it almost made me forget her mission and the two grim notes.

"You still got them nice manners. Yes, sir. I will accept your kind invitation to spend the night." She shot me an unreadable look. Whether it was mockery or gratitude — or both — I couldn't quite tell.

"Come and choose a room then," I offered. "This place has as many as a hotel."

"Spooky. Nice, but spooky," Queenie concluded, as by flickering candlelight, I escorted her down a long corridor to the room she'd chosen. We'd shared an improvised supper beside the fire and toasted our long-standing friendship with plastic glasses of canned juice.

The camaraderie of our meal changed my resolve. Somewhere in the course of our after-dinner conversation, it had become apparent to us both that I *would* go down to the city with her the next day. Before she went to bed, she told me, "Melia's husband found that note in their room. That's all I know about it."

When the fire died away and there was no sound from the room at the end of the hall, I extinguished all the candles but one. In my room, I pulled from its hiding place the strong plastic bag in which I kept those few things most important to me. I opened a small leather portfolio that I had found in one of the rooms of the lodge and put the two notes inside.

In the light from my candle, the bold, uneven handwriting seemed to writhe. But I did not find that nearly as frightening as the fact that there were not two such notes in the portfolio. There were six. I had been receiving them for months.

CHAPTER TWO

We set out into a world so bright with snow, the eyes blurred. The pines surrounding the lodge drooped under the burden of it. Blue jays and cardinals swooped from tree top to bush looking for a few red berries peeking out from the heavy whiteness. The rosy sun of dawn lent a patina of pearl to the scene.

We could have pooled the few dollars we had and bought tickets for a bus or a train to take us to the northern terminus of the subway system. We might even have found a way to hitchhike on some side road away from the major highway and Christmas shoppers heading downtown. Instead, we walked.

"The long way is sometimes the fastest," Queenie said as she guided me along the combination of paths and roads she had taken the day before. As we went, the sun lost its softness and the sky became a hard, bright blue against which the mounds of snow glowed with clean abundance.

I left everything behind except the plastic bag that held my important possessions. I'd burned my blankets and my few rags of clothes except for the one good set I was wearing. I was careful to make sure the fire was out before we left. I didn't ask myself about the apparent finality of the arrangements. Nomads don't look back.

"I thought you was helping put the plants back in the valley after that flood two years ago. I thought the city was paying you good money," Queenie commented as we trudged through the snow.

"You're right. And I managed to save a lot of that money since I could live at the unused hatchery as long as I cared to. That was part of the arrangement with the valley restoration team at City Hall. I didn't mind the daily commute downtown. Even after the contract ended, the solitude up here was great for awhile. But lately I guess I started missing having people to talk to every day."

"You're a good talker. Always were," Queenie answered. She didn't seem to sense any contradiction in the fact that we then lapsed into a comfortable silence that lasted for the next couple of hours.

The further south we walked, the less deep the snow. The landscape of early winter was, to my eye, as rich as that of any season. Hardy nonhibernating insects scuttled across the untouched snow. The dried remains of summer's plants — the curling gray wings of burst milkweed pods, the hard black seed-pods of the lily with their little round chambers like those of a revolver — rose above the snow into the windless air. It was cold but pleasant and I thought, as I think every year, that snow that falls before the winter solstice or after the vernal equinox is almost a sort of tropical snow — warm, moist, heavy and lush.

It took almost seven hours to walk the thirteen or so miles, and as the hours passed, we went from woodland to suburb to park to residential street until finally, late in the afternoon, we reached Queen and Sherbourne at the bottom of the city. Queen Street runs for six miles from the eastern edge of Toronto to the western edge parallel to Lake Ontario. In its run, the street passes through a beach-side bohemian village, aging working-class neighborhoods barely gentrified, patches of rooming house/doughnut shop streetscapes, into the downtown core and out again past Old City Hall Criminal Court where I used to work, then the storetop studios of young artists, stretches of ethnic restaurants, art galleries, the mental hospital, shops, then finally, beach again.

Queenie's house was on Pembroke Street close to the city core. The house had seen better days and was only a little less ramshackle than my lodge in the woods.

"Stow your stuff here and we'll go down to the shelter for supper," Queenie suggested.

"I might still be banned from there," I reminded her. I had been thrown out for violent behavior long before, but then sneaked back once or twice without incident. I didn't want to press my luck.

"Forget it. They got a new director now. He won't even know who you are."

The "shelter" was a community center close to Queenie's place. It was jammed full of people when we got there. I was overcome first by the roar of the crowd. It had always been that noisy. I just wasn't used to it. Then there was the smell: the unmistakably human scent of warm skin and seldom-washed hair. Overlying that was the aroma of coffee and an institutional, cheap supper cooked in pots that had been scoured with disinfectant. I surprised myself by breathing deeply, eager to have the sad, familiar odors in my nostrils.

"We could find out a whole lot right here," Queenie said

as we set our bowls of stew on a communal table. "We could start finding out about Melia because that's her husband."

She pointed to a small, seedy-looking man whose thinning black-and-gray-hair was greased back over his shiny scalp. He'd not taken the risk of removing his jacket while he ate. It had once been black leather but now was so scratched and scuffed as to appear mostly beige. He was hunched over his stew, protecting the bowl in the crook of his arm and shovelling the concoction into his mouth in big, slurping spoonfuls.

"Come on," Queenie said, picking up her bowl, "We don't got no time to waste."

Reluctantly, I followed her. I left my stew behind. I had lost my appetite.

Queenie sat down close to the man but not touching him. "Jack," she called softly. "Jack, listen to me. I got a friend here who's gonna help us find out what happened to Melia."

"Melia made a mistake, that's all," the man answered. He stopped slurping, but kept his eyes on the floating masses of carrot and potato in their dark, murky gravy. "I told her time after time, 'Don't go out except to work.' She never listened to me. I told her, 'The courts close, you come right home. Eat, give me my medicine, go to sleep. That's all you got to worry about.' "

"How did Melia give you the medicine?" Queenie asked. "With a spoon or . . ."

"Sometimes a spoon. Sometimes a shot. It depended." He became agitated. "What am I gonna do now? Huh? You just tell me how I'm gonna get my medicine now."

He pulled the bowl closer and lifted his spoon. But he put it down before it reached his mouth. "The night she died, Melia went to that park where the minors play ball. She used to play ball herself — real good. In the old days when they allowed women. I said to her, 'It's the middle of winter. Why do you want to go to a ballpark?' She said she was talking to somebody at the court who told her about a book on teams they used to have for women. Melia said the talk made her want to see the Christie Pits again. She used to go in the summer all the time. She said the park was part of her past. I said to her, 'So what?' I went to sleep. The next thing I know it's morning and there's a cop banging on my door."

"Jack, what medicine do you take?" Queenie insisted. "Melia never told me she *helped* you take your medicine."

"Medicine. Yeah. So now I'm up shit creek without a paddle. How am I gonna get my medicine? The government's not gonna help. You can't count on nobody for nothing these days."

"I had enough of this. Let's get out of here," Queenie said. Her voice was suddenly hoarse and her fingers shook as she buttoned the top layer of her clothes. "This place stinks."

I took Queenie's sudden irritation to be exhaustion from having walked twenty-five miles within twenty-four hours. I was exhausted myself. In my shopping bag was a handy slice of plastic known as a bank card. I used the card to open the door to the foyer of a nearby bank branch. I slept there all night. And in the morning, I used the card to withdraw enough for a decent breakfast and two weeks' rent in a rooming house.

The little run-in with Melia's grieving widower had pretty much robbed me of any ambition to discover what had happened to his wife. Yet, for no apparent reason, I found myself near the Christie Pits later that morning.

Though there was less snow in the city than there had been further north, the park was full of children sliding down its steep slopes on pieces of cardboard and plastic, the almost fluorescent blues, purples and pinks of their winter jackets making a bright confetti-splash of color against the snow. When I'd been a boy, I'd slid down those same slopes, only I had a fine wooden sled with iron runners that cut into the snow with a sound that I could still voluntarily call to mind after more than fifty years.

I had grown up not far from this park in a section then called Little Italy. It became unfashionable to use such terms for the ethnic communities of Toronto but I saw that the street signs in this part of town were crowned now with little decorations in red, white and green, the colors of the flag of Italy, and said "Little Italy" in bold black letters above the actual street names. "What goes around, comes around", the street people are fond of saying, and it is true.

As I wandered in the snowy Sunday afternoon through the neighborhood of my youth, I began to look for a place where I could stay for more than just a night or two. Something of the indefinable pain I'd felt before Queenie had arrived at the lodge had returned when I'd said goodnight to her. I did not want to name that pain, but I could. Loneliness. A person can live alone for a time and love it. But loneliness is a worm. And once it turns, there is no peace.

The streets near the Christie Pits are some of the most typical in the downtown core. But the long tidy stretches of three-story row houses show personal style. Some have trellises in front, bare in November but covered with flowering vines all summer. Some have little stone grottoes enclosing plaster statues of the Virgin Mary. Some have storm doors with brightly painted metal cutouts of the saints, St. Francis of Assisi being the most popular. Others along the same stretch are cleanly renovated with front yards paved in brick and decorated with flower urns.

A number of the houses had "Room for Rent" signs posted in the front windows. I was contemplating one of them when I realized I'd once owned that particular house myself. A feeling of loss hit me like a punch to the stomach.

When my wife Anne had been pregnant with our first child, Ellen, thirty years earlier, we'd given up our small apartment overlooking a ravine through which ran the Don River and moved back from the suburbs to this neighborhood because Anne, whose own mother was dead, wanted to be near my mother. I had hated the idea. Though I worked nearby in a law office that served the Italian community, I was full of ambition. I wanted better circumstances for my family and myself.

But we had some happy times in that house and the memories flooded back unbidden. I saw Anne, her long blond hair, her pale skin rosy, sitting beside the fireplace in the little front room, working on some piece of needlework my mother had shown her how to do, some impossibly small garment growing beneath her fingers the way Ellen was growing beneath her heart.

"Hey, mister, you got some sort of problem?" The sharp voice jolted me out of my reverie. The front door of the house was flung open and poised in its frame, in absurd contrast to St. Francis who had only moments before been visible there among small animals, stood a pasty-faced, dark-haired, solid-looking teenager.

Her lips were blood-red. She was dressed all in black

from her zippered leather blouse to her heavy boots that appeared to be fastened by the sort of hardware I associate with the pipefitters my late father, the bricklayer, used to work with in the construction trade. The girl looked to be about sixteen and the silver rings that pierced her left nostril matched the ones that pierced her right eyebrow. "Why're you standing there with your mouth open? You lose something?"

"I'm — I'm looking for a room."

"Yeah, well — you got cash on you?"

"What?"

"Money. Rent. You know, like what you pay to live in somebody else's house?"

Her voice was full of saucy contempt. I asked myself why I should stand there and be subjected to her insolent attitude. But she reminded me of girls who had come before my bench when I was a judge. Sauciness, I'd learned, was sometimes a sign of intelligence. Intelligence in the young never failed to intrigue me.

"Of course I've got money, and if you'd please get your parents, we can talk about my taking the room you've got advertised."

"What have my parents got to do with it? I own this house. I'm the landlord. The room's a hundred and ten a week. Cash."

Where would somebody your age get the money to buy a house like this? I wanted to ask. But I just nodded and she gestured for me to step onto the roofed porch.

"You get to use the kitchen and the living room. You could eat in the dining room if you want. No guests allowed."

When I saw the inside of the house, I questioned

whether it was my old home after all. It was now cut up into six or eight rental units and little remained of a single-family dwelling.

But despite this, the place appeared to be very well-kept. The wooden floors were waxed. There were cheap but clean curtains on all the windows and the bedroom that she showed me, on the third floor overlooking the back garden, was furnished with a serviceable bed, a chair, a dresser, a small table and a lamp, each of which had been carefully selected from a used furniture store on Queen Street. Of course I'd never seen any of it before, but the total effect was one of haunting familiarity.

The two bathrooms, one on the first floor, the other on the third, and the renovated kitchen were spotless and modern. Beside the stove was a shelf and on it were six neat piles of dishes and cutlery. A sign on the refrigerator reminded tenants not to touch food that didn't belong to them.

"You run this house?" I asked.

"Yeah. It's like my own small business or whatever. I'm the owner-operator." She stuck out her white hand with its black fingernails in a businesslike way, obviously expecting me to shake it, which I did, careful not to squeeze too hard lest one or both of us be injured by the twenty silver rings she wore.

"Tootie Beets — not my real name," she introduced herself.

"Ellis Portal — not my real name, either."

"Cool — you got the hundred and ten?"

So I had a room and within a week, between Wal-Mart and the nearest thrift store, I also had my own pile of dishes and cutlery, two sheets, four towels, shirts, pants, a jacket, underwear, a winter coat and a small library of books.

I also had a phone and a number of calls from Queenie. "They didn't even give Melia no funeral," she told me. "They just buried her like it was some dog they needed to get rid of. And nobody checked her body for poison, either."

It seemed strange to be talking to Queenie on the phone, because we'd always talked in person, but I could picture her at the pay phone at the end of the dingy hall of *her* rooming house, which was far more downscale than mine. "Queenie, I think you're going to have to put this all behind you."

"No! Melia was murdered. If you don't help me find her killer, I'll get somebody else who will!"

Reluctantly, I agreed to meet Queenie in an hour. I hung up and checked the clock in the hall outside my room. Noon. It was a grandfather clock. A nice looking one. I was once more wondering where Tootie Beets had got her money — and her name — when I heard my phone ring again.

I picked up the receiver. "Hello, Ellis."

I drew in a sharp breath and immediately regretted that I had exposed myself by even that small indication of the shock I was feeling. The deep, cultured, commanding voice on the other end of the line was the last I would have ever expected to hear. It's not often, I suspect, that a Justice of the Supreme Court has occasion to place a phone call to a rooming house.

"Hello, Stow." It was our old nickname for John Stoughton-Melville and it had stuck despite all that had happened since we'd been in law school together.

He was as peremptory as ever, using the tone he'd use with a secretary or a servant.

"Ellis, I need your help at once. Harpur has walked away from Riverside Institute and they think she may have wandered into the valley."

How did Stow know I was back in town? How did he know my phone number? I didn't even bother to ask. He was like Sherlock Holmes's arch enemy, Professor Moriarty. His agents were everywhere and splendidly organized.

"I want you to help. They think Harpur's been missing for at least twelve hours."

There was a lot of history between Stow's wife Harpur and me, desperate love for thirty years on my side and casual dismissal on her side. I hadn't seen her for a while but that didn't matter. Once the most beautiful, the most brilliant of the five of us who graduated from law school together, she had inexorably slid into Alzheimer's disease and violence two years earlier.

"I'm not legally permitted anywhere near Harpur . . ." I began to argue.

"Ellis, you know the valley better than anyone else. You lived there. If you don't help out, Harpur could perish."

Stow knew very well of my hopeless infatuation for his wife. Apparently he was willing to set aside his anger about it for the time being. Despite my better judgment, I agreed to meet the team of search volunteers at the Broadview subway station, about half an hour away. I left within minutes, passing Tootie working at the dining room table, a big book with long columns open before her. The sight of her young head bent intensely over the house ledger touched me in an unexpected way. I thought about my daughter Ellen and emotion filled me. But there was no time for that now.

Riverside Institute for Long-Term Care had once been a public hospital but had been sold to a consortium of doctors who turned it into a private facility for well-to-do Alzheimer's patients. As the wife of Supreme Court Justice John Stoughton-Melville, Harpur deserved the best and got it, even at those times in which she couldn't tell the best from the worst, which was most of the time.

The Institute sat on Broadview Avenue, overlooking a wide vista of park, then the river valley, and beyond, the downtown neighborhoods of the city. Although the snow that had fallen the previous week had melted, a new light dusting made everything crisp, clean and slippery. Harpur had walked across a corner of the hospital grounds adjoining the park to reach the bridge directly below the hospital, a bridge from which an open-mesh metal staircase descended onto a path that led north and south along the river.

"The police are afraid she might have wandered into the brush," the volunteer leader explained. "There are plenty of places where it's thick enough to get lost in." He instructed the others to fan out but asked me to stay with him. He knew me from my work in the valley for City Hall. "What do you make of this situation?" he asked me.

"It's impossible to guess her reasoning," I answered. "I think she'd be likely to stick to the path." I didn't want to admit I was afraid she might have slipped and fallen. Despite the light snow cover, it was much colder than it had been a week before. It wouldn't take much time for hypothermia to rob an unwary person of consciousness, especially if she were on medication.

"We have a big team looking for her," he told me as we carefully negotiated the metal-grill stairs. I didn't let myself look down because it made me dizzy to be able to see the frozen ground far beneath us through the grid of the steps. "Some of the volunteers are kids."

"Kids?"

"Yeah, teens. They're young offenders on community service. They know the valley well because they've been doing clean-up work down here."

I had little use for social service agencies, especially since my last "case" had exposed a halfway house for pregnant girls as a front for a scheme to provide questionable medical services to Harpur. But if young people were helping out in the valley instead of lingering in jail or loitering on the street, I was willing to set aside my grudges.

The leader and I followed the icy path north over an old wooden bridge that echoed our footsteps as we crossed. "The kids are up by Chester Springs Marsh," he said.

In just two years, the carefully reconstructed marsh had become indistinguishable from one that nature would have created. Even the clearly audible traffic on the highway that ran parallel to the river couldn't spoil the feeling of the wilderness. The pond-like enclosure was ringed with snow-dusted bushes as high as our shoulders. I was just about to mention that the bushes were growing fast, when I caught a glimpse through their twisted leafless branches.

Crouched near the ice-glazed shallow water were two figures. One of them was a dead ringer for Tootie Beets. I wondered how she had got here before me and whether she was a reforming delinquent as well as a landlord. Then I saw that this person was male. The other figure was a woman whose natural elegance was not disguised by squatting on the ground. The startling beauty of her red hair was only a little diminished by the few silver streaks that shot through it. She was as old as I. Her delicate paleness seemed but a more subtle shade of all the whiteness of the snow.

"She's here," I whispered to the leader as he came up behind me. "And one of the kids is with her."

We watched them in silence for a moment, trying to decide what to do. I didn't want to risk startling Harpur or her rescuer. For all his black leather and shiny metal, the young man spoke in a well-modulated voice, and I saw that he remained a little distance from Harpur, as though he realized that if he got too near, she'd run. "You can come back with me," we heard him say gently, "I can guarantee no one will hurt you. They know me. Even the police know me." He smiled ironically, "And I'll tell them that you're my friend and not to punish you for running away. Everybody runs away sometimes."

I was only about twenty feet from them, close enough to see the fearful doubt in Harpur's eyes as she raised them to the face of the youth. "You promise?" I heard her ask.

"Yes. Come on. I'll help you walk."

"I'm cold," Harpur said. She stood and I saw she was wearing nothing but a long white nightgown. Against the starkness of the winter valley, the black clothes of the boy and the colorless paleness of this garment of Harpur's, her hair, which I was amazed to see fell nearly to her waist, was the only color in the landscape.

"Let's help them," I whispered.

"Who the hell's out there?" Harpur called, in an entirely different voice from the one in which she'd said she was cold. This was a demanding voice. Hard, arrogant and familiar.

"Take it easy," I said, stepping out from cover and moving closer to Harpur and the boy.

Harpur's face registered shock and confusion. "Gelo?" she asked, softly, plaintively.

She had not used that nickname since we'd been children, and it shook me. "Gelo?" she said again. But she was addressing her young rescuer.

"It's okay, Ma'am," he said, "We're going to take you home now."

In the end, it was the police who brought Harpur home, if the Riverside Institute could be called home. She insisted on having the boy remain at her side, and she kept calling him by my nickname, which sent an absurd dart of jealousy into my old heart. I reached out and shook "Gelo's" hand. Like Tootie Beets, he was wearing a lot of rings. But unlike her, he noticed my crested ring. I thought he looked surprised and it crossed my mind that maybe he had designs on it — might steal it if he had the chance.

It was a cruel thought about somebody who had just saved a life.

"You're four hours late," Queenie said, "and I been waitin' here the whole time."

"Don't be mad, Queenie," I begged, sitting opposite her and digging into a fat doughnut-shop tuna sandwich. I would have thought the shock of seeing Harpur in her sad condition would have taken away my appetite.

"Go ahead, eat," Queenie said. "I got all the time in the world."

32

"Look, Queenie, I'm sorry I haven't done more about Melia. I know how you feel and maybe . . ."

"Oh, this is gone way past being about Melia now," Queenie said evenly.

"What?"

"I been sittin' here for hours waitin' to tell you. Somebody else just got murdered while you been foolin' around, passin' the time of day."

CHAPTER THREE

"I never knew the victim's name till now that she's dead and I only seen her once."

Queenie kept her eyes off mine as she spoke. She seemed to study her reflection in the greasy doughnut-shop window. Or maybe she looked beyond the glass across the street to the corner where a few people straggled into the evening service of a large old church. Or the opposite corner where a few of the "early girls" were bouncing up and down, cold already, although it was only the beginning of a long night of hooking on the Track.

"What *was* her name?"

"Paulina del Mario. She had a real bad problem. Like I said, I only seen her once, but it was enough."

Queenie pulled one of her sweaters a little tighter, despite the fact that in contrast to outside, it was sweltering in the shop.

"What was her problem?"

"She had a terrible accident to her face. After I seen her, I asked Melia what was wrong with her because Melia knew her for a long time. Melia told me she used to be real beautiful. Spanish or Portuguese or Italian. Anyway, one day she was minding her own business, driving to work and this car comes out of nowhere and bangs into her. The windshield gets busted into a million pieces that fly all over the place. Two big pieces cut this Paulina woman across the face real bad."

Queenie shook her head, lifted the styrofoam cup she'd been cradling and took a sip of tea. "She figured she could at least get a whole lot of money if her insurance company sued the people who made the windshield."

"She would have had a good case," I interjected.

Queenie's eyes flashed into mine for an instant and I could see she was trying not to laugh. I couldn't help acting like a judge once in a while.

"The whole world is full of people who could have a good case in court — or think they could, Your Honor. Maybe she could have, except she made a mistake."

Across the street, one of the hookers leaned into the open window of a late-model Cadillac. She laughed, shook her long hair and stepped back onto the curb away from the car, which peeled off with an angry squeal that I could hear even through the thick glass of the shop window and over the din of the customers. "What mistake?"

"She put off getting her face fixed — waited too long. Melia said Paulina told her that she'd get more sympathy from a jury if they could see how bad she got cut up. Only it didn't work that way at all. The jury just got kind of scared or disgusted or something. Instead of giving her millions like she thought they would, they only gave her a few thousand and the lawyer got it all." She paused. "After all," she continued, "it ain't like Paulina had to pay

35

to get her face fixed. The government pays for things like that."

"The government" was Queenie's phrase for every program, service or institution provided by the taxpayer.

"That's true, Queenie. So what *was* the problem?"

"Because she waited so long, her face went permanent. Nothing could fix it. That, plus the fact that she didn't get no big money like she deserved, made her go crazy. She started hanging around the courthouse all the time. One day I went to bring something to Melia. She told me to go inside and take a look. Paulina was sitting in the back of a courtroom listening in on a trial something like her trial was. She was real quiet — else they would have thrown her out — but she had this big bag of papers with her. When the court took a break, she came out and talked to Melia. She said she had 'documents' to prove that she really won her case after all. She said all she had to do was get a judge to read them and the judge would see that the jury meant for her to be a millionaire. She thought that sooner or later she would luck out and run into one of the judges in the hallway and make him read the papers."

I hadn't thought about it for a long time, but suddenly there returned to me the memory of sneaking out of Old City Hall Criminal Court, praying that some poor soul or other who had haunted my courtroom would not notice me as I left the building and headed for my car. It had happened so many times. The courts were full of spectators and some of them came every day as if they had no other life.

"How did Paulina die, Queenie?"

"She was outside, just like Melia."

"You mean she froze to death in the Pits?"

"Not exactly. She went to court on Friday, like she

always did. She was there all morning. At lunch time she had some soup in the cafeteria. Then she went back into court at 2:15 when the trial she was watching started up again. But the court ended early and she went home. Only when she got there, she found out she was evicted. It happened to her a lot of times. All her things was on the sidewalk. I guess she just laid down on top of a bag of stuff and closed her eyes and that was it."

"Who said she was murdered? It sounds like she simply died from misadventure."

"What?"

"By accident, Queenie. It sounds like a tragic accident."

Queenie shook her head vigorously. "No," she insisted. "She was healthy. I got the whole story from Melia's husband. He knew Paulina. Melia said they used to talk about medicine all the time because they were like . . ." She wrinkled her brow in thought. "What do you call somebody that always thinks they're sick?"

"A psychosomatic?"

"Huh?"

"A hypochondriac?"

"Yeah, that's it. Melia's husband and Paulina was hypochondriacs. The husband said the same police officers that asked him questions about Melia came back and asked him questions about Paulina. The police told him it was a suspicious death and that the coroner was going to check into it and all."

"The coroner would have to be called for any sudden death", I explained. "That doesn't mean it was murder."

"First Melia is found dead in a park in the middle of winter, then Paulina, her best friend." Queenie shook her head slowly, "I know these people, Your Honor. These wasn't accidents."

The door opened and a tall young pimp, handsome in an expensive-looking fedora and long designer camel's hair coat stalked in, followed by a sweet-faced blonde who looked about fourteen. Despite the cold, she was wearing nothing more than high-heeled platform shoes, white lace tights and a little pink leather dress that barely reached the tops of her lean thighs. She looked about ready to burst into tears. "Sit," the man told her and she sat.

"If it's the same killer, then there's gonna be one of them notes," Queenie said, dragging my attention away from the pimp who was spoon-feeding his "investment" from a cup the waitress had put in front of him.

Queenie stood and picked up one by one the faded sweaters and worn jacket she had tossed on the seat beside her. As she dressed, she told me, "I know how a judge thinks. I ain't never been a court groupie like Paulina del Mario or Melia, either. But I ain't been your friend all these years without learning nothing. I'm going to prove those women was murdered."

I hadn't forgotten my own little collection of threatening notes. I hadn't had any mail whatsoever at my new address. And I hoped to keep it that way.

But before I could tell Queenie that the last thing I wanted to see was another one of those notes, she was walking toward the exit. Following her was the pimp and his blonde girl. I saw him pinch the girl hard to make her move faster. She gave a little yelp and hurried out the door.

"A guy with a briefcase came by and your phone's been ringing off the hook," Tootie greeted me when I got home.

"A man with a briefcase on a Sunday?"

"He could have been one of those religious people," Tootie speculated. I noticed she changed her clothes often but everything she wore was black and every accessory was metal.

"Except he asked for you by name. Specific, like."

"Next time he comes," I said, passing her to climb the stairs to my room, "tell him I don't live here."

"I don't lie," Tootie said, pursing her amazingly red-black lips. For the moment, I believed her, though I couldn't say why. But I still wanted to know more.

"Then tell me how a youngster like you got the money to buy this house."

"Just because I don't lie, doesn't mean I don't have secrets," she answered, and she had the temerity to wink at me.

It had been a long, complicated day and I was ready for a shower. I stuck my head out my door. Silence. I hadn't actually met any of my housemates yet, though I had caught glimpses of them scurrying in and out and I had certainly heard them splashing around in the bathroom. I gathered my towels and fresh clothes.

But I didn't make it out the door before the phone rang. "Hello?"

"Hello, Ellis. Harpur tells me you helped her today. She'd like you to come by tomorrow." Stow didn't identify himself. He didn't have to.

I was surprised at the notion of Harpur being in good enough shape to have recognized me. But maybe she and Stow were able to understand each other despite the ravages of her disease.

I wasn't just surprised by this call; I was apprehensive. "Look, Stow, I'm uneasy about breaching the conditions of my peace bond."

"Forget it."

Forget that I had almost gone to jail for physically assaulting Harpur one night when I was drunk? Forget I could land in jail if I were caught anywhere near Harpur now — or Stow, for that matter? Of course, I *had* ignored the peace bond this afternoon but that had been an emergency.

"Tomorrow's Monday. I can have the bond lifted in the morning," Stow said.

"Notwithstanding the fact that it's been in effect for seven years?" I asked. "I remember your saying then that you could incarcerate me for the rest of my life if I so much as looked at your wife." The peace bond had stipulated that I stay away from Harpur and Stow. Except for one sad and dramatic moment when I'd confronted them about their part in my last "case", I had obeyed it.

"Ellis, calm down. You're becoming quite overwrought. Just listen, will you? I'm hardly likely to have you jailed when I need you to help me."

I couldn't imagine why Stow thought I could help him. He had everything that exceptional intelligence and undeniable charm could bring to a man. Maybe he thought the only thing I hadn't tossed away was my cunning. Why would he need *that*?

"I want you to visit Harpur. I've checked up on that young man who found her in the valley. He was in line for a scholarship to Oxford. Then he ran afoul of the law."

"I know nothing about him."

"That's not the problem. He's from a reputable family and has behaved himself perfectly except for a silly prank that went wrong and caused a lot of damage. I don't object to his visiting Harpur."

"Then why do you need me?"

There was a silence — uncharacteristic, I thought. I had never met a more self-possessed, self-controlled man than Stow. In fact, in more than thirty years of knowing him, I had seen him angry only twice. My infatuation with Harpur had been the cause both times.

"Ellis, she seems to have you and the boy mixed up in her mind. As if she doesn't always know which is which. She said your name over and over again. And she said, 'Please. Please make Ellis come.'" He paused as if to gather his wits. "This request doesn't necessarily imply the imposition of a long-term obligation," he resumed stiffly.

"You mean she might just want to see me once, to tell me something?"

Or to demand something, I wondered.

"Yes."

I thought about it for a moment. When I'd been a judge, I'd sat on the boards of group homes, including those for the mentally and emotionally ill. The stress of volunteering plus my busy schedule had possibly contributed to my burning out. Still, there had been times I would not have refused a complete stranger if one had asked me to visit him in Riverside, so how could I refuse a woman I had once thought I loved more than myself — more than my wife?

"All right, Stow. But not until I have a signed document to the effect that the peace bond has been lifted."

"You'll have it first thing tomorrow."

Stow was as good as his word. "Fax came for you." I heard Tootie call through my door at 10:05 A.M., minutes after the courts opened for the week.

"How could somebody send a fax to me? I never gave

41

anybody your fax number. I didn't even know you had a fax machine," I called back.

"It's by my bed."

"Shut up!" somebody yelled from down the hall.

I opened the door and nearly jumped to see a total stranger standing on the threshold. Tootie was dressed in a long flannelette nightgown, like a choirgirl's outfit. There was not a speck of makeup on her fresh, young face. Her skin was smooth and rosy, and her lips were a soft, sweet pink. I had to remind myself that she was my landlady and young enough to be my granddaughter and that — even though I hadn't seen her in seven years — I still had a legal wife. I felt a stab of pain and I didn't know whether it was for Harpur, Anne, Tootie or the old fool Ellis Portal.

She handed me the fax. It was a court order rescinding the peace bond. "All they have to do," Tootie said, "is find your address from your phone number. From that they can find out whether there are any other phones at the same address. And from that, whether any of those phone numbers are for a fax machine. If it *is*, bingo. Piece of cake!"

"You have a fax machine in your *bedroom*?"

"Among other things, if it's any of *your* business," Tootie said sharply. Clearly her tough little self was alive and well under all that clean-faced sweetness.

I decided to hurry even though I didn't relish the thought of going to Riverside Institute. How different from my feelings during the long, long years in which I would have given anything to be in the same room with Harpur Blane, Harpur Stoughton-Melville, Harpur as she had been and would always be somewhere deep in my heart — too deep to change, too deep even to hurt.

Once it was no longer public, Riverside Institute had shed its old image as quickly and completely as an ambitious woman who snags a rich husband. Gone was the concrete drive that had taken such a sharp turn off busy Gerrard Street that cars making the turn ran the risk of crashing into westbound Carleton streetcars. Now an intricate brick drive, something like the ones I used to help my father lay when I was a boy, made a graceful shallow half-circle in front of the building.

Gone were all those 1970s metal-armed chairs with pea-soup fake-leather upholstery. They'd been replaced by genuine antiques in mahogany and rose-toned silk. I found Harpur, when I'd been shown to her room, sitting in a pale-gold leather wing chair. She didn't acknowledge my presence but stared out the window toward the valley where I'd found her the day before. Her wild red hair was now carefully coifed in an upsweep that showed the years had not slackened the fine lines of her jaw and chin, which seemed set like a child's in determination. She was dressed in a slim suit the color of butter. I saw she was wearing the ring like mine. I saw, too, that she was not alone.

"Hi, I'm visiting Harpur today. She asked for me to come back. She keeps calling me 'Jello'. It's bizarre!"

The young man I'd met at the marsh the day before stood up and offered his hand. He had remarkably fine manners for a delinquent. He was still wearing the same clothes — an outfit I was beginning to call, in my own mind, a Tootie Beets suit.

"Are you Italian?" I asked him. With his dark curls and olive skin he could have been from any of the hundreds of ethnic groups of Toronto.

"Yeah, I am. What's that got to do with anything?"

"I'm Italian, too." I didn't explain how and why I had changed my name. It was a long story and since it had to do with being ashamed of my roots, I didn't pride myself on it. "I've known Harpur since we were kids. When I was a kid, 'Gelo' — I spelled it for him — was my nickname. Harpur's a little mixed up. That's probably the only name for an Italian teenager she can think of at the moment."

"Let me get this straight," the young man said in his pleasant and well-modulated voice, "Harpur doesn't think I'm a bowl of sugary, solidified green slime, but instead she thinks I'm somebody she knew fifty years ago. Far out!"

"Forty," I said with a smile. "Forty years ago."

"Impure cocaine."

It was Harpur who'd uttered the words, seemingly out of nowhere. I was mystified, but Gelo seemed delighted.

"That's it!" he cried, "That's the right answer."

He picked up a folded newspaper page and carefully filled in the squares of a puzzle.

"What's that?"

"It's a cryptic crossword puzzle. Ever do one?"

"No."

"Well, it's my hobby. And I'm showing Harpur how it works. She's amazing. You think she's totally spaced out but sometimes she can figure these clues as well as I can."

He handed me the puzzle. It looked like any other crossword. About half the answers were filled in. At the top was printed "Good King Wenceslas". "The puzzle's got a name?" I asked.

"Not always," Gelo answered, "but this one does because it's got a theme. All the clues have to do with the Christmas carol. See, here's the one Harpur just figured out."

He pointed to a clue that said, "Snow lay dinted."

"That's impure cocaine? I don't get it."

"Cryptic clues aren't like regular crosswords," Gelo said. "It's kind of hard to explain but you have to go through extra thinking before you get the answer. See, this says 'Snow lay dinted.' First you have to figure out that dinted means 'dented.' Dented snow. A footprint. In other words, stepped-on snow. 'Stepped on' means that a drug was cut with something — you know, mixed with something that makes it less pure. Snow is coke — cocaine. Therefore, 'Snow lay dinted' is 'impure cocaine.' Harpur is right!"

He laughed, and she did, too. But it wasn't her old, rich, teasing laugh. It was more of a high-pitched cackle. The sound of it caught me off guard. I sought her face. Her green eyes were suddenly locked on mine. But before I could even think what she might want to ask of me, the light in those eyes faded. She turned back to the window and never looked at me again.

The next morning, a Tuesday, I took Queenie out for breakfast at a little diner near her house. There are still quite a few genuine old diners left in Toronto — and a lot of fake ones. This one was the real thing. We feasted on home fries and eggs and bacon and toast with lots of coffee.

"You're gonna get a little pudgy again, Your Honor," Queenie said, "but it'll look good on you. You'll be just as handsome as in them pictures of you from the old days."

"What did you find out about Paulina?" I asked Queenie when she'd finished everything but her toast, on which she was now spreading jam with ladylike finesse.

45

"I found out that part of her insurance settlement deal was free drugs for life."

"What?"

"Yeah. Free prescriptions. She had this card from that big insurance company Rushmore-Something, the one that has that mountain on its writing paper. The way I found out is sometimes she let other people use the card if they needed medicine real bad and didn't have no money."

"Who told you that?"

"Melia's husband. He didn't say so in so many words but I think he might of used it once or twice himself. Which reminds me, he said he used to have a rash like yours and he gave me this free sample of an ointment." She dug through her sweaters to find an opening to her jeans, then presented me with a small white box. The end of the box was open but the safety seal on the tube inside was still intact.

"You think it's okay to use this?" I asked.

"Sure," she said. "The tube ain't been opened. Course it won't be as good as what I done for your rash. You want me to make some more wood-dust powder?"

"No, thanks." I broke the seal, opened the tube and spread a little cream on my hand. I felt an immediate sensation of cool comfort. "Were you able to find out whether there was any note like the one that Melia received?" I was hoping the answer would be no. I hadn't received any more myself.

"I'm still working on that angle," Queenie answered, and I tried hard not to smile.

"You sound like a real detective."

"Your Honor, you've got to get going on this," Queenie said and there was no mistaking her seriousness. "This ain't no coincidence. Two people that know each other die outside when it's hardly even cold, at least to people used to being outside all the time. Somebody's gotta check it out."

"The police are working on it; you told me so yourself."

"They don't care about a couple of down-and-outers like Melia and Paulina. Look, Your Honor, them deaths are connected because Melia and Paulina knew each other from court. You could just go and look around — the way you looked around that halfway house when Moonstar asked you."

"It's not the same thing at all. For me to hang around court would be totally inappropriate. I'm a disgraced judge, for heaven's sake!"

"You ain't a disgraced nothing! It's just in your own head. Lots of people are a former this or a former that. What's the big deal? All you gotta do is look around. I'm asking you as a friend."

She reached across the table and touched my sleeve. It was just the slightest brush of her fingertips against the cloth but I could feel the heat of her body and could feel also that my skin seemed to tingle in response. I was touched so seldom. "Maybe you could just take a little look around the outside of the court. You could go right now. It's eleven o'clock. Everybody will be inside, won't they? Just try it."

I drank the last of my coffee and signalled the waitress to bring the bill. As I counted out the money, I wondered whether this whole matter might not be some sort of ruse. I didn't doubt that the women were dead but I did wonder at Queenie's insistence that they had been murdered. And to use that insistence as a way to get me back in the vicinity of the court might be her way of manipulating me, of reminding me that I was once again without any gain-ful occupation to, as she would say, take my mind off my troubles.

But I couldn't distrust her. One of the great things about having Queenie as a friend was that she was never devi-ous. What she said was what she meant.

"You don't need to be scared," she said. "It ain't the same court."

"I know it's not the courthouse in which I used to work," I answered. "But that's not the point. Somebody might see me."

She rolled her eyes and clicked her tongue. I knew what she was thinking. It could be summed up in two words: so what?

I left Queenie and walked west along Queen Street for a few blocks until I came to the huge Victorian building of dark red stone that had been Toronto's third city hall but was now a courthouse referred to as Old City Hall. It was there I had spent ten years on the bench. Old City Hall was a "lower" court, which meant cases were tried there for misdemeanors, called "summary convictions", and arrangements were made for felonies, "indictable offenses", like murder, to be moved to the "higher" court, often to the courthouse at 361 University Avenue, where Queenie's friends Melia and Paulina had spent their last days.

Contrary to what Queenie might have suspected, to be near Old City Hall didn't bother me that much. There I fit right in, a criminal among criminals. The lawyers and judges with whom I'd worked would have moved on to bigger and better things in the seven or eight intervening years. So would the crooks.

But the higher criminal court — "361" — was a different matter. Ninety judges sat here in the Ontario Court, General Division, at 361 University Avenue. These were plum appointments. In this higher courthouse, there were distinguished justices before whose benches appeared the best-known lawyers. Any one of these people might recognize me, might remember that I'd blown my career by an act of violent stupidity. The thought of running into one of them made me sick to my stomach.

Nevertheless, I kept walking west past Bay Street and crossed Nathan Phillips Square, the plaza in front of New City Hall, a twenty-story structure formed of two curved concrete towers surrounding a low circular pod. A few skaters in bright coats circled the ice rink in the square and my attention was momentarily caught by their lazy, happy movements. But I pressed on. At the western edge of the plaza sat elegant Osgoode Hall, modelled after an eighteenth-century English stately home. Directly north of that lay the 361 courthouse, eight stories of gray cast concrete in a vertical-rib design that made the building resemble a gigantic jail cell. Abandon hope all ye who enter here.

I could clearly see signs that homeless people were squatting on the courthouse grounds. Beneath one of the graceful porticoes of Osgoode Hall, a pile of old blankets partially hid a suitcase and a plastic water jug. There were sleeping bags stashed here and there — under the wide arch that joined the law library to the courthouse, beneath a stone bench by the southern door where a few court constables gathered for their morning cigarettes, behind a low wall that separated Osgoode from the courthouse.

But I saw none of the owners of those sleeping bags nor did I see anyone entering or leaving the court. Nowhere did I detect any sign that the building might figure in the deaths of Queenie's friends. I was thinking that I was wasting my time when I passed under the law library arch from the east and found myself facing the United States Consulate directly across University Avenue.

The sight of the building shouldn't have surprised me. I'd been in the Consulate countless times. My wife was an American citizen. In fact, when I met her thirty years earlier, her father, once Consul General to Toronto, had still been in the diplomatic corps.

But suddenly standing there facing the Consulate, I was overcome with guilt. I had made no effort to find Anne, to straighten out the matters between us, nor to do the thing which most needed doing — to apologize for all my shortcomings.

Depressed by coming face to face with my past, I decided to tell Queenie that I was sorry but my mystery-solving days were over.

A couple of hours later, I was standing on her doorstep rehearsing a speech to that effect, when the door opened and Queenie was standing in front of me.

"Your Honor! I went by Paulina's place after I left you this morning. Somebody else has her room now and they put all them bags with her stuff in them in a dumpster. But I went through them bags one by one. I think I found the note that would connect her to Melia."

"You *think* you found it? What does it say?"

She dropped her eyes and kept them down as she answered, "I don't exactly know, Your Honor, on account of, I don't know how to read."

CHAPTER FOUR

"*The Lord that delivered me out of the paw of the lion, and out of the paw of the bear, he will deliver me out of the hand of this Philistine.*"

"That's what the note says?" Queenie seemed to be having trouble keeping pace with me as we hurried to the familiar warmth of our favorite doughnut shop at the corner of King and Church.

"Another quote from the Bible," I responded. "I just wish I knew the Bible better."

"I know the Bible pretty good," Queenie said, settling onto a stool at the counter and cupping her hands around the mug of tea I handed her. "I'm Anglican."

I glanced at her in surprise.

"Lots of Cree are," she explained. "Moosonee, where I come from, is an Anglican Diocese with a bishop and all."

"Then you know the source of this quote?"

She shook her head. "No. What could them words mean, anyway?"

I studied the bold handwriting. It looked as though it were done with a calligraphic pen. The ink was dark black and the letters were large and well-formed. But again I noticed that for all its boldness, the writing bore unmistakable signs that the hand that had written it had been rendered unsteady. "Maybe it refers to the victim's disfigurement," I offered.

"You mean like how Paulina's face was all messed up?"

"Yes. The paw of a lion or a bear would disfigure a person. And 'Philistine' could refer to the insurance company who failed to give her what she felt was her due or it might refer to the judge who heard the case." I didn't relish the thought that the writer of this note bore a grudge against a judge, or should I have said another judge in addition to myself?

"What's a Philistine, anyway?"

"A good Anglican should know," I teased her. "In the Bible it means an enemy of the people of Israel. But it can also mean somebody who is crass or uneducated or who doesn't appreciate fine things or understand a complex situation."

She wrinkled her nose in a way I was surprised to find endearing. "I'm not sure that fits exactly," she concluded. "But you know, Your Honor, it's funny. We have a saying in Cree: 'The bear is putting his paw over your eyes.'"

"What does that mean?"

"It means the bear is doing something to the hunter to make sure the hunter can't catch him."

I don't know which of us was first to suggest seeing Matt West but I do know Queenie was much more enthusiastic about it than I. At any rate, we decided to walk to Yonge Street, the main north-south street of the city. Its sidewalks were crowded as rush-hour travellers did last-minute shopping and made their way home. The grayness of the weather had given way to the grayness of encroaching night as we headed north to College Street. A few flakes of snow loitered in the still air but they disappeared whenever they touched something solid like a newspaper box, a store window or Queenie's silver hair.

At College Street we crossed to the northwest corner where people richer than we huddled over cappuccinos and lattes at Starbucks. Unlike the dazzling fluorescence of the eateries Queenie and I frequented, the coffeehouse lighting seemed as dark and exotic as the coffee. "You can smell it right out here on the sidewalk," Queenie said. "Smells strong."

As we passed the coffee shop, she nodded to an apparent acquaintance standing on the corner. He grasped a fistful of sticks about two feet long, each one holding a flag. Their bright oranges, yellows and greens seemed to blur in the light haze of snow. "Any country — you name it, I got it," he cried out as he waved his wares, keeping one eye on the crowd and the other on his mobile rack of shelves, with its neat piles. "Invest in the Economy (My Economy). Buy a Flag," his sign claimed.

We trudged on through the crowd. "I used to like that old police headquarters on Jarvis Street way better," Queenie commented when we'd walked past a pub, a restaurant and an office building to get to the new headquarters. "This place looks like a kid built it by piling up a bunch of brown blocks."

"Why do you know so much about police headquarters?" I asked her but it was a foolish question. She'd said all she intended to say on the subject.

"I hope they don't close at five or nothing," she said as we approached the duty desk. The clock said 4:55. At a little distance behind the marble counter, two uniformed officers chatted quietly while a third studied a document. There was no rush here, no bustle; the atmosphere was restrained. The spacious lobby was a cool shade of pink marble. A wide staircase in the same marble swept down from the upper floors where the real police business was conducted. Queenie asked for Matt West and within minutes a tall, muscular black man was walking toward us. I had never met Matt West but because of my previous experience as an amateur detective, I knew more about him than he could possibly be aware of.

Queenie knew him, too, from his days in the Youth Bureau, when he'd made a deal with her daughter, Moonstar, to keep the kid out of jail. Unfortunately for both Matt and Moonstar, the alternative — a stint in a halfway house called Second Chance — had failed to save Moonstar from death in the streets and had indirectly cost Matt his right hand.

Not that one would know by looking at him. He had a way of carrying himself, of holding his right arm so that his sleeve covered his missing hand. It seemed natural that only one hand was visible, the other always in his pocket or behind his back.

"I heard you're in charge of the homeless now," Queenie said.

Matt smiled. When he did, his whole face lit up with warm generosity. But there were other things in that face, too. I could see wary sorrow in his dark green eyes. And I could also see the toughness of the man, as if behind the smile his teeth were clenched and his jaw frozen. He looked like the kind of person whose every private moment was spent thinking about a puzzle he was determined to solve.

He was a man who kept his distance. "Mrs. Johnson, how can I help you today?" he asked formally.

I was so taken aback at the thought of Queenie's legal name being something as prosaic as "Johnson" that I didn't even listen to the presentation of her story to the police officer.

My attention was further drawn away by the decor of his office. I hadn't had any preconceived notion of how it might look, but if I had, I would have expected it to be stark, functional and done in some neutral shade. Instead, Matt West's office resembled the homeless shelters that both Queenie and I had known in less flush days. A threadbare rug that might once have known the fingers of Persian weavers lay over the police-issue broadloom, visible here and there through a number of holes. The rug complemented Matt's desk, an old kitchen table with a blue-and-white enamel top and spindly wooden legs still in their original blue-and-cream paint, chipped and battered by the years. For all its shabby appearance, though, the table was covered with tidy piles of pristine file folders, each neatly labeled in small, clear, precise writing that matched the writing in his open memo book. The writing told me that the hand he'd lost was not the one he wrote with. I wondered if he considered that a mercy.

In the corner of the office, another battered old wooden table held a small institution-type coffeepot, a box of doughnuts open beside it.

On the wall, Matt had tacked dozens of articles and photos from magazines and newspapers, all about the homeless being so often the victims of crime. But there was something unpredictable about the pictures. I studied one of a striking, dark-haired man crouched under a blanket as though he were on his haunches. Anybody seeing that photo in the office of a task force police officer would have thought the photo was modern, a potential client down and out on the Toronto streets. But I knew differently. The photo was a reproduction from 150 years ago. The "homeless" man was really the great Victorian explorer, Sir Richard Francis Burton, and his wanderings without shelter were in the deserts of the Sind.

I was thinking about that when, among pictures of people clearly from the streets of today's Toronto, I caught a glimpse of another crouching man. This one stared out at me from a photo torn from the *Toronto Daily World*. He squatted beside a tar-paper covered packing crate beneath a tree. Visible behind him was a stream running through a wood but through the trees at the top of the photo, a few highrise buildings could be made out in the near distance. I knew the location. I knew the picture and the man in it. It was me.

"Melia and Paulina," Queenie was chattering on, "they had friends that hung around the 361 courthouse all the time, like they had nothing better to do. They go there every day, these people. There's a name for them. I heard the matrons and the deputies call them something but now I can't remember."

"Groupies," I said. "They are referred to as court groupies."

Matt West shot me a look. "How would you know that, sir?" he asked.

"Common knowledge."

"You see, officer," Queenie interjected, "somebody's just got to go into that court and interview those groupies. They would have the clues you need to figure this all out."

"You, sir," Matt began. He had that cool voice I had once

heard day after day from the police officers testifying in my court, "Who would you recommend we interrogate?"

I thought he was baiting me. I had just accompanied Queenie to give her a vote of confidence. The last thing I needed was police attention. It was true I now had a faxed court order saying that my peace bond had been lifted, but I still didn't want to take any chances. Not to mention the general feeling I had, the kind that never leaves a person who has once lived on the skids, that contact with the police was best reserved for dire emergencies.

"I just came with her. I've got nothing to do with this."

Matt West said nothing for a long minute. He played with a large paper clip, turning it end over end in the adept fingers of his left hand. I suddenly had a flashback to the day I had seen his other, severed, hand for the first and last time. I noticed he wore no rings.

"Mrs. Johnson," he finally said, "I appreciate your coming by with this information. You can be sure we'll check out anything we feel might be helpful in this case. In the meantime . . ."

He pulled open a little drawer in his desk, a drawer I couldn't help reflecting must have been designed originally to hold silverware. He took out a business card with the distinctive red-and-blue design incorporating the seal of the Toronto Police. "You call me right here at this number if you think of anything else."

I had used that ploy a million times in the old days when I needed to give somebody the brush-off. It doesn't do a bit of good to give a person a private number if that number hooks right back into the main number after four rings. And I never knew a cop who answered his or her phone in four rings. In the old days, such callers would have been bounced back to an operator. Now they get lost in an endless loop of non-existent conversation called "voice mail".

Queenie smiled and took the card. I didn't like the look of the smile. I was pretty sure I knew what was coming. We slid our way down the handicapped ramp in order to avoid the snow-covered stairs and started to walk eastward on College Street, past her friend who greeted our return with a lazy wave of the flag of Portugal. "Half price," he said.

But Queenie didn't even hear him; she was gearing up to let loose. "Some head of the homeless he is! We might as well rot in the streets. He didn't even ask to see them notes when I told him! Can you believe that? He don't care at all!"

"Queenie, he doesn't think it's murder. Homeless people freeze to death every winter."

"If this ain't murder then what do those notes mean? Answer me that."

It was a good question. One I'd asked myself more than a few times. "Obviously the police don't think the notes were meant as any kind of threat," I answered. Despite the dampness and the arthritis in her legs, Queenie was stomping down the street, even pushing other people out of her way. I got the feeling she'd crossed some line I'd never seen her on the other side of before. "You have to consider the possibility that the notes aren't threats."

"You don't sound like that's what *you* believe about them notes," Queenie challenged. "At least it ain't how it sounded when you read the one about the bear paw and the Philistine."

"There are all sorts of reasons why someone might write down a quote from the Bible," I responded. "There are all sorts of reasons why they might give or send such a quote to another person. Maybe they were just prosely-tizing."

"Huh?"

"Trying to convert somebody to a particular religion."

Queenie thought about that for awhile. The sidewalks were still thick with people. I realized it was only a month until Christmas. I usually didn't keep track of such things. Christmas was just another day to me.

We wove our way among the shoppers and the com-muters, the fresh snow rapidly turning to slush beneath the crush of people's feet. I was thankful for the luxury of waterproof boots. I had not always been so lucky.

"Your Honor," Queenie said as we stopped for a moment in front of the Hudson's Bay store at Yonge and Queen. She seemed to be looking at a large mechanical mouse that moved toward and away from a piece of *papier maché* cheese to the tune of "Deck the Halls," audible through the loudspeakers that broadcast over the side-walk. "Your Honor, you got to do me just one favor."

"Queenie, I . . ."

"Please? Just poke your head in at 361. Take a look at them groupies and see if any of them look like a person that would write them notes. You're a court expert. And don't tell me you're scared or ashamed. You ain't such a baby as that. And don't tell me you're busy, either. You been sittin' on your duff since you left that job at City Hall. Just when you were pullin' yourself up, like, too. You ought to do this for your own good. Plus to catch a killer."

I wanted to tell her no, again. I tried to work out an excuse in my mind. But suddenly the last three notes appeared before me. The bizarre notion struck me that maybe the handwriting was God's. *". . . the Lord raised up judges ..." "Behold, I send an angel ..." "... he will deliver me ..."*

I shook away the thought. But I couldn't shake away my guilt at stalling, refusing to tell Queenie that I was too old, too tired.

By the next day, I had a whole new view on the matter. When I got home, there was a letter waiting for me. It was in the familiar bold but shaky hand. And it had come to my rooming house by Priority Mail.

Whoever was writing the notes had found out exactly where I now lived and hadn't wasted any time in resuming the threats.

"Precious in the sight of the Lord is the death of his saints."

CHAPTER FIVE

Toronto police today confirmed that another female "street person" has been found dead under suspicious circumstances, the third in less than a week. The body of the third victim, Anmarie Marsh, was found propped against the fence in front of the Forest Hill mansion she shared with Dr. Hamilton Marsh, a prominent plastic surgeon, before their divorce three years ago. "Foul play has not been ruled out," Detective Sergeant Mattheson West said, "but we are not considering any alleged clues placed in newspaper puzzles."

West was referring to phone calls from the public about a so-called "cryptic crossword" in the weekend edition of the Toronto Daily World, *a puzzle based on the Christmas carol "Good King Wenceslas". "We've had people connect one of the victims who had been a baseball player with the clue 'a good league hence,'" West said. "Others pointed out that Rushmore-Secure, a company with a mountain as its logo, was associated with a victim 'underneath the mountain.' We believe these are mere coincidences."*

* * *

"I told you. I knew it. The police won't listen to us because they're up to something."

"Please, Queenie, I'm not quite up yet."

She was standing outside my bedroom door, Tootie Beets beside her in a strange ensemble of flannelette pajama bottoms, a black leather vest, earrings shaped like spiders and pink rollers in her ink-black hair. "I tried to keep her out, but she pushed me," Tootie explained. "I don't know why anybody in this house has to get visitors before 8:00 A.M."

"I'm sorry," I said to Tootie, "we'll be more considerate in the future."

She nodded and shot me a look that seemed to say that she expected no less from people who lived under her roof. I couldn't help but smile.

I ushered Queenie in. I was in a state of semi-dress myself. Blue Jays sweatshirt, boxer shorts and wool socks. Grim as her message was — Queenie had come to shove the *Toronto Daily World* article in my face — she still managed to take careful note of my appearance. "You sleep in that get-up?" she asked.

"It didn't occur to me I'd have to receive visitors before I had a chance to dress." I didn't like the testy sound of my voice. It's taken me a lifetime to learn patience, and now that I've nearly succeeded, I don't like even small lapses.

"This ain't a visit," Queenie retorted. "It's business."

"Whose business?"

"Yours."

I shook my head but I motioned for Queenie to take a seat. There was only one chair in the room, a straight-backed 1920s kitchen chair that seemed to have had a thick coat of glossy white paint applied to it every couple of years.

I sat on the bed. It too was vintage, from the forties. I admired the stylish thrift with which Tootie had decorated the house. *How did she learn to run a rooming house?* I thought for the tenth time. As I studied the newspaper Queenie had handed me, the pink light of dawn was turning to the yellow light of morning through my only window. It glinted on the few items I'd collected for my personal grooming, lined up on the windowsill: a shiny black ceramic mug, a small glass that held my toothbrush, a hairbrush and comb I'd bought at Shoppers Drug Mart on St. Clair.

I was about to ask Queenie whether she knew Anmarie Marsh when my eye fell on the sentence, "Anmarie Marsh spent a brief period behind bars following a conviction for credit-card fraud."

I put two and two together. "She's another one of the hangers-on at the court, isn't she?"

"Yeah. But it ain't the 'public' that's come up with the idea that this person's death is connected to Melia. The cops did. And you can bet there's more to it than what the police tell the papers."

There was. Including the note I'd added to my pile the night before. I wondered whether there'd been a note discovered on the body of the latest victim.

I shot Queenie a glance but she wasn't looking at me. She was at the window watching the sky as the last traces of pink disappeared into brilliant blue. The bare tree branches of early winter framed a cityscape of rooftops and backyards. "It ain't really winter yet," Queenie said, "but soon it's gonna be real cold. When that happens, a few people are gonna freeze to death. I wonder if the cops are gonna think that's some kind of puzzle, too."

I rose and stood behind her. The top of her head came up to my chin. Her hair smelled of sweetgrass smoke, and I knew that meant she'd been "smudging", ritualistically burning fragrant dried grasses and herbs, then directing the smoke over her body so that the spirits could enter and guide her. That these beliefs did not spar with her Anglican beliefs was a mystery to me. Her fingers absently traced the peeling paint on the windowsill. "Somebody wrote words here," she said.

"What?"

"Here on the windowsill, a long time ago. They're covered in paint but you could still see the letters."

I leaned closer. I adjusted my reading glasses to make out the faint tracings she was pointing to, and when I saw what the two words were, I started.

"Hey — you jumped. Like somebody was walkin' on your grave. What's wrong? What do them words say, anyhow?"

"It's a name and it *is* from a long time ago, more than twenty years, I'd say. The name is Ellen Portal."

"Your girl?" Queenie was astonished. "How can that be?"

"I used to live here. I used to own this house. Ellen was rambunctious — not like her brother Jeffrey. She must have carved her name."

"Wow," Queenie said. "You used to own this house, now you rent a room? You really ought to get it back together, Your Honor."

She was right. "Queenie," I said, turning from the window, folding the newspaper and handing it back to her. "You've got a point. I can't promise you anything but I'm

64

willing to try and get into the courthouse. In the meantime, I want you to tell me something."

"What?"

"How did you find out where I live? I didn't tell anybody."

A strange look passed swiftly over her features, as though she suspected I'd intended to insult her, then decided I wouldn't do such a thing. She smiled, "You think I used some kind of Indian trick to track you? Smelled your footsteps or something like that?"

"No, of course not. I'm sorry. I didn't mean . . ."

"Forget it. It's got nothing to do with the old ways. I got your address from the Internet."

"The Internet!"

"Yeah, they got it at the shelter. You can pretty much get the address of anybody that's got a phone."

She was already out the door and halfway down the block before I thought to wonder how a person could get information off the Internet when she was unable to read.

I suppose a lot of people wonder why I just walked away from being a judge. I can explain it in two words: criminal conduct. But of course, whenever a thing can be explained in two words, there's a lot more to it than meets the eye.

Be that as it may, by the time I stepped down from the bench, I'd been a judge in the "Provincial" or lower criminal courts for ten years, and I was used to, as they say, "the powers and privileges thereunto appertaining." A half-dozen years of roughing it have dulled my memory but I do recall how it felt to walk into a room and have a momentary breath of respectful silence descend upon the crowd, almost a gasp of surprise. And I remember how it felt to be driven up to the sculpted stone portico of the Windsor Club with Stow, who had proposed me for membership, and have a bevy of service people attend to one's arrival, moving in the way good domestic workers always move, seemingly able to run and stand still at the same time.

And, absurd as it may be, I remember the "uniform". Not only the heavy black silk judge's robe with its scarlet sash that hung from my shoulder, crossed my chest and fastened at my waist, but also my own personal attire — the tweed and camel's hair of my coats, the soft mellowed linen and silk of my handsewn monogrammed shirts: E.G.P. Ellis George Portal. A self-made name for a self-made man.

I remembered these things as I stood in the thrift shop at St. Clair near Bathurst in a bustling neighborhood where Italians, Chinese, Jamaicans and other ethnics patronized rows of small shops bursting with cheap produce, clothing, flowers, office supplies. The thrift shop was busy even on a Wednesday afternoon, and I felt the familiar odd sense of urgency one has in shopping at an establishment where everything is incontestably one of a kind.

I poked around in a large wooden bin and pulled out the item I'd come for: a hat to pull down over my brow in order to avoid meeting the eyes of anyone when I walked the halls of the court house. The hat I happened upon was a fine one, a dark brown Stetson fedora, not much different from the one I'd seen on the pimp. It was a little the worse for wear, having spent who knows how long at the bottom of a heap, but I punched it and pulled it back into a semblance of its original shape, paid two dollars and wore it out of the store.

To a person as used to long treks as I, the forty-five-minute walk down Avenue Road past the Provincial Parliament building at Queen's Park and onto stately University Avenue was a mere stroll.

As I crossed the busy plaza in front of the courthouse at 361 University, I fought back a sudden wave of nerves-induced nausea. I pulled down my hat brim and scanned the crowd. Though it was only a month until Christmas Eve, there was plenty of outdoor activity. In a round yellow tent, a hot dog vendor skillfully juggled hot sausages, buns, drinks and money. A long line of teenagers, students from high-school law and civics classes, filed through the front revolving door of the building. A slender woman with dark hair and sultry beauty in a stylish gray wool coat breezed out another door. She seemed to be headed right toward me, and for a panic-stricken minute, I thought she might be an old associate. When she looked up, I was relieved to see she was a complete stranger.

As busy as the front plaza had been, the courthouse itself was even busier. But its spacious modern halls seemed somehow to absorb the bustle. Built in the early 1960s when everything new was considered better than anything old, the building had none of the art nouveau charm of Old City Hall where I had sat in judgment on petty crooks. Old City Hall dated from the 1890s and was three stories of perfectly preserved turn-of-the-century extravagance. Curving sweeps of carved wood, contrasting shades of parquet flooring, intricate curls of floral-motif wrought iron, cage-type elevators, marble staircases, windows of all descriptions, including stained glass two stories high. The public areas of "361", in contrast, were completely devoid of ornamentation. The walls were cold white marble, the floors white terrazzo.

Up the center of the main lobby ran two stainless steel escalators. There wasn't a window or a staircase in sight.

Every lawyer who appears in the courthouse at 361 University Avenue is required to be robed. The robe consists of gray trousers for men, a skirt for women, in "legal stripe", a wide stripe of darker gray. Over the trousers or skirt, legal counsel wear a tight-fitting long-sleeved black jacket that reaches the waist and buttons down the front. From beneath the jacket peeks a white linen shirt with a small stand-up pointed collar. White "tabs," short pieces of linen descending from the collar, add a touch of brightness. Over all this is a flowing black robe with big sleeves adorned with a row of buttons at the cuff. The robe's wide smocked yoke gives the appearance of very broad shoulders. Lawyers, like warriors, need to seem larger than they really are.

Attached to the back of the left shoulder of the outer robe is a peculiar Y-shaped piece of matching black fabric. Ask a lawyer and he or she will tell you that they have no idea what this piece of fabric represents. I once asked a court hanger-on, however, and he told me that the legal robes date from medieval times when lawyers wore back shoulder purses into which clients put payment. By pretending to be surprised by recompense, the lawyers kept the appearance of serving justice without serving themselves. I don't know how true that is, but it makes a good story and there is no place in which a good story is more welcome than a court.

I have never seen a man or woman whom the lawyers' robe did not flatter. It makes fat men look thin, skinny women look shapely, tall people look short and short people look tall. However, fashion is a secondary consideration. A robe is worn to maintain the dignity and honor of the court. A lawyer cannot be "heard" unless he or she is fully robed. An unrobed lawyer is ignored by the judge and treated as if simply not there.

The lawyers seemed more of a threat to my anonymity than the students, until I saw how young they all were. Once in awhile, I saw a face I thought looked familiar, but after awhile, *everyone* began to look like someone I'd seen before. What was familiar was not any one person, but the feel of the place. The courthouse bristled with a kind of hopeful and purposeful energy. People hurried into and out of little knots, often centered on one of the robed men or women, as if everyone had a stake in something big. Everyone wooed the law and sooner or later, the result of their devotion would become known to all. The courthouse was like a gambling casino. The losers went to jail. The winners walked free. The innocent called winning "justice". The guilty called losing "luck".

It was just after 2 P.M. when I glanced at a clock on the wall over a long desk to the top of which the day's "sheets" or court schedules were taped. Spectators and students scanned the sheets while lawyers and clients lounged near the escalators or sat on the blue plastic chairs bolted to the marble walls, waiting for the uniformed court staff to unlock the courtrooms.

I thought that I'd take things slowly. I thought I would just go in, sit down, look around and see how I felt.

There were no courtrooms on the first floor, so I went up to the second and buried myself in a small crowd, hoping to slip unnoticed through the main door at the rear of a courtroom. Though uniformed staff unlocked the doors with an official flourish of jingling keys, there was no security check. Nobody asked me a question or even looked at me that closely. Nor were any of the court staff armed, including the special police officers, "blueshirts", who guarded the glassed-in prisoner's dock in the center of the courtroom.

Despite the stark modernity of the courthouse, I had to admit that the courtroom was imposing. Seventy feet long, fifty feet wide and thirty feet from carpeted floor to white-painted ceiling, the room was panelled in wide sheets of matched oak from a single tree. The judge's bench was raised ten feet on a dais. Behind it, a gold-veined marble slab twenty-five feet wide rose from floor to ceiling. On the slab, a white unicorn and a golden lion flanked the royal shield of Great Britain. For some reason, the white unicorn was in chains.

Although a spasm of nervousness rippled through me, I felt almost at ease as a spectator with no duty in the court, no function except to watch. I sat as near to the rear as possible, on a hard oak bench. Before my bottom even touched wood, however, I felt a rush of air against the nape of my neck and heard a whispery, mature female voice in my ear uttering a single syllable: "Hat!"

I jumped. How could I have forgotten something even the most callow of students would know? A courtroom is like a church: A man is not allowed to wear a hat.

I took it off, smoothed my hair. I glanced over my shoulder at the whisperer. The main door was now being guarded by a "matron". She wore the uniform of a "Court Services Officer": gray trousers, white shirt, blue-and-gold striped tie, blue blazer. But her blond hair was glamorously curled and her long red nails shone incongruously against the business-like cuffs of her shirt. I suspected working in the courts was her second job.

My attention was diverted by a sharp knock at the front

of the room. A door to the left of the bench opened a crack. "Order! All rise!" I heard a deep, gruff voice declare.

I had not heard those words in that majestic tone for the better part of a decade. It sent a thrill through me — not sorrow or regret, as I had feared, but a feeling less personal and more profound. Respectfully, I stood. The aging deputy, also in the uniform of the Court Services Officer, opened the door fully and stepped back. There was a flash of black, red and white. To my astonishment, the judge who entered was a woman much younger than myself. She did not wait for the deputy to seat her but sat herself as the court clerk, also robed in black, announced that court had resumed.

The matron with the scarlet nails led a witness to the stand. No jury had been summoned, and I realized I was watching a case tried by judge alone. The judge wore only slightly less makeup than the matron and she had piercing eyes that scanned the courtroom. I felt a moment's apprehension when her gaze seemed to seek mine but I assured myself she could have no idea who I was.

I studied the people in the courtroom. Those in robes — Her Honor, the prosecutor for the Crown, the Defense, the clerk or registrar — seemed unlikely to know the court groupies. The uniformed staff — the blueshirts, the matron and the deputy — was a better bet. It was their job to keep an eye on the room. Almost by definition groupies were regulars. Anyone who worked the courts every day would know regular court watchers.

Short of becoming a groupie myself, an appalling thought, I didn't see any way of getting close to the court staff.

Nor did I have much luck observing the observers.

Long lines of high school students, remarkably silent in their expensive heavy boots, filled the wooden benches, listened for ten minutes until they were bored and tiptoed out again. No one was allowed to sit in the front row directly behind the prisoner's box. But, at the front to the side, a woman in a thin, cloth coat and poorly bleached hair sat as near as she could to the far wall, an angle from which it was easiest to catch the eye of the accused without risking a reprimand. In my court I had seen whole families huddled in such a spot, wanting that small contact with a loved one in custody. But a judge tries not to notice such things lest pity pollute justice.

It was nearly 4 P.M. before the main door cracked open, its squeak silenced by the matron's hand, and a genuine groupie slipped in. It was a woman I recognized from my Old City Hall courthouse. Involuntarily, I slid down in my seat. The years had served the woman better than they'd served me. She must have been in her seventies but she had the slim build and upright carriage of a younger woman, and her auburn hair was unmarked by gray. She wore a suit and only those who knew how to look carefully would know she was poor. I saw that she wore no boots despite the winter weather, that her shoes were misshapen by dampness, that try as she might, she had been unable to completely remove their salt stains. I saw, too, that she carried a tattered notebook into which she wrote with meticulous attention. I noticed that for the sake of avoiding undue attention, the matron didn't ask her to stop taking notes, even though it was against the rules for anyone except lawyers, police and reporters to write when the judge was on the bench.

During the long days of my life as a vagrant, observation had become my hobby, my passion. But it was a trap.

Who might be watching the watcher? I had not felt the eyes of the matron on me, but as she resumed her position at the door after escorting a witness to the stand, she flashed me a look. I saw that little dawning of interest pass over her features, that revelation that the eye is about to call deeply upon the memory. It was time to leave.

I had learned nothing that afternoon and I didn't relish admitting it to Queenie. I was framing excuses when I turned onto my street and saw that three people were standing on Tootie Beets's front porch.

One of them was Tootie herself. I saw her shrug her shoulders, evidently in answer to a question. She was dressed in her accustomed manner but her gestures lacked her usual sharp belligerence. I understood why almost at once. The man to whom she spoke was well-groomed and tall. He was also black. This was no boyfriend. This was Detective Sergeant Matt West.

Matt and Tootie were not alone. A smaller man in a fine camel's-hair coat listened intently to what they were saying. He wore tan leather gloves and held a slim leather briefcase. I could tell even from the distance of half a block that the coat was Armani and the briefcase Gucci. I would have guessed the gloves, too, but I had no intention of getting any closer.

Instead, I turned and fled to the one place I knew I'd be safe from all these people who had suddenly crowded into my solitary life.

CHAPTER SIX

By the time I got to the stairs into the valley, there was nothing left of the sun except an angry orange gash behind the twisted black branches of trees and the distant silhouettes of skyscrapers.

I felt as if everything were spinning around me: Queenie and her dead friend, little Tootie Beets and her odd male twin Gelo, the city with its horde of hard memories, the court with its stolid reminders of what I once had been.

When I had first come to the valley, I had been not only the perpetrator of a criminal assault, I had been the victim of my own grueling ambition. Ruthless, driven and driving, I had risen from my Italian immigrant roots to the upper echelons of the legal profession. For my pains I had reaped money and respect. But like so many others, I had lost as much as I had won. By the time I ran away from the bench, I was a stranger to my loved ones and a grim familiar of alcohol, cocaine, sex and regret.

The day I came to the valley half a dozen years before, I was probably, as the courts would have it, "incapable of forming intent." That is, I was the confused ex-patient of a mental hospital just finishing six months of living on the streets. I had come that day as I came now just to get away briefly from the kaleidoscopic sights and sounds of the city. Without really intending to, I had stayed and made a strange new life for myself in company with the homeless that live hidden among the 1000– acre forest that stretches along the river valley north from the lake toward the headwaters in the vast reaches of rural Ontario.

But, I was relieved to realize, a walk of an hour or two was now sufficient to bring calm clarity back to my mind. Over my shoulder, low in the east, I could see the most beautiful constellation of the winter sky, Orion, with his belt of stars. To me, he was a hunter banished to the sky, but Queenie knew a different tale. To her, the constellation was the stern paddler of a great canoe of which Polaris, the North Star, was the bow paddler. In their canoe they carried the whole sky and all the creatures made of starlight. They seemed to watch over me until I turned back and headed up from the depths of the valley.

As I mounted the stairs and took the footbridge to Broadview Avenue, I glanced south and saw that the lights in most of the rooms of Riverside Institute were still shining brightly. I had lost track of the hour but I knew Alzheimer's sufferers often do not distinguish night from day. I decided on impulse to see Harpur.

As I slipped through the revolving doors at the main entrance of the hospital, I caught a glimpse of my reflection. Before I'd gone into court, I'd stopped off for a quick haircut. My hair was trim at the sides and fashionably long on top. The style seemed to set off my face in a way that reminded me that I had once been considered a handsome man, solidly built with olive skin and dark hair that was now completely gray. My thrift-shop coat was neither camel's hair nor tweed, but it sat easily on my shoulders. I flattered myself that it made me look rather lean and, though not as muscled as I'd looked when I'd worked out every day, at least not as emaciated as when I'd been a homeless bum.

There had been a time long ago when the thought of entering a room in which Harpur waited would have filled me with terror. Terror that I would look wrong, say the wrong words, be the wrong person, maybe even the last person she wanted to see. I found my fingers shaking a little when I raised my hand, knocked gently on the door of her room and softly cried, "Harpur?"

I jumped back when, instead of hearing her voice, I was suddenly facing Harpur herself, her beautiful face pale, her startling green eyes vivid. As if I had flown back through all the years in which she had been the stunning, unreachable wife of Stow, I stood before her as I once had — young, awkward and as hopeless in my manners as in my love.

"Don't just stand there like an idiot. Come in." She gestured with a broad sweep of her hand as if the pathetic sickroom were a mansion. "And hang up that dreadful coat."

As I passed, I smelled her perfume. The fruity, rich French scent that I had always associated with Harpur had been replaced by something light with a hint of lavender. It was too old a fragrance, too passive. Someone else had to have chosen it for her. She wore a robe of dark green silk, wide at the shoulders and narrow at her waist. Her red hair was bound in a black silk ribbon and she had a flawless manicure. Her embossed gold ring, just like

76

mine, looked gigantic on her frail fingers. My heart knotted with pity and old longing.

"Where's your young friend tonight, Harpur?" I asked, not knowing what else to say.

"I don't know. Maybe it's time for bed."

"You seemed to be enjoying his visit last time."

She didn't answer and a shadow crossed her face. She began to twist the gold ring around absently on her slender finger.

"Ellis," she said softly, her deep voice little more than a murmur. In the background I could hear hospital sounds: voices, carts and chairs being wheeled, loudspeaker music now and then interrupted by officious voices. I leaned closer and caught again the weak, sad scent of lavender.

"Yes, Harpur?"

"Do you remember the day Stow gave us these rings?"

I fought the urge to reach out and stop her twisting hands. I could never touch Harpur, not since I'd gone to jail for attacking her. And besides, I didn't want her to see the rash on my hands. Instead, I nodded. "Of course I remember. It was the day that Stow, you, William Sterling, Gleason Adams and I became lawyers, more than thirty years ago."

"We were so beautiful," she said almost in a whisper.

"You're still beautiful, Harpur."

I meant it and she saw that I did and her face lit up with a teasing light. "You're in love with me, Gelo. Always will be. That young man who comes to see me — I call him 'Gelo', too. It confuses him."

"Yes. But *you* know what the name means. You called me that long before the day that Stow gave us these rings."

"Promises came with them," she said, twisting her ring even more feverishly. I glanced at the space next to her on the bed. I wanted to sit beside her. But she was the wife of a Justice of the Supreme Court. And she was Harpur. My old hopeless love flared with a pain dulled only slightly by memory and age. I pulled the chair a little closer to the bed.

"And all the promises were the same," she recited, in the way in which a child recites an often-told tale. "We each promised that all the others could ask us once and only once for a favor that could not be refused, no matter what."

"It seemed like such a simple thing to say, didn't it, Harpur?"

"Stow got you out of jail," Harpur said, raising her eyes and letting them meet mine.

"Yes. I still owe Stow a favor."

"You owe *me*!" Harpur almost yelled. "Don't you forget that. People have to pay their debts or they will learn a lesson."

"And there will be no more favors from William and Gleason."

"Forget about dead people, you fool. Stow doesn't owe you. I don't owe you. But you owe us. You owe both of us."

She stood abruptly and pulled tight the belt of her robe. I noticed again how very thin she was.

"Get my girl in here."

"What?"

"Wake up, Ellis! Just call out the door and tell one of the nurses that I *need my girl*!"

I didn't know what she was talking about. I opened the door and looked down the corridor, hoping to catch the attention of a nurse. The only person I saw was a volunteer wheeling a cart of books along the hall. "Yes?" she said. "Can I help you with something?"

She was a plain, pleasant, soft-spoken middle-aged white woman, the archetypal hospital volunteer.

"Mrs. Stoughton-Melville needs some assistance," I explained. "Could you please get a nurse?"

"No need for that. I can help her myself," the woman said sweetly. I was rather surprised at this, coming as it did from someone with no authority. But then, I had no authority there either. Or anywhere, for that matter.

"I know what Harpur likes at this time of night," the volunteer said. "Let me."

She wheeled her cart into the room, parked it beside the bed, walked over to where Harpur was standing and took both Harpur's hands in her own. "Sit down, Mrs. Stoughton-Melville. Relax. Be calm. Everything is just fine."

"Get this man out of here and get my girl this minute," Harpur insisted. "The party is tomorrow and we have to make the list."

"Everything is all arranged, Madame," the volunteer cooed. "Sit down quietly here and I'll read to you. What would you like to read tonight?"

"The same one as last night," Harpur answered. It dismayed me to hear that while she was definitely calming down, her voice seemed to have deserted her with her lucidity. Instead of the strong, teasing tones tinged with mocking arrogance, I suddenly heard the voice of a child. But not of the child Harpur. No. I heard whining submission and I hated it, though it didn't seem to bother the volunteer.

"Which book?" I heard the volunteer ask Harpur as she

smoothly and simultaneously handed me my coat. I took the hint.

"This one." In a whining baby tone Harpur added, "Not *that* one. I don't want *that* one."

Just before I stepped into the hall, I turned back to glance at the women. It was then that I saw the two books that Harpur was choosing between. One was a children's book with large garish illustrations of monsters and elves.

The other book was the Bible.

CHAPTER SEVEN

Somewhere in the distance a great orchestra played. I strained to hear it but the harder I listened, the more the music was marred by a discordant drum. I decided to find the orchestra, but my way was soon blocked by a rushing torrent of water that threatened to rise higher than my head. I could feel the wetness against my chin, my cheek, my bottom eyelids. I blinked hard and opened my eyes on what at first seemed total darkness. Then I turned my head toward my window and saw a tiny sliver of red cutting the black sky.

I have not spent much of my life waking up in rooming houses, thank God. I found the sounds of morning depressing. The tinny music from a cheap radio. The hacking cough of a smoker. The rushing water of somebody else's shower, which almost certainly meant that my own shower that day would be frigid, despite Tootie's excellent skills at managing the house she had somehow contrived to buy. For one fleeting instant I wondered whether Matt West might be "on the take". Whether Tootie and the man with the briefcase might be involved in drug trafficking. And whether the three of them might be thinking that a disgraced judge would be a handy addition to their team.

It was a mean thought. Exactly the sort of self-protecting negativity I sometimes engaged in when I was growing fond of somebody like Tootie or wished I could confide in someone like Matt.

I turned over and tried to push myself back into sleep. I had never been much of a sleeper until I became a bum. I lay in the warmth of the bed and let myself remember other awakenings. A bitter winter morning, only a thin sheet of styrofoam between me and the snow, breathing air so cold I could feel it all the way to the bottom of my lungs. In a way, that was easier than waking here in such close proximity to strangers. How clean the air of the valley seemed then, though it was only slightly less polluted than the air in the city.

I remembered the sweet satisfaction of steaming hot coffee brewed from ice melted over an open fire. I even relished the memory of having slept with my breakfast bun in my pocket so that my body heat would keep it from freezing during the night. I used to laugh to think that I was lucky that I had no butter and was spared the problem of keeping it from freezing in winter and going rancid in summer.

But sweeter than those memories were others that I tried to push away when they came unbidden after so many years. Memories of waking in this house when it belonged to me. My wife Anne's porcelain-pale cheek tinged with morning's rosy light, her hand beneath her sleeping face. And downstairs, in the kitchen that now housed the cheap utensils of transients, our two children had laughed and bickered and managed to cook us all a decent breakfast. Bacon and coffee. Nothing so peaceful, so hopeful as those mingled aromas first thing in the morning.

I thought of calling Queenie to tell her about my visit to court. It had been nearly a week since she had come up to implore me to leave and I had gotten nowhere. Now, not only had Melia died in the Pits, but Paulina had been found dead on top of her scattered possessions and Mrs. Marsh outside her former mansion. Much as I hated to admit it, if these three deaths were indeed connected, the strongest clue *was* that all the women appeared to have frequented the courthouse. Melia had begged there. Paulina had loitered, determined to snag a judge to listen to her pleas. The Forest Hill wife had gone through the rigors of a criminal trial for fraud; the *Toronto Daily World* article had confirmed that.

Nervous as I had been that someone might recognize me, my little jaunt to the courthouse the day before had whetted my appetite for more. Even seeing the one woman who could be described as a "groupie" made me feel that Queenie might be right about the necessity to observe the regulars.

Later that day, when I went back to the courthouse, I purposely avoided the second-floor courtroom I'd been in the day before because I'd been so sure that the woman who guarded the door had eyed me knowingly. I rode the stainless steel escalator up the center of the lobby to the fourth floor and, in an abundance of caution, walked west along a wide corridor, took a sharp turn left and entered the more remote of two courtrooms that were nestled together off a small hallway. I thought that being in a more intimate courtroom would make observing the observers easier.

I needn't have bothered. First of all, this room was just as large as the one I'd been in the day before. The same expanse of oak panelling met my eyes. Beyond the long rows of wooden benches stretched the bar — a solid wooden railing nearly as high as a man's waist. Inside it stood the glassed-in prisoner's dock with its bolted-down chairs and its iron rings in the floor to secure the shackles of the dangerous.

Between the dock and the judge's bench were large oak tables for the Crown and the Defense. A man about my own age was busily arranging two tiny paper doilies on each table. Between the doilies, he placed a small plastic tray. From a box he took four drinking glasses wrapped in white paper bags. He positioned each glass carefully in the center of a doily.

He and I were the only people in the huge courtroom and he didn't seem to notice me. He kept his eyes on the implements of his trade, which now included a number of stainless steel water jugs, two of which he centered on the trays between the glasses. In the old days, all the court jugs and trays had been sterling silver.

Within minutes, a door beside the judge's door opened and two blueshirts, a slim young man and a sturdy-looking young woman, led the accused into the "box". Without being told, the prisoner turned his back to them and the woman unlocked his handcuffs and hung them on her belt where they dangled beside her mini-baton and holstered can of cayenne pepper spray.

Shortly after 10 A.M. the judge took the bench and summoned the jury. A jury trial would be more interesting to the general public and, I reasoned, more likely to draw spectators than a case tried by judge alone.

The room quickly filled with observers, and they soon had their eyes trained on the third of three doors behind the bench. This door swung open and a tidy line of men and women filed slowly into the jurors' box at the judge's left. For the most part, the jurors were dressed as if at a ballgame — jeans and sweaters. There had been a time in which male jurors were required to wear suits and females to wear hats and white gloves.

As the last juror took his seat, a blue-blazered Court Services Officer stepped through the jurors' door and noiselessly closed it behind her. It was the same carefully made-up woman I'd seen the day before. She bowed in the direction of the bench, then took the matron's chair at the end of the jury box.

I was surprised to see the same matron assigned to different courts. I was used to each court worker permanently assigned to a particular courtroom. If workers moved from court to court as need arose, I might have a hard time avoiding recognition.

Though I had come to watch the spectators, my interest was drawn by habit to the testimony of the witnesses, especially when the accused took the stand. The case was one of assault causing bodily harm; the perpetrator was the grandson of the victim, accused of having broken her arm. He claimed that he had accidentally put pressure on the arm while adjusting a tray on the old woman's chair.

I had no interest in the facts of the case. I had long ago realized that an assessment of so-called fact was not necessarily what yielded truth. I watched the posture of the witness, the way he tilted his head away from the jury, the way he occasionally leaned toward his own lawyer as if he could hardly wait to answer his questions. Was he a little too eager to tell his side of the story? A little too afraid of the men and women called upon to judge what had really happened?

I watched the jury, too. Their faces were unreadable. That was a good sign. It meant they had not yet made up their minds. It also showed that none of them had an emotional investment in the outcome. The judge would soon warn the jury not to consider the consequences of its verdict. Each of us has the power to wreck the lives of other people but few are so aware of that power as the twelve members of a criminal jury.

I was harboring these lofty thoughts when the judge called a recess and was led out of the court by his deputy.

I noted the ponderous grace of the old judge as he slowly exited the court, his black robe not at all ruffled by his movements. He must be, I thought, one of the superannuated justices, a man already retired but returning to do a few months' work now and then. When I had been elevated to the bench, almost all the judges, civil and criminal, had been old men. Appointed at the age of forty, I'd been one of the first of a new breed. Now the courts were full of young judges, many of them women. And a man past fifty-five, as I was, was considered almost too old for such an appointment. The thought was depressing until I reminded myself I had no need to care.

I decided to try another court. The observers in this one were mostly law students — older, more intense and much better dressed than the highschoolers. No one unusual as far as I could see. I was about to turn to head out the door when I felt a tap on the shoulder and heard a hearty voice declare, "Ellis — Ellis Portal. Imagine seeing you *here!*"

My first thought was to run. Behind the bench were the judge's, jurors' and prisoners' doors. If I made a sudden move toward any of those, I'd be apprehended by the guards. They weren't bearing firearms, but they were strapping young people and their mini-batons could do significant damage to my old bones. As for their pepper spray, a shot of that in the face would render the strongest man blind for hours.

There was also a barristers' door but a gaggle of black-robed lawyers was gathered in front of it. That left the main door of the court. There was no escape out that door either, because I soon realized that the person who had called my name was the monitoring court officer.

Was he about to throw me out, or worse, embarrass me by announcing who I'd been and who I now was? Could I, like Simon Peter, pretend I was not the man he thought I was?

"Ellis, it's so good to see you," the officer insisted, and I suddenly recognized him. I turned toward him in astonishment. The last time I'd seen him had been the day I had been interviewed as a prospective member of Stow's club, the Windsor.

I had to struggle to remember his name, but it came. "Harry," I said, "Harry Carleton." I tried to hide my shock at seeing the former president of The National Merchants' Bank in the uniform of a Court Services Officer.

As if he realized what I was thinking, he smiled and gave his head a little shake. "Lo, how the mighty have fallen . . . ," he said.

Was he insulting me or deprecating himself? Whichever, he certainly didn't seem in any way humiliated by the reduced circumstances in which we both found ourselves. In fact, he appeared downright amused.

"Last time I saw you, Ellis, you made quite an impression, as I recall. You used to be an exceptional tennis player. How's your game these days?"

And then he winked.

"Court's down for twenty minutes, Ellis. How about joining me for a break? We can slip down to the cafeteria in the basement, have a cup of coffee, catch up on old times."

It was less embarrassing to accept than to explain why I thought it was a good idea to refuse. I let Harry lead the way.

The cafeteria was crowded with lawyers in their robes, students, jurors in jeans, blueshirts in their police-like uniforms and court service staff in their blazers, gray trousers and white shirts. We squeezed in at a long table with a couple of empty seats at the very end. Everyone greeted Harry as he sat down. They resumed their boisterous conversation without giving me a second glance. "Great bunch we've got working here," Harry said.

I ventured, "The last time I saw you, you were —."

"Ellis," he interrupted, tapping my arm with his index finger in a gesture that I took to be one of friendly confidence, "how do you *think* I got here?"

"I have no idea," I answered, not sure I really wanted to know.

"It's simple. I retired. And like a lot of other people who work here, I got sick of retirement in two weeks. I heard about this job from friends. The pay is a third of what I pay my housekeeper but it keeps me out of the house, gives

me something to do all day. Plus I meet all kinds of people I never met at the bank."

"Cops, criminals?"

"Yes. And decent people in search of justice."

There was a moment's silence. We both sipped our coffee, rather self-consciously, I thought.

"You could work here, too," Harry said, as if he'd had
to think about it before making the suggestion. I guessed
then that he knew exactly what had happened to me.

"Are they hiring?" I didn't know why I asked the question.

"No," Harry said, leaning closer to me. The gesture
reminded me of the way the accused at bar had leaned
toward the Defense. It hinted at something underhanded.
"They're not exactly hiring, but there's a job that's going
begging."

"What?"

"Look, Ellis," he said, "you hit a slippery patch a while
back. Can happen to the best of us. I know things have
been rough. I saw you here yesterday. I was surprised.
Touched, I think you might say. It occurs to me that you
might miss the court life."

He took another sip of coffee. Around us the noise of the
cafeteria was almost a roar but I could hear him clearly
despite the fact that his tone was low. I realized that a
banker must have as many confidential conversations in
his career as a judge has.

"Now that I've been working here a couple of years, I
see things differently. A person comes here. Maybe he is
accused of something and is innocent. He tells his story.
Justice sets it right. Or maybe a person hurts somebody
and thinks she's going to get away with it. But she
doesn't."

"What are you suggesting, Harry?"

"I can get you a job here if you want one."

I laughed and leaned back.

He leaned closer. "No, I mean it. I mean right now. Today. You could walk in here tomorrow morning in uniform. You could be one of us. Nobody would give it a second thought. We have people retired from all kinds of positions. We've even got show people who work here as a day job."

Harry glanced down the table as if to see whether anyone was paying attention. Nobody was. "Ellis, this is a big place. The way the hiring works is that you have an interview with the personnel officers. If they decide in your favor, they put your name on the hire list. Later you fill out your papers and hand them in at the Court Services Office. That's the office that gives out our assignments. First day on the job, a person just shows up, reports that he's been hired, fills out his papers, gets his uniform and goes to work."

"Are you suggesting that I *pretend* I've been hired?" I asked in amazement.

Harry smiled. "In a way," he answered, "but it's not quite as simple as that."

"Then what *are* you suggesting?" I tried to sound indignant. But I was actually excited. As an officer of the court, I would have a much better opportunity to keep my eye on the hangers-on.

"About a month ago, they completed the fall hiring of court officers," Harry explained. "Everybody has started work except two. One is a young woman who wanted to finish a course she's taking before she starts. The other is a friend of mine. He's supposed to start on his fifty-fifth birthday. That's tomorrow. I can call and ask him if he would let you have his place."

"But I can't just show up instead of the man they really hired!"

"Ellis, take my word for it. Nobody will ever know. They'll ask you to fill out a lot of forms, including a contract. You just put down your own name and your own bank account number for payroll." He gave me a furtive glance and I wondered if he were surpressing the urge to inquire if I *had* a bank account — even, perhaps, whether I'd considered taking one out at the bank at which he'd been president. Old habits die hard.

But they do die. I was not as honest as I'd once been. Desperation rounds a man's edges. "Harry, you really think this will work?"

"Trust me. By the time the paperwork gets back to personnel, they'll be unsure who you're supposed to be."

"But if they *do* find out, they'll fire me!"

"So what? At least you'll get a few weeks' work. It's not like you need a good reference for your next job. Besides, if they fire you, you can always grieve it with the union."

"But I don't belong to a union!"

"You will if you fill out the union membership form."

My years of living rough had taught me even more about lying than my years as a judge. I didn't feel the slightest bit apprehensive when I smoothly handed the Court Services manager the employment form with my own name at the top and my own signature at the bottom. So far I'd done nothing illegal. Or even dishonest. I hadn't pretended to be anybody I wasn't. I had just turned up in her office at 2 P.M. that same day and said that I was going to report for duty the next morning and that I had come in ahead of time to fill in the forms and to get measured for my uniform.

"Marnie Alliston," she said, holding her slender hand out for me to shake. I did feel like a scoundrel when she said, "Welcome. I hope you'll enjoy your time with us."

She led me down the hall, turned a corner, held a white plastic card up against a small box mounted on the wall beside a steel door. The box clicked and a little red light turned green. When the door opened, it revealed a stairwell leading in one direction only: down. The heavy steel door snapped shut behind us and the second it did, I was filled with the awful sensation of entrapment.

Had she already figured out that I was getting the job under false pretenses? I had never been in the subbasement of 361 before but I didn't need to be told what was down there. The same thing that is in the lowest reaches of every courthouse in the city: the cells.

It seemed to take forever, but it was actually only minutes before I glanced over Marnie Alliston's shoulder and saw her hold her plastic card against yet another box, this one mounted on the wall at the bottom of the stairs. There was a grinding sound and a section of the wall moved aside. She turned to face me before the panel had slid all the way open. Behind her I caught a glimpse of long rows of gray metal gym lockers not quite as shabby as the rusty, beat-up metal lockers in the public baths I used to frequent.

Marnie smiled at me. "I can't go in there," she said. I thought she had a sweet voice for a public servant. "It's the guys' locker room. I have to wait outside. Tomorrow you'll be photographed for your own passcard, but for now, I'll wait outside."

"I'm not sure why I'm here," I said hesitantly.

Still keeping her back to the open door, Marnie nodded toward the lockers. "My understanding is," she said, "that there is a long rack of spare uniforms against the wall at the back of the room. Pick out a blazer and a pair of slacks to wear until we can get the tailor to come for measurements." She wrinkled her pretty face. "People are supposed to have things drycleaned before they turn them in, but I'd check to make sure if I were you."

On the way home, I stopped at Wal-Mart and bought myself two white shirts to go with the blazer, slacks and necktie I'd carried home from the courthouse. I felt an odd exhilaration at the prospect of having a job. Of course, I *had* worked for the valley restoration crew at City Hall since my fall from grace. But this was different. This was my own turf. Instead of the shame I had expected to feel, I felt excitement. I had been so concerned about not being recognized that I had failed to look around me. When I did, I saw that Harry Carleton wasn't the only distinguished retiree working at the courts. I even saw another ex-judge, a man whose legal career had been more exalted than my own, now working as a defense counsel. And judging from the look of his client, he wasn't handling the top cases of the day!

It had never occurred to me that there *was* life after death; it was called taking another job after retirement. And it certainly sounded a lot better to be a retired judge than a disgraced one.

There was nobody waiting for me when I got home.

And no phone messages, either. I felt a little disappointed. But I hung up my coat and began to unwrap my new shirts. Before I could get the first one on a hanger, there was a knock on my door.

It was a man who identified himself as living in the room next to mine. "Get your butt downstairs now for the monthly house meeting or Tootie will throw you and everything you got out in the street."

Not wanting to face the ire of Tootie Beets, I got my butt down there, and for a little while, I forgot everything else.

CHAPTER EIGHT

No visitors before 8 A.M. or after 11 P.M. No taking other people's food or leaving communal pots and pans behind for others to scour. No going down into the basement to adjust the heat or up into the attic to escape the noise. No excess noise. I was definitely moving up in the world. Tootie Beets's place, she reminded us fervently, was no flophouse. It was, as she put it, "Like, a community thingie."

I was seriously contemplating another hike into the cool quiet of the river valley when I opened the door to my room and saw the red light on my phone flashing eerily in the blackness. I had accepted the phone company's offer of a month's free answering service. I heard Queenie's deep, almost raspy voice when I punched the "speak" key. Recorded, she sounded harsher than in person. I wondered whether machines intimidated her.

"Where you been all day?" the voice said. "I been by for you twice and that tough landlady of yours says she don't know where you got to . . ." There was a pause, almost as if Queenie had expected an immediate answer to her question. Then she drew a big breath, audible on the tape, and dove into her message.

"You and me, Your Honor, we gotta go someplace tonight. Don't worry, it ain't dangerous or nothing." She added the last too quickly for my comfort. Where did Queenie and I *have* to go?

There was another pause and I thought she'd hung up, but I was wrong. There was more to the message. "Bring some cash, will you? We gotta buy something to take with us."

I peeked out my door at the clock down the hall. Seven forty-six. I hoped the ten dollars I had in my wallet would be enough. I grabbed my coat and headed downstairs, nearly knocking over one of my more surly housemates. "Watch where you're going, you stupid old fart!" he snarled. So much for the one big happy "community thingie".

I couldn't see Queenie on the porch. I was halfway down the walk when I felt a tug at the back of my sleeve. I jumped.

"Calm down," she said. "Nothin's wrong. And I ain't sneakin' around. I was just waitin' for you in the shade."

"You mean in the shadows?"

"Yeah — the shadows on the porch."

"Why didn't you just knock on the door?"

She shook her head and raised her hand in a quick, dismissive gesture. "Forget it, Your Honor. We got more important things to think about. We gotta go to a feast."

Queenie had never been a fast walker; her legs always seemed to give her trouble. But my day in court, plus our house meeting, plus all the mystery surrounding this little excursion had tired me out. I had trouble keeping up with her as we headed for the Christie subway station, and I was breathless when we got there. Queenie peeled off three gloves to reveal two small, shiny subway tokens nestled in her palm. "My treat," she said proudly.

We hurried down to the eastbound platform. There was no use asking Queenie to explain if she wasn't prepared to, so I simply followed her, jumping out behind her to change to the southbound train when we arrived at Bloor.

We got off at College station and Queenie used six of my ten dollars to pick up some fruit at a convenience store in the underground level of a shopping mall called College Park. We walked up a wide marble staircase, through a bank of glass doors, and out onto the street. This was the same block police headquarters was on and we even gave a flying greeting to our acquaintance, the flag seller.

As soon as we passed him, I stopped in my tracks and gently pulled Queenie into a doorway. "Enough is enough, Queenie. I've got to know where we're going."

She glanced up at me. A nearby store sign illumined her face with the soft light that cancels shadows and lines. For the first time I saw that Queenie was a pretty woman. She had a way of hiding her face, swinging her hair in front of it or keeping her profile to people when she talked. She had lived with so little privacy for so long that she avoided looking at people straight on. But she was looking at me straight on right now. The prettiness was fleeting, however, and when it vanished, it was replaced by embarrassment tinged with fear.

"Queenie," I said gently, reaching down to push a strand of her hair away from her slightly open mouth, "what exactly is going on?"

She pushed my hand away but her touch was as gentle as mine. She kept her eyes downcast. "Today is American

Thanksgiving," she said. "I know you don't celebrate no holidays, especially if it ain't really a holiday here, but I thought maybe you wouldn't mind coming to a feast — you know, a special supper."

"Are you inviting me?"

"Your Honor, this here feast is a Native thing. Like I told you, I'm Cree. But I got lots of friends from other nations. Tonight we got a bunch that come up from the Tuscarora Reserve down in New York State. Every Thanksgiving, American and Canadian, we share a feast with our American neighbors. This year the Oneida are the hosts. We're gonna have food and stories and prayers."

"Queenie," I said, wishing I could lift her chin and get her to look me in the eye again, "I'm honored to be asked."

She bowed her head even lower and the odd light caught the sheen of her silvery hair. Though she tried to hide her face from me, I caught the trace of a smile crossing her lips. But she willed the smile away. And when she lifted her head and turned her face toward the street, the usual Queenie, guarded, hard almost, said, "Don't get me wrong, Your Honor. This ain't personal. It's business. I asked you to come because we got to get back to work on figuring what happened to Melia."

"What does this feast have to do with that?"

"It ain't the feast that has anything to do with it; it's this place."

She gestured to the glass doors in front of which we stood. The door revealed what looked like the lobby of an ordinary office building. I could see a carpeted area with a row of elevators at the back. In front of the elevators was the semicircular desk of a concierge and sitting behind the desk was a security guard.

Queenie waved. The man waved back and I heard

another one of those clicks I had heard at the courthouse all day. I wondered whether the world would soon be totally without door keys.

"This here is the head office of the New Confederacy of Ontario. A lot of the chiefs of all the Indians in the province got together an organization to fight for rights and things like that. They also do stuff to keep our heritage going."

As we spoke, we headed up in the elevator. Queenie continued, "Two days ago when we saw Sergeant West, he told us that if we remembered anything to get back in touch with him. He said people forget things all the time because they get upset when something bad happens to a friend of theirs, but then later they remember again. Well, I did remember something. I remembered that one day Melia asked me a whole lot of questions about the old ways. She said Paulina was interested. I think they wanted to know about medicine, like herbs or something. So I told Melia about this place. That's because people who know the old Indian languages teach them here. And they teach how to do beads and work with porcupine quills and make baskets and that. I thought maybe they might have some lessons in the plants that the people — I mean the Indians — use for medicine. I thought maybe Melia and Paulina might want to come here."

"And did they come here?"

"Yes. I remember because Melia told me that when she was here she seen a poster about a scholarship for Native girls and she said she felt sad because the poster reminded her about Moonstar and that Moonstar never had no chance for things like that."

Queenie paused for a moment, and I respected the momentary silence to the memory of her dead daughter.

99

"Your Honor," she resumed, "to tell the truth, that's all I remember. But I keep thinkin' that Melia must have been poisoned because she didn't die accidental. She wasn't beat or strangled. She wasn't shot or cut. So what else is left? And if she was poisoned, whoever poisoned her would have to know exactly what Melia was used to eating and taking, don't you think?"

Before I could tell Queenie that she had a point, the elevator door opened. The office of the New Confederacy was modest — standard metal desks and chairs and filing cabinets — but outstanding in its decorations. The Ontario Cree, like Queenie, were Indians of the frigid North. But there were other areas of the province shown, like Point Pelee in the south, where the weather was often mild and the vegetation lush. A bold depiction in oil of three gray wolves swimming in white-and-blue icy water was so realistic as to send shivers along my shoulders. Next to it hung an abstract in brilliant color, the deep greens, lush browns of the forest in summer. Sculptures of bears, wood carvings of hawks, woven tapestries of families of deer showed a deep and abiding respect for creatures that shared the physical world with man. And from the realm of the other world came the ethereal "dreamcatchers" — hoops strung with wire and thread on which shone pale iridescent beads in greens and blues, silvers and pinks, all set off with the fluttering grace of long, soft feathers.

But most amazing to me was the beadwork that recorded the history of the people and, reverentially displayed in a glass case all its own, the notched stick a yard long and two inches in diameter that recorded the entire legal code of an Indian nation. I thought of the court and its majesty. I felt as humble in the presence of this wooden staff as I had felt in the presence of my esteemed brethren on the bench.

"Just keep your eyes open," Queenie whispered, "and your ears, too."

She might have added, "And keep your mouth shut." I wasn't exactly sure whether Queenie suspected someone at the feast but the possiblity of being in the presence of a poisoner dampened my appetite. Though I was led to a table groaning with the richness of the harvest, I didn't feel like eating anything. Which was a shame. Clearly a great deal of work had gone into the preparation of the meal. Gourds, the green and red apples Queenie had bought, squashes and other brightly colored fruits and vegetables decorated the table at intervals. At its center sat a huge steaming pot of rabbit stew, full of chunks of meat, multicolored beans and cubes of squash, carrots, potatoes and turnips. Plates heaped with fat cornbread muffins and thick slabs of homemade whole wheat bread accompanied the stew.

A visiting elder, a woman a little older than Queenie but with a short, stylish haircut, prayed briefly and, as everyone stood in a circle, burned a bit of dried sage in a ceramic dish. I stood awkwardly not knowing what to do. But I soon saw that as the smoking dish was carried by the elder's assistant from person to person, the guests removed their jewelry and also their eyeglasses, then cupped their hands as if to direct the sage smoke toward their faces, over their throats and chests, finishing by holding their hands over their hearts. When the dish came to me, I did the same but I did not take off my ring. Nobody seemed to notice.

I accepted what the women served in what I soon learned was the traditional manner, clockwise around the circle. Queenie, at my elbow, kept up a running commentary on the food. She also told me that the next time I "smudged", I should take off anything that would deflect the spirit in the smoke away from my body.

I pretended to eat, pushing the food around on my plate, still thinking of poison. I watched the other guests at the table, a single slice of one huge tree trunk. They were of both genders and all ages. Not all were Native, but everybody seemed to be wearing small reminders of Native culture — a beaded shirt, a woven headband, a hair ornament of twisted white leather and white and black feathers. In physique the people, both tall and short, seemed solid, and I couldn't keep my eyes off the shiny masses of their black hair. Once Queenie's hair had been that raven color, I thought with a twinge of regret.

Had I seen any one of these people on the street in ordinary clothes, I might have had to look twice to figure out that they were Cree or Ojibway or Oneida or Tuscarora, but seeing them gathered in the context of this festive circle, I felt their dignity, their elegance and the power of the long generations of their practices and beliefs.

"Rabbit stew," Queenie said, offering me a bowl. "Cornbread. Baked squash. Bean casserole. The Oneida call beans, corn and squash 'the three sisters'."

If there were any poison suspects among this jovial, decorous group of people, I didn't notice them. In fact, by the time the meal was over and we had listened to several traditional stories about the coming of winter carried in the great canoe of the sky paddlers, I had nearly forgotten our mission. It wasn't until we had been bid "on^ ki' wah", goodbye, having been warned that the elevator was about to shut down for the night, that Queenie and I were able to talk with one of the workers at the Confederacy who knew about the courses in herbal medicine. "I volunteer here," she told us. "But I only started a few months ago. I don't remember anyone named Melia asking about herbs." She showed us a poster listing the most common plants of the Ontario forests, meadows, beaches and marshes.

"I know a lot of these," I told Queenie. "I used them in the valley. Broad-leaved plantain; that's called 'soldier's herb' because you can use it on wounds. And Pineapple-weed — you can make tea out of that and drink it when you have a cold. And here's Shepherd's-purse." I pointed to a picture of a plant with seedpods in the shape of little valentines. "That they call 'poor man's pharmacy' because it has so many uses."

"But none of those make poison," Queenie pointed out.

"Poison?" the woman repeated. She seemed shocked by the word. But she gathered herself. "We'll be starting a course again next month." She handed Queenie a brochure just as the elevator door closed. Queenie was wearing her heavy winter shawl. Any chance of reaching into a pocket of hers in the near future was slim. So I wasn't surprised when she slipped the brochure into my pocket.

"Hang on to that," she said, "and we'll go have a coffee and talk about it."

"How about the Starbucks down the street on Yonge?" I asked her.

We got our coffees and sat at a small table at the back. Like the other tables in the place, it seemed to be set in a little pool of light all its own.

"Let's see that brochure," Queenie said. "Maybe we can

figure out whether Melia and Paulina took that course. Unless it cost money. Them women never had two cents to rub together."

I reached into my pocket. I pulled out the brochure. Something else came with it, a piece of newsprint folded several times to form a square hardly more than an inch on the side.

"What's that?" Queenie asked.

"I don't know what it is or how it got into my pocket."

Carefully I unfolded the little square and laid the creased paper on the small round table between us. I smoothed the newsprint with the heel of my hand. I had certainly seen it before.

"It's a puzzle."

"Like the one about Good King What's His Name?"

"It's that puzzle exactly," I answered.

"It's all filled in. Why would somebody give you a puzzle that's already filled in?"

"I can't say." But I recognized this as the puzzle I'd seen in Harpur's room, the one she and the boy she called Gelo had been working on. Harpur had plenty of opportunity to slip it into my pocket. Poor Harpur! Hiding objects without any notion why.

Then my eye caught a line of faint writing at the bottom of the piece of paper. The puzzle itself had been worked in ink. Harpur and Gelo were extremely confident puzzle solvers it would appear. The other writing, however, was in pencil. It was so faint I had to dig out my glasses and hold the paper to my nose.

What I read was a single sentence. It said, *"Hope that is seen is not hope"*.

"You look like a ghost just walked over your grave," Queenie said.

I handed the paper to her. I completely forgot that she was unable to read. She took it nevertheless and appeared to study it carefully. I remembered with a pang of pity how many times when I was on the bench I had seen people who were illiterate pretend they could read. Sometimes they guessed what a document said. Sometimes they even guessed correctly. More often, they would study a paper for a very long time, then raise their eyes and say, "I'm sorry, Your Honor, but I forgot my glasses at home."

"What do them words say, Your Honor?"

I took a breath. "They say, '*Hope that is seen is not hope*'."

"*Romans*. Chapter eight. Verse twenty-four," Queenie said almost in a whisper.

"You know this verse?" I asked, surprised.

"Yeah. I go to church every week now. That sayin' is one of our pastor's favorites. He preaches about it all the time. It means you just never know where help is gonna come from." She glanced at me furtively. "It could also mean that when God helps you, you can't expect to be able to see what he's doing."

I didn't appreciate sermons and Queenie knew it but I was impressed.

"There's something about this that scares you, right, Your Honor?"

I tried to find the words to deny it but I wasn't fast enough. Queenie kept talking.

"Because if this ended up in your pocket, it ain't so different from the notes that ended up on Melia and Paulina."

"No."

"So that could mean that whoever gave them notes coulda also gave this to you?"

"Maybe."

"A killer coulda put it in your pocket." Queenie said. It wasn't a question.

We were both silent for a few minutes. A thin wail of recorded jazz cut through the coffeehouse chatter, the clink of china mugs, the hiss of the milk steamer and the espresso maker.

"Nobody in the Confederacy coulda put that note in your pocket. You were practically sittin' on your coat the whole time we were in there."

"Queenie," I reached across the table and touched her hand. She didn't pull away. "I agree. I don't think our being at the feast had a thing to do with this note. I think it's been in my pocket all day."

"Where were you all day, anyhow?" She asked as if she had just remembered how hard it had been to get in touch.

"I was in court."

"You were?" She didn't try to hide her pleasure at the news. "You went there to check things out?"

"I did better than that. I'll tell you all about it. But I don't want to lose my train of thought here. I have to try to remember every place I've put my coat. Last night when I took it off, there might already have been something in the pocket. I had just visited my friend, Harpur Stoughton-Melville, at the hospital. The most logical explanation is that Harpur put the paper in my pocket."

"But who wrote it? Aren't there all kinds of people around a hospital all the time, nurses and that?"

"Yes. And I think I put my coat down on a chair or the bed. I wasn't there for long but I might have hung it up. I just don't remember."

"But what if the note is from the same person and that person is a killer?"

"No matter who the note is from, there's one enormous problem with this theory about somebody murdering Melia and Paulina and that other woman."

"What enormous problem?"

"There was no motive. No reason to kill them. In murder mysteries, characters kill other characters for all kinds of reasons."

"I'm glad I don't read them mysteries." Queenie declared.

"Right. In real life, however, there are only three reasons why people kill. Greed, anger and insanity. What did Melia and Paulina have — or that other poor woman who went to jail for fraud — that anyone would want enough to kill them?"

"Nothing," Queenie conceded.

"And who was angry at them? Not Melia's husband. People like him think only of themselves. I doubt he could get angry enough or interested enough in others to kill them. Oh, he might get worked up about not getting what he wanted when he wanted it, but his type usually only has enough stamina to throw a little tantrum and that's the end of it. As for poor Paulina, *she's* the one who was so angry, not the other way around."

"Maybe it was that way with the other one, too. That she was mad at her husband for marrying somebody else when she got in trouble."

"Right."

"So that leaves crazy," Queenie observed.

"And who did Paulina and Melia know who was crazy?"

I meant the question sarcastically but Queenie seemed to take it with the greatest seriousness. I could almost see her running through all of Melia's and Paulina's acquaintances.

"There's a lotta weirdos in the courts, Your Honor. You know that better than anybody." She looked me right in the eye and said, "All we gotta do is find a crazy person who hangs around the courts and figures they got a motive to kill *you*."

CHAPTER NINE

I told Queenie about my new job. I still felt uneasy about having acquired it under false pretenses, but not Queenie. She was a street fighter whose attitude was what you can get is what you ought to have. She thought I was a genius to have achieved the job the way I did, but then, she thought I was a genius, anyway.

And I was beginning to think quite highly of her mental powers, too. Which is why I was reckless enough to agree that the two of us should work together in keeping our eyes on the courthouse at 361 University Avenue, or more precisely, at *who* was frequenting that courthouse and what they were doing there. Within the first week of my commencing my official duties and Queenie commencing her unofficial ones, we already had identified a core cadre of groupies. Not all of them were destitute; not all were mentally unbalanced; not all were people without any education or profession. But there wasn't a totally "normal" person among them.

Queenie and I soon worked out a system. I was technically in training, which I had thought would mean some sort of classes or at least monitored observation of what I was doing in court. Since my supervisor had no notion who I really was, she could have no way of knowing that I needed neither classes nor monitoring, which was just as well because as it turned out, there were none. Instead, my training consisted of being plunked into and hauled out of as many courtrooms as could be managed in a single day. I've never been a watcher of television, but I began to feel as if I were at the mercy of a remote control that could stop my viewing just when the show became engrossing.

Court Services Officers were authorized to enter the heavy security doors on each floor by means of their plastic keycards, but the area behind those doors, where the jury rooms, the prisoners' elevator and the internal staircase were, would be out-of-bounds to Queenie. Each courtroom had separate doors for the judge, jury and prisoners behind the bench, and a barristers' door just past the bar. The public entered only by the main door at the rear. Outside the courtrooms on each floor, the public was pretty much confined to the central area by the escalator and a corridor with witness rooms running along the north of the building.

Since most people used the escalators, that left one public area of the courthouse relatively untravelled. This was the so-called fire stairs, an enclosed stairwell that ran eight floors from the cafeteria on the basement level up to the most modern courtrooms, the new ones on the seventh floor. All anyone had to do to gain access to this stairwell was to open the fire door, which was never locked. It seemed the perfect spot for Queenie and me to meet.

"I got three," she told me on the Tuesday of my first week on the job. "One seems like some sort of minister or something. He's got that do-gooder kind of voice — you know what I mean?"

I nodded, "Sugary?"

"Yeah. Soft and sweet like he's gonna reach up and give you a smack on the cheek!" She brushed an imaginary kiss away from her dusky skin. "Wears a suit every day, too. I don't think he's a priest. More likely a preacher. Maybe even a Baptist."

"Why would you say that?"

"Oh, they always got this little smile on their face like everything's just dandy because we're all going to heaven just as soon as we see the light."

"Maybe we are, Queenie."

"Only if God is a Baptist!"

I smiled but that was the extent of my response.

"You said three, Queenie. Who else have you got?"

We were leaning side by side, our backs against the wall, on the landing between the second and third floors. I thought I heard a heavy door whoosh open and snap closed above us. Queenie started, too. I had been told there were cells above the seventh floor even more closely guarded than the ones in the sub-basement, but I hadn't met anyone who had actually seen them.

We waited in silence for a minute, but nobody came and there were no further sounds.

"The minister, he may be temporary," Queenie explained, "doing some kind of mission work or something. But the other two are permanent for sure. One is a middle-aged woman. Looks like a librarian or a teacher. They call her 'The Nice Lady', because she's one of them what they call 'professional volunteers'. She does volunteer stuff all over the city — the food bank, the humane society — you name it. One of the CSOs told me 'The Nice

111

Lady' used to be a nurse. She must have gave that up 'cause she's here too much to have a job. Somebody said she was always real nice to Melia. Maybe gave her things to take home, I don't know. Don't mean nothing, though."

"Why?"

"Because 'The Nice Lady' was nice to *everybody*." Queenie shook her head and let out a low laugh that echoed in the empty stairwell for an instant, then quickly died away.

"And number three?" I asked.

"Somebody a little off," Queenie answered. "And she's been that way for almost twenty years. She's got a nickname. It don't sound mean, but it is."

"What do they call her?"

"Brenda. She's tall with dark red hair. There used to be a redhead called Brenda Starr in the comics, wasn't there? I remember her pictures. The reason they call this groupie Brenda is the poor fool thinks she's a newspaper reporter covering cases, like Brenda Starr. You're gonna be seein' her around for sure because she tries to get to every single court every day — all forty of 'em. She acts like she's writing. Only if you get a look at her notebook, you see that she just scribbles crazy. The blueshirts and CSOs are pretty good to her. You see her jump up in the middle of a witness's testimony and run out to the pay phone and dial. You can hear her talk and talk like she's got this big story to tell a newspaper." Queenie glanced up at me for an instant. "But there's one thing you don't never see her do."

"What's that?"

"You never see her put no quarter in the phone."

I wanted to tell Queenie I had seen the reporter, too, but I only had a ten-minute break.

I was working in one of the smaller courtrooms on the third floor. I was grateful for that because, unlike the large courts, this one had a judge's bench only slightly elevated above the desk of counsel. I only had to take one small step up to reach the judge's water jug. I did not know what my feelings would have been had I needed to mount the stairs and ascend to the grand height of the bench in the larger courtrooms. Would I be overcome with regret that I was no longer a justice of the Queen's Court, useless against the shame of the circumstances that had robbed me of the title? Or would I feel relief that I no longer held the fate of my fellow citizens in my hands?

The matron on duty in this court had told me she liked to keep a jug of water on the low window sill behind her chair at the end of the jury box. I was just replacing that jug when I glanced out the window and saw that some-one was striding out the front door of the American Consulate directly across the street.

I studied the solid but slim figure for a moment before I realized who it was. She stopped on the top step as she pulled a pair of gloves from the pocket of her black wool coat. With abrupt gracefulness, she pushed her fingers into the gloves, tugged at the hood of her coat and shoved her dark curls back until only a few of the most stubborn were visible. Against the dark cloth, her pointed chin and wide cheeks made her face look like a heart.

I was observing all this from three stories up across a wide street. It was not the sharpness of my vision that allowed me to trace these details. It was the depth of my knowledge of this woman, of Ellen, my daughter.

Her mother, my wife Anne, was an American citizen. Ellen might be having a document notarized or picking up a form. As I watched her descend the steps and walk

113

south, her gait smooth and confident, I felt lonely. My daughter was the only person in my family with whom I still had contact, but it had been months since I'd called her. Guilt always made me hesitate and hang up the phone.

I had known for more than two years that Anne had never filed for divorce as I had requested when I had my breakdown. I had sometimes thought about the fact that we were still legally married. Everything having to do with my life as a husband was so far away, so different from my present life, that it seemed like a work of fiction.

I wished I could call out to my daughter, shout through the thick bulletproof window of the courthouse, through the heavy winter air, through the rushing traffic on University Avenue, shout out, "Ellen, I'm sorry and I am going to fix this. I am going to fix whatever remains of the family that we once were."

But she slipped into the crowd on Queen Street and disappeared from view.

During the next few days, Queenie and I identified at least ten more hangers-on. We met at our usual spot in the stairwell to discuss our observations. Four of the people comprised two elderly couples who seemed to have decided that watching this live drama where so much was always at stake was more entertaining than television and cheaper than cable. These four didn't seem worth spending much of our time on, and of the other six, three proved to be undercover police officers, which Queenie verified by eavesdropping in the basement cafeteria. The men were discussing a case in which they would appear as witnesses. "Police detectives always give themselves away," Queenie said with the smile of the knowledgeable. "They talk a certain way, they walk a certain way, and sooner or later they all put on one of them black raincoats, just like in the movies."

It was common wisdom on the street that any perceptive person could spot an undercover cop a mile away. But it was a myth. There were police officers so deep undercover they didn't recognize *themselves* in the mirror. I had known it as a judge, I had known it as a bum, and I knew it now. But I didn't want to argue with Queenie because she was right about the particular three she had seen.

We were tempted to forget about Brenda, too. She seemed more like an old friend than a potential killer. So, besides the minister and the nice lady, we now had another three groupies to keep our eye on.

"The first one's what I call a mad perfesser," Queenie speculated. "He's got long dirty blond hair, a straggly brown beard, old-fashioned glasses with a black frame. He wears a gray shirt and gray pants, all kind of wrinkled. And big brown shoes. And he's got this row of pens in his pocket."

"I know the man you mean," I told her. "He carries a battered leather satchel full of books."

"Yeah. A beat-up old school bag. But he's a smart one, I'll tell you that. I heard him talking to the preacher. Big words from both of them. I also seen him reading in the cafeteria. Thick books about numbers."

I also had noted a Native woman and, in another court, a teenage girl. "They weren't witnesses, Queenie, because there was an exclusion order in effect, which means I had to check at the door whether they were to give testimony. Both said no. Later, I saw them together in two more courts — two different cases. So they're not friends or relatives of accused people."

"Was there anything funny about them? Suspicious?"

I hesitated, wanting to frame my answer carefully. Before I had found refuge in the valley, I had spent some months in a mental hospital, followed by six months of wandering the downtown streets. I slept in flophouses, missions and shelters when I was lucky, in garages, doorways and parks when I was not. Gradations, one might almost say a hierarchy of the homeless, were my companions. At the bottom were those whose ragged distress was most blatant, whose helplessness was the most obvious yet somehow the least able to attract help, possibly because they had given up all pretense of being members of ordinary society. Their hair was matted with grime, skin peppered with embedded soot; their shoes flopped when they walked in concert with the flapping tatters of their clothes. These were men and women whom others gingerly assisted with spare coins and gratuitous cups of coffee, but whom most people accorded wide berth, even outdoors. In enclosed spaces, like subway cars, reminders of the presence of such people lingered long after they had left. When they fell asleep on the subway, the greasy imprint of their slumber marked the glass partitions, the vinyl upholstery of the subway car. Anyone familiar with the transit system was familiar, too, with the sensation of inadvertently walking into a subway car that had not yet relinquished the smell of clothes and skin saturated with sweat and the exhaust fumes of underground garages, of breath that reeked of garbage-can food, rotting teeth and — on lucky days — alcohol.

At the other end, at the top of the hierarchy, were those who carefully washed every day in the restrooms at the bus terminal or the train station or shopping malls, who never wore the same outfit two days in a row, alternating the ones on their backs with the ones hanging to dry in some secret place. These souls could spend the afternoon reading in the public library because they still had a valid library card and could be quiet for long periods of time. These men and women didn't smell of the street, not yet. But already their faces were etched with a weary, wary wisdom.

"You ain't sayin' nothing," Queenie commented, "because you figure they're homeless and you don't want to judge nobody to be suspicious just because of that, right?"

"Right," was all I replied.

CHAPTER TEN

Toward the end of my first week on the job, I saw Harry Carleton sitting alone at a table in a far corner of the cafeteria. I bought a coffee and sauntered over as nonchalantly as I could manage. He was reading but his face lit up when he saw me.

"Ellis," he said, "how's the training going?"

"Fine," I answered and took a sip of my coffee to hide the sarcastic smile that seemed to want to twist my lips.

Harry laughed, "This place never ceases to amaze me," he said. "They more or less leave you alone to train yourself. The best way is to find some deputy who's willing to let you follow him around like a pup."

"I got a question for you, Harry. Why would a retired bank manager or a man who was a major in the army or a woman who taught at a university stick it out in a job like this?"

A little nod in my direction, a barely perceptible sigh of satisfaction showed me that Harry appreciated the fact that I was already getting around on my own. "So you've already met a few of us?" He closed the book he'd been reading, as if readying for a long chat. I glanced at the cafeteria clock. It had been years since I'd had to pay attention to the time. It made me nervous.

"That's the reason right there, Ellis," Harry said.

"What?"

"That clock. That's the reason why a lot of us retired people work here."

"You mean because our lives are ticking away?"

Harry laughed heartily. "Good heavens, no! Quite the opposite. When you're sixty years old and you have nothing to do, when you wake up every day wondering how you are going to fill the hours, that clock becomes far more of an enemy than it ever was in the days when you were trying to beat it all day long. You'd think that filling water jugs and minding doors and telling people where the restrooms are would be an embarrassment for a man who used to manage a major division of a multinational financial institution, but to tell the truth, I love it here. I love being part of the bustling world of the young instead of an anonymous, cast-aside 'senior'. I love the drama. Every day I hear one more incredible tale of love, violence and all the disasters in between."

"A lot of witnesses *are* incredible, Harry. I'll grant you that."

"It's life that's incredible, Ellis, and here in court it just parades by me every hour of the working day. I could have worked harder on my golf or bridge or tennis, but nothing gives me as much satisfaction as watching the wheels of justice turn in their creaky old way." He paused and smiled wryly.

"Anyway, most of the men — and the women, too, I guess — will tell you that working here keeps them off the street. That's a joke, of course, but what they mean is that after a long working life of being under constant pressure, a job like this gives you all the fun of working with none of the bother!"

I didn't want to tell Harry that the job really was keeping *me* off the street. In fact, I didn't think I should tell him — or anybody else for that matter — anything about myself that they didn't already know. I didn't have much trouble in that regard, since years of living rough had taught me that keeping your mouth shut could be a matter of life and death. No, the way in which I began to be careless was in forgetting just whom I might run into.

By Friday of the first week, I was already settling into the routine of minding the door. At the morning break, the retired army major Harry and I had mentioned took over as the deputy in my court. He came up to me as I was replacing a water jug and said, "After I bring His Honor into the court and seat him, I have to leave for a few minutes to go down to Room 241, where they process the paper work for the court orders."

"Okay," I said. "What should I do?"

"I want you to keep your eye on the judge. It's unlikely His Honor will adjourn before I'm back, but in case he does, come up here, ascend the steps to the bench, help him out of his chair, take his bench book where he records his notes, stand beside him and announce 'Order' in a good loud voice. It's best if you come up as soon as I leave. If he adjourns, you escort him down the steps and out the door. He walks first, you behind. He'll tell you where he wants to go — either his chambers or the judges' lounge. Stick with him. Don't get too close, but don't get too far behind, either. If he wants to go up to the lounge, you'll have to take the private judge's elevator. You know where that is?"

"Yes," I lied. If I were walking behind the judge, he'd surely head to the right elevator.

"One more thing, constable," the major said, "you can't just come traipsing up across the whole court to the bench. You have to go around the long way — outside. You've got to exit the court by the front doors. Go past the escalator to the door to the back corridor. Use your plastic card. You have one, don't you?"

"Yes." Fortunately, I'd been issued a card that morning.

"Good. Once you're in the corridor, keep to your left until you get to the set of double doors in the middle of the hall. Go through those doors. You'll know you're in the right place when you see the elevator that comes up from the cells. Keep going past the elevator. To your right you'll see the doors to two courtrooms. Ours is 4-6. The judge's entrance leads to the back of the bench. It's just a few steps to the deputy's seat. You got that?"

My head was spinning but I told him I understood.

"Good man," he said, and left to get the judge to open the court.

The major had not yet returned with His Honor and I was sitting in my place beside the main doors when the barristers' door flew open with unusual energy. I jumped out of my chair and headed for that door, partly to tell whatever lawyer was coming in not to make so much noise because the judge was on his way, and partly to assist him with the huge files the lawyers always carry. As I stepped up to the door, the trim little female lawyer in her black robe over a short gray skirt and black stockings recognized me the same instant I recognized her.

Her dark blue eyes flashed with an instant, intense fury, the quickness of which she had inherited from her father.

"Daddy!" she hissed. "What are *you* doing here?"

I should have known that I'd run into Ellen. I should have remembered that when I'd last seen her in the autumn, she'd told me that she was being considered for a position as prosecutor with the Crown's Office. Of course I'd known for a long time that she was a lawyer. It had been through her connections at law school that she'd been able to find me hidden away in the valley when I'd lost all contact with my family.

I should have put two and two together and figured out that Ellen would have ended up here in the high court where the Crown argued its most important criminal cases.

But Crown prosecutors worked all over the city, all over the province, really. Ellen had never told me where she was assigned. Now, not a week into the job and faced with the nearly impossible task of finding my way through the maze of hallways in order to get to the bench, possibly to escort a judge I'd never met to an elevator I'd never seen, I also had to sit in the presence of my own daughter while she argued her case, knowing she'd be distracted by my being there. She'd be angry. I'd be nervous. The major announced, "Order!" sending us both scurrying to our proper places.

The judge, a steely-eyed man who looked around the courtroom as if he already sensed unusual emotion there, nodded to the Defense and the Crown and asked if they were ready to begin. Ellen turned and gave me the signal to bring forth the first witness. The papers in her hand trembled. I called the name in the public hall, escorted the man to the stand, presented him with the Bible and stood beside the witness stand as the registrar swore him in.

This put me face to face with Ellen, who stood at her podium beside the Crown table not fifteen feet away. In order to get back to my chair, I had to pass her. I kept my eyes down but I could feel hers on me.

She began her examination in chief. Despite her apprehension at seeing me, her voice was steady, her questions precise. I felt a swirling wave of pride seeing her up there, so professional in her robe, so sharp in her examination.

I was so enthralled that I didn't see the major get up from his seat beside the judge. It was only when I heard the door gently close behind him that I realized I had already lost valuable seconds.

I rose as quietly and quickly as I could. I slipped out the front doors but I had to wait until they were closed all the way, keeping my hand on the big brass knob until I was sure the door would shut without a sound.

Then I flew past the escalator at the center of the floor, dodging the usual crowd of witnesses, lawyers, students, family members and even one of our groupies.

I managed to get to the door to the secure corridor just as another CSO was walking through, but she didn't see me and the door slammed in my face. I heard the lock click shut. I fumbled with my plastic card, but no matter how I turned it over and over, the little red light on the box beside the door refused to turn green and that click — that click that was replacing all the keys in the world — refused to sound.

I don't know how long I would have stood there playing with the card had not another CSO come flying out the door, allowing me to enter.

I ran down the corridor, mercifully in the right direction, but a prisoner in shackles was being led to the cells' elevator and no one walks more slowly than one whose ankles are bound by iron. I had to wait until he was safely in the elevator before I could pass. As I looked down the hall to remember which door I was supposed to enter, one of the doors opened. All I saw at first was the bright red slash of the judge's sash. He stood immobile outside his door. His robes were slightly askew, disarranged perhaps because he'd had no help getting up from his chair. He held his red bench book in his hand and his knuckles were white where he gripped it.

Clearly he was furious at having had to suffer the indignity of descending the bench unaided, at leaving the courtroom unescorted.

But his was not the fury I most feared.

CHAPTER ELEVEN

She flew and I followed.

Out the wooden doors, down the escalator, into the basement, past the cafeteria, through a tile-lined tunnel, up in a small elevator and out into the sacred precincts of Osgoode Hall, home of the Law Society of Upper Canada, seat of the Ontario courts of appeal, site of the barristers' private dining room. She was like some swift black bird, a muscular, mobile personification of anger. But she was also my daughter.

"Ellen, I'm going to have a heart attack if you don't slow down."

I knew her anger was part of her love. She was angry — had been for one solid year — because I was not living up to her expectations. When had I ever?

"And I'm going to have a heart attack if you don't straighten out, you foolish, infuriating man!"

She *did* slow down though, as the elevator opened onto a small hallway, its deep red carpet a startling contrast to the cream of its painted, panelled walls gently illumined by discreet crystal chandeliers. Her heels barely clicked on the Byzantine mosaic of the floor as we passed under an arch into the first section of the double lobby, where life-sized portraits of retired twentieth-century justices stared down at us. The Honorable R.S. Robertson. The Honorable Dalton C. Wells. The Honorable J.C. McRuer. Beneath these worthies, tall chairs with high carved wooden backs and worn dark blue leather seats ranged against the wall. A law student snoozed in one, indifferent that she slept in the chair of a retired Chief Justice.

Portraits of great justices of the 19th century gazed down from the second section of the lobby. There could be no approval from Sir Adam Wilson, The Honorable William Hume Blake or Sir Matthew Crooks Cameron for me or my daughter, I imagined. Who among those stern men in their robes would have forgiven my disgrace or accepted the women who now had joined their ranks? There was but one portrait of a woman on the wall of the lobby of Osgoode Hall, and it was the largest and most lush of all: Queen Victoria.

"Are you sure I'm allowed in here?" I dared to ask as we screeched to a halt a few steps from the door of the barristers' dining room.

"You're with me. And if anybody asks what you're doing in that CSO uniform, tell them you're researching a book. Listen, Daddy, I've got to disrobe. That's my table over by the window. The waitress's name is Sheila. She has standing orders to give my guests whatever they want."

She was gone before I could utter a word of protest. It was I who had taught Ellen how to go after what she wanted. Her actions bordered on rudeness but who was I to complain? I couldn't quell the pride I felt in her spirit, her accomplishments, her strong dark beauty, so different from that of her mother. I was glad she'd railroaded me into lunch. I had missed her. I was full of questions. And besides, I was starving.

But I was not eager to enter that room with its twenty-foot white ceiling decorated in plaster ornaments of massive, intricate, floral wreaths, and I hesitated on the threshold. The sound of crystal and silver mixed with a recorded melody, some calming strain of violin accompanying oboe. The table Ellen had pointed to was beside a tall window draped in sheer white. Beside it stood the aforementioned Sheila. Gingerly I took a step toward her.

Once such rooms had been commonplace to me. I had strode into them without noticing the fineness of their architectural detail or the decor, indifferent to the splendor that surrounded me.

But now I walked carefully with my head down. At best, the legal eagles would wonder what a CSO was doing in their private room. At worst they would be startled to see old Ellis Portal so reduced.

But then, I had been much more down on my luck than this!

That cheery thought sustained me as I proceeded through the room, steering my bargain basement shoes clear of the edges of linen tablecloths.

"Sorry, Daddy, I didn't mean to take so long," Ellen said as she slid into the seat opposite me. She plunked down the velvet bag she, like all the barristers, used to carry their robes. It was a deep hunter green, and her initials — the same as mine, *EGP* — were monogrammed in white silk script, the letters four inches high. I wondered whether the bag had been a gift from Anne or perhaps from Ellen's husband. Many years before, my father had given me mine but I had discarded it because the initials on it were the wrong ones. He had always insisted that my name was Angelo Portalese, Jr.

Sheila was at Ellen's side in a moment and Ellen told her to bring us both the usual, whatever that was.

"I'm sorry I got so upset," she said, "but the last time we talked, you said you were going to keep in touch. That was in October. Now it's almost Christmas and I haven't heard from you once, not once. Then you show up here in the same courtroom as me, dressed like that."

She grabbed a roll from a silver filigree basket and tore off a hunk of bread in a way that was so characteristically Italian, so like her grandfather, the late Angelo Portalese, Sr., that I couldn't suppress a smile.

"What are you grinning at? This is serious. I need to know what you're up to."

"I'm smiling because you remind me of somebody, that's all. And as for how I'm dressed, I have a job, an honorable one. It's better than spending my time staring at the walls of my room." *Or a deserted government building*, I might have added, *or a packing-crate hut covered with stolen tar paper and hidden among the trees.*

Ellen shook her head in a gesture of impatience. "You know, Dad, I'm only in the profession because of your inspiration."

Her imminent diatribe was stymied when Sheila put the appetizer down in front of me.

"What's the matter, Daddy? You look like you've never seen shrimp cocktail before. You always loved it."

Too many pigeons, squirrels, dandelion leaves and wild roots separated me from the days when I had enjoyed the tasteless things I once called delicacies. I stared at the cold, worm-like objects. Their sickly-looking white flesh was veined with coral splotches. They hung over the side of a crystal goblet as though they were skinned fingers hanging onto it for dear life. And each finger sported a crusty orange nail. In the bowl of the goblet, a pool of viscous dark red liquid puddled in a cup of some sort of wrinkled greenery, atop which a thin, bright sliver of lemon grinned with a lunatic smile.

"I guess I'm not hungry."

Ellen called the waitress back. "Take these away. Cancel the rest of the order. Bring us each a bowl of vegetable soup."

She turned her attention back to me. "Tell me what's wrong, Dad."

I didn't want to worry her by confessing I had hardly eaten in days because I couldn't stop thinking about poison. I didn't mind telling her I'd let Queenie believe I was willing to help "solve" another "case", but I didn't relish admitting that I had no clue to any potential murderer and couldn't figure out why any killer would pick such pathetic victims. Most important, I also did not want Ellen to know I had received threatening notes myself. I didn't want to endanger her or give her yet another reason to think I needed to be saved.

"Daddy," she said, breaking the sudden silence, "I never meant to imply that being a CSO isn't a valuable and dignified thing to do. It's just that I cherish the dream that someday you'll straighten out your situation with the Law Society. Get back into things in an appropriate way."

"Return to the judiciary! Ellen, you're joking."

"Maybe that *is* too big a step. But you could check into your status as a lawyer. You've never been disbarred." She stopped, poured herself a glass of water from the crystal pitcher that seemed to glow in the soft light filtering through the gauzy curtains. Where they did not quite meet, I saw a few fluttering snowflakes dance lazily in the wintry air. "And the legal trouble you got into could be struck from the record. It's been more than five years. You could get a pardon and have the record sealed."

"Ellen, listen, I'm in court for one purpose and one purpose only. I gave my old friend Queenie reason to believe that I could help her again. She was a friend of one of those three women who were found dead. And the only thing that links the murder victims — if that's what they are — is 361 University. Instead of concentrating on the remains of my legal career, how about really helping me?"

"What do you mean?" She looked alarmed.

"Ellen, I need you to find out what the police have on those deaths."

She opened her mouth as though to offer some sort of objection but I knew I was on solid ground. "You're a Crown prosecutor. You can get Matt West to give you anything you ask. It's just basic information anyway. Do they have suspects? Motives? Is the m.o. the same in all three deaths, in their opinion? And what about the puzzle clues written about in the newspaper? 'A good league hence', did that refer to Melia, Queenie's friend? 'Underneath the mountain', was that the mountain on the logo of the company that insured Paulina del Mario? Was Anmarie Marsh found 'right against the forest fence', meaning Forest Hill?"

"Why should I encourage your sleuthing, Daddy? Are you starting a new life as Sherlock Holmes?"

I glanced across the table. She was smiling. Of course she was. As soon as she'd said Sherlock Holmes, I knew she was with me. How many hours had she spent sitting in my lap reading the exploits of the Great Detective, even anticipating his conclusions at an age when most children could not make head or tail of those mysteries?

"Don't get smart with me, Ellen," I said with a grin. "Just find out what you can, will you?"

She didn't agree but she didn't disagree, either.

I would have been a few minutes late had I made it back to the courtroom that day. I'd been assigned for the afternoon to the seventh floor. However, I never got past the fourth.

It was so crowded on the escalators at lunch time that I always headed for the deserted stairwell to get there faster. I was still in good enough shape to climb seven flights to set up before court resumed at 2:15.

As I entered the stairwell, I noticed a barely perceptible odor. Years before, when Anne and I had lived in an apartment building overlooking the Don Valley, we had occasionally found nasty specimens of animal and human waste in our stairwell, but in my experience, such unwelcome discoveries were a fairly rare occurrence in downtown Toronto. However, in the courthouse stale air did *not* seem unusual. People were constantly complaining that the air was "sick" and giving them headaches and nausea. They also attributed the air as the cause of the epidemic sleepiness of the place but that allegation remained unproved.

The odor, which was strangely metallic as well as having a warm, animal-scented undertone, became stronger as I raced up from the first floor to the second and from the second to the third.

I climbed the stairs between the third floor and the fourth. I thought I heard a sound. Because the isolated stairwell was so cut off from the bustle of the courthouse by doors on each floor, even the slightest sound seemed magnified. What I heard sounded like a breath, a groan, even the arrhythmic beating of a heart, though later I thought I must have imagined that.

Suddenly, as I raced to the point at which the fourth landing became visible, I saw a man lying on the floor.

He was slouched in a corner, his shoulders propped up against the wall, his gray shirt showing every wrinkle in the harsh fluorescent light. At first, I thought he might be stoned or just asleep. His head was inclined toward his right shoulder, and his long, dark blond hair fell over it. The hair was not especially clean. The face, which I now saw was lightly pocked with old scars, was the face of a man not yet out of his thirties. He wore dark-rimmed glasses, behind which his eyes were peacefully closed. But as I looked longer, I realized that his posture suggested pain. His knees were drawn up and his arms encircled them, his strong-looking hands clutching each other and crushing the already creased fabric of his trousers.

I had no idea what my job required under such circumstances, but since I had already wakened several people in court during my brief tenure, I thought it was probably wise to rouse this man and to get him to pick up his briefcase, carefully placed beside him.

When I mounted the final stair and stood over him I was shocked to see he was not merely sleeping. From beneath the rumpled folds of his slacks, past the thick soles of his Orthopecs-Footease, a dark puddle was silently forming. Though there was not a visible wound, the man was sitting in a spreading pool of rich red blood incompletely mixed with some other fluid. It took me a moment to make out that that fluid was liquid feces.

And then, inexplicably, the odor I'd been smelling all along suddenly became so overpowering that I gagged and added half a bowl of vegetable soup to the mess on the floor.

Vomiting cleared my head. I reached toward the man and touched the side of his neck. I could feel a faint pulse. As I pulled my hand away, my glance fell on his briefcase, one of those school bags that opened at the top. It was stuffed with books and papers. At the very top was one of the court Bibles.

I knew it was wrong to touch objects at a crime scene — if that's what this was — but my fingerprints might already be on that Bible and surely it was covered with the fingerprints of countless others. It would have been useless as evidence. So I picked it up and flipped through it. I saw at once that one single passage was highlighted in bright pink. Like many of the court Bibles, this one had a paper clip at the end of the fifth book of the Old Testament, Deuteronomy, so a CSO could swear Jewish witnesses on the Torah. But the book that bore the pink highlighting was not one of the first five. It was Proverbs, the twentieth book of the Old Testament. The highlighted passage said, *"He will not regard any ransom; neither will he rest content, though thou givest many gifts."*

My hand shook as I carefully placed the Bible back where I'd found it. I took the time to examine the tidy row of pens in the man's pocket. There was not a highlighter among them.

I dashed to the nearest courtroom and alerted the first blueshirt I encountered, who set in motion a fast, complex series of emergency procedures that soon had the stairwell full of ambulance personnel, police and court emergency staff.

I kept to the sidelines as they carefully lifted the victim and placed him on a stretcher. Wisely, the ambulance attendants wore orange vinyl suits impervious to liquid.

Then came the police detectives to cart away the poor man's briefcase after cordoning off the landing for further examination. I had no intention of mentioning what I'd seen in the Bible but I also had no hope of escaping their questions. Mercifully, they accepted my statement that I had simply come upon the victim in the course of my duties, that I had neither seen nor heard anyone near him or anywhere in the stairwell, and that I had alerted the authorities at the earliest opportunity, which was nearly true.

By the time the police finished questioning me, reporters had arrived and were scribbling away, no doubt trying desperately to describe the scene, which was now a bloody mess caused by moving the victim out of the confined landing. Cameras were never allowed near the courtrooms so the reporters had to rely on words without pictures, something ordinary courthouse reporters were accustomed to. It wouldn't be long, though, before those reporters were shunted aside by celebrity reporters, who, I understood, often usurped the regulars when a major story broke. This was a big story, judging from the large number of police on the scene, including Matt West who was coming up the stairs just as I was escaping down. He didn't notice me among the crowd in the stairwell.

I was less successful in avoiding Marnie Alliston, the Court Services Manager. "I've been looking for you," she said as I nearly collided with her on the first floor.

I felt a jolt of fear but it passed the second I realized that it didn't matter if she'd discovered I hadn't really been hired. All she could do was tell me to turn in my uniform.

She extended her hand as if to shake mine, but drew back before touching me. "You did a good job up there," she said. "You acted fast and you alerted the right people. You may have saved a life here this afternoon."

"I'm glad I could help," I said feebly. Next thing I'd find myself saying "Aw, shucks, it was nothing, Ma'am," and posing for a picture as Employee of the Month. All I wanted was to go back to Tootie's house.

As if she'd read my mind, Ms. Alliston said, "Of course you can take the rest of the afternoon off. And you can fill out whatever reports are necessary first thing Monday morning. Unless you think you might not be able to remember."

I'd be able to remember all right. In fact, I figured it would be a long time before I would forget that sight of yet another court groupie — the mad professor — on the brink of death from causes natural or unnatural for reasons unknown.

"So now you're some kind of hero again. Just like when you saved that little girl from the flood in the river two years ago."

"No, Queenie. I'm no hero. I just happened upon someone who was sick, that's all."

She had been waiting for me at the northern exit of the courthouse on Armory Street. It never ceased to amaze me how long and how patiently Queenie could wait.

"I'm starved, Queenie. Want to go for some Chinese food, my treat?"

"Sure," she said, and though she wasn't looking at me, I could almost feel her eyes light up.

Hundreds of thousands of Chinese make their home in Toronto. There are at least three "Chinatowns", the oldest of which stretches for many blocks northwest of the court-house.

Queenie and I trudged through the snow that had fallen all day. It was already twilight and the blue shadows contrasted with the warm light from the windows of take-out places where barbecued ducks and squid and hunks of pork hung from hooks. We turned a corner and dipped into an alley. At the far end was a little restaurant where you could get a pile of rice, meat and vegetables at any hour of the day or night for four dollars.

The service was friendly. As everything was simply ladled out of huge pots in the kitchen, it was fast, too.

But not fast enough for me. By the time the steaming platter of savory beef thinly sliced in a dark sauce and served with broccoli, Chinese greens and water chestnuts arrived at our table, my hunger disappeared again. There was plenty for two but only one ate it.

"Another feast you ain't touched," Queenie commented.

"I don't know, Queenie, I'm just not hungry lately. I mean, I'm hungry all the time but every time I actually see food, my appetite goes."

"Well," she said thoughtfully, "it ain't no surprise considering how we been thinking about poison. And I bet what you seen today ain't helped your appetite."

The sight of the "professor" sitting in his bodily excretions flashed back into my mind as if I were still looking at it. "Yeah," I said and bile rose in my throat.

"Your Honor, what exactly happens when a person takes poison?"

I thought about that. In the Criminal Code of Canada a section prohibiting "the administration of a noxious substance", caused us as law students to joke that the phrase could be used to describe certain people's cooking. But I couldn't remember details of any significant cases relating to poisoning. Like all judges, I was well aware of many "private" crimes that never come to the attention of the law. Acts committed in the name of the relief of suffering, for instance. The deformed child who becomes a victim of crib death. The elderly man whose wife finds him unaccountably entangled in smothering bedclothes. The nurse who mistakenly administers pills at shorter intervals than prescribed.

But I also knew, as a person who'd eaten things few others had eaten, that the healthy human body has remarkable powers for ejecting dangerous substances. Poisoning a healthy person is no easy task, especially in an age in which many "noxious substances", including cocaine and heroin, are under the control of what Queenie would call "the government".

"I don't know, Queenie," I finally answered her. "Different things can happen. The only case of poisoning I remember from my days as a judge was one in which a man was accused of raping a woman who ran a health food store. She was convinced that she couldn't get away from him, so she told him that she wasn't going to resist and that she'd like to make him a cup of tea before they went to bed. He agreed. She used sweet-tasting herbs to make the tea, which put the man into a coma. Then she escaped and called the police."

"Did that guy ever wake up?" Queenie asked.

"Yes. In jail. When I came upon the man today, I thought he was just sleeping or stoned. When I saw blood, then I thought maybe he was sick. But what kind of sickness would cause symptoms like his? We've all had food poisoning once in a while. I can't help thinking that what I saw today was like the results of that greatly magnified."

Queenie looked puzzled. "You're saying you think he *was* poisoned."

"I'm saying he might well have been."

"And now you're afraid somebody's gonna poison you, too?"

"Yes." I thought about the notes I'd received. . . . *delivered them out of the hand of those that spoiled them . . . Hope that is seen is not hope. Precious . . . is the death of his saints.* I did not want to be labelled a victim. But it was hard not to admit my fear when directly questioned by Queenie.

"I can fix that."

"What?"

"Let's go. I've ate all the Chinese I can stuff in." She pushed away the plate. "I can buy *you* something. My government check come today and I been to the check casher."

Like many people who received monthly welfare payments, Queenie never set foot in a bank. She made other financial arrangements.

"You been nice enough to do for me. Now I'm gonna do for you. And while we're at it, I wanna know more about this dead guy."

"He's not dead yet, Queenie."

"He's almost dead. And he's another groupie."

"Yes."

"What did they say about him, anyway?"

"They?"

"The police and all them reporters that was hanging around."

I had been so intent on getting away that I had only heard a few of the questions that were being tossed around. "Well, they found out his name, which was Carl Madison. And one of the reporters mentioned that puzzle again."

"The one in the paper?"

"Yes."

"What did that have to do with the perfesser?"

"I don't know, Queenie. The reporter said something like, 'Here's another saint.' He could just have meant another victim."

"Yeah, well, we're all gonna be saints someday but your day ain't come."

She took me to a fruit and vegetable grocer on Queen Street. She made me watch every single thing she bought: a few tomatoes, an onion, two kinds of peppers. Then we went to a neighborhood market and I stood beside her as she randomly selected a very fresh-looking piece of fish well wrapped in plastic.

She let me carry the packages. And when we got to her room in the boarding house on Pembroke Street, I accompanied her down the hall to watch while she got water from the faucet in the restroom. "It's real clean in here," she said. "I clean it myself." I watched as she filled a pot, then emptied it to rinse and fill again. "No poison here, Your Honor," she announced, giving me one of her smiles.

As well as having no sink, Queenie's room had no stove, but that didn't stop her. I looked over her shoulder as she deftly juggled three pots on two burners of her hotplate. When she was finished, she'd produced braised fish and a sort of vegetable ragu, which she combined in one of the pans. I understood that this was how she intended to serve the meal. "I don't use no dishes," she explained, "so I don't waste soap havin' to wash extra things."

Her room had only a bed, a chair and a little table on which were displayed a few of her meager belongings: a picture of her late daughter, Moonstar, as a smiling little girl with huge dark eyes and straight black hair; a necklace of silver strung with coral and turquoise beads; a copy of the Bible. Queenie cleared a place for me and set down the dinner. She had washed a fork and shook it dry. I sat on the chair and ate my fill without fear or nausea.

When I was done, she made me tea. And started questioning again. "What happened to that guy — the blood and all — how can we find out if it was poison? Do you think we could ask Detective West?"

"No. Tomorrow after work I'll go to the library and see if I can find a book about the effects of common poisons."

"Common?"

"Yes. Things that might be found anywhere."

"I know what common means," Queenie said softly. "What I was wondering was why you think that if it's poison, it has to be common."

"Because if this is murder, I can't imagine why a killer would go to extraordinary means to —"

"You mean because the people that got killed are nobodies?"

"Of course I don't mean that. What I mean is the killer has nothing to gain, at least as far as we can tell. So why would he go to the expense and danger of procuring unusual substances?"

Queenie nodded, seeing my point. "What about the Bible? You said those words were highlighted. It's the same thing as if it was a note, right?"

"Yes. Yes exactly. But I still can't figure out what those Bible quotations mean. Part of the problem, Queenie, is that there are copies of the Bible everywhere and people quote the Bible for all sorts of reasons."

"Yes. Except there ain't that many religious people around these days, are there?"

"Queenie, I think that wherever there is trouble — courts, prisons, hospitals, shelters — wherever there is trouble, there are religious people."

We sat in silence for a little while, just sipping our tea. "Poison, puzzles . . ." Queenie finally said. She shook her head. She lifted her gaze, caught my eye for a second, then seemed to study the photograph of her daughter. "I can't figure out no quotes from the Bible and no puzzles. I'm sorry that perfesser guy got hurt. I only seen him a few times. He was kind of pathetic. What I really want is just to know what happened to Melia."

I risked reaching out and taking her hand. I feared she would pull away. Instead, she gave my fingers the slightest little squeeze. "Queenie," I said softly, "I will find out who harmed Melia and why. I promise."

"Killed," she said, "not harmed, *killed*."

It was after 10 P.M. when I got to Tootie's house. Nobody in my new domain ever seemed to have an engagement in the evenings. They all seemed to stay home all night every night. Walking through the hall to my own room, I heard five noisy attempts at entertainment from five separate rooms, a cacophony of TVs, disc players, videos, radios. It was depressing.

But not as depressing as realizing that I had not had a single phone call that day, or any of the past several days for that matter. And not as depressing as noticing that somebody, probably Tootie Beets, had propped a little card against my phone. I had no privacy. I had nothing to hide or steal so I shouldn't have cared that Tootie came into my room when I wasn't there, but I did care.

And I cared about the card. It was from the postal outlet in the local drugstore. A little box was ticked. A registered letter was waiting for me.

A registered letter could only mean more trouble. Impulsively, I tore the card to shreds. Surely I had trouble enough. My friend Queenie wanted me to find a murderer. My daughter Ellen wanted me to be the man I'd once been. My boss wanted me to work a job that I'd taken by lying. And a person who'd already killed three — four, if the professor didn't live — almost certainly wanted me dead, too.

CHAPTER TWELVE

I awoke before sunrise. It was too early for my fellow house rats to be stirring. I imagined them in their individual stupors and wished them further hours of peaceful slumber, enjoying the wonderful absence of communal noise.

Unlike Queenie's landlady, Tootie allowed no food preparation in the rooms, not even boiling water. I couldn't stand the thought of starting my Saturday in that kitchen, so I ventured into the dark December morning for my first coffee.

I wound south through the neighborhoods until I reached College Street. In the early morning light, the Christmas decorations lacked the luster they'd had the night before when the street with its quaint shops must have been ablaze, judging from the strings of lights everywhere. I was glad to have missed it.

Things had changed so much in the fifty years since I'd grown up in the streets not far from this one. Though they might look like ethnic enclaves, downtown Italian neighborhoods now had shops and restaurants that numbered among the most sophisticated in the city.

I ducked into a little cafe that smelled of fresh bread and just-ground coffee. Its few round tables were already taken by men who chatted in voices not yet as loud as they would become later in the day. Some read the paper. Most smoked. There were no women.

When I had been a boy, my father had often dragged me into such places, never paying attention when I complained about the aging relics of the old country.

But now, surprisingly, I felt warmed and comforted by the hushed tones of the Italian tongue, the hiss of the milk steamer, the rustle of the Saturday paper, the week's thickest edition. I took a seat by the window where I could watch College Street coming awake.

I went up to the counter and bought a paper. There was nothing on the front page about the man I'd come upon in the court stairwell. I scanned the Table of Contents at the bottom of the page. When I saw the listing for the cryptic crossword, it occurred to me that it had been two weeks since the appearance of the Good King Wenceslas puzzle.

I opened the paper. What had happened in the stairwell was buried at the bottom of a routine report on cases too unimportant to rate a major story but not unimportant enough to ignore. According to the report, Carl Madison, retired professor of computer science at Toronto City College, had taken ill while in court. His condition was listed as "critical".

Without my willing it, the youthful face of the man sprang into my memory. How could a person in his thirties be "retired"?

I turned to the puzzle page and studied the cryptic. I wondered how the person who created the puzzles for the

Toronto Daily World managed to come up with a new theme every week and how the puzzle-maker thought of all the double, triple, even quadruple clues with which he or she teased faithful followers. I was about to turn the page when I noticed that the answers to the previous week's puzzle were displayed along with a few brief explanations of the more obscure clues. Maybe the Wenceslas puzzle also had been explained. I asked the man behind the counter whether he kept papers from previous weeks. After digging through a pile, I found the previous Saturday's *World*. There *were* explanations for some of the clues, including the three saints mentioned in the carol, St. Stephen, St. Agnes and St. Wenceslas himself.

The clue to the St. Wenceslas answer was a simple anagram. And I could also understand the reasoning behind the St. Stephen clue. Rather unimaginatively, it relied on seeing the saint's name in two separate parts, "step" and "hen".

I remembered then what I'd heard on the landing. "Here's another saint." What might that mean? Agnes was the only one I couldn't figure out. In this case, the saint's name had not been an answer to a clue but part of the clue itself. The answer was "Lambert's Cascade". Whatever that was. The clue, which the solution had reprinted, read, "St. Agnes's computer falls". Beside it in parenthesis was the number 15, indicating, of course, that the answer had fifteen letters. All the explanation said was "Agnes equals lamb. Fall equals cascade".

I had never been much for puzzles and games, though I knew many highly intelligent people used them to hone the powers of their minds. I preferred to hone mine on the hard flint of reality.

With this self-satisfyingly arrogant thought in mind

and with the whole day ahead of me, I decided to set out in search of the only two people among my acquaintances who would know to what Lambert's Cascade referred.

At first I believed I was out of luck. I discovered that on Saturday morning at Riverside no visitors were allowed. Then I hit on the idea of claiming to be a volunteer from Courthouse Outreach Services nicely verified by my plastic security I.D. Signing the volunteer register as requested, I provided Tootie's address and added my phone number for good measure.

"We have some others from the court with us today," the coordinator said. I hoped I wouldn't run into anyone I knew as I made my way through halls crowded with square-dance performers in bright swirly skirts, a bevy of craft instructors toting giant bunches of what appeared to be basket-weaving rushes and a string quartet of men as aged as some of those for whom they'd come to play. I stopped for a moment to help them hoist their cello through the narrow aisle between the folding chairs set up for their concert, but I politely declined when they asked me to remain.

There once had been a time, I was sure, when Harpur Blane Stoughton-Melville would have greatly enjoyed a chamber music performance. She had held memorable parties where such musicians played. But she was audience only to her own distant thoughts on this December morning. All idea of asking her to help me figure out the puzzle clue fled when I saw her.

Someone had whimsically placed a Christmas corsage in her hair. Like everything else Harpur wore, this little bouquet of red silk poinsettias, real holly leaves and golden ribbon was well-crafted and tasteful. Nor did its festive brightness mar the cool grace of Harpur's dark green brocade robe. She sat in her chair by the window, and her hands, empty of all adornment, were folded in her lap.

I stood watching her, a portrait of motionless beauty against a backdrop of lively whiteness outside her window. Past her immobile profile, I could see that children in their multicolored winter jackets were tobogganing down the big hill at Broadview Park.

She did not move when I entered the room and let the door close with a click behind me. She did not turn when I called her name. She did not blink when I came around the bed and sat on the edge opposite her not two feet away. Once I would have considered myself the happiest man in the world to have been able to sit this close. Now it filled me with nearly unbearable sadness. I realized that to get something you have longed for in the wrong season or the wrong way is far worse than never having it at all. This was as true of Harpur's present calm as of my nearness to her.

I don't know how long the two of us would have sat there in stillness had not the door sprung suddenly open. Harpur's young friend, Gelo, stood poised in the doorway. How he had become exempt from the "no visitors" rule wasn't much of a mystery. A single phone call from Stow would have done it. Gelo wore the same black leather jacket, black tee shirt, black jeans and black boots as before. But he also wore something else, which I saw at once. On his finger was a heavily embossed golden ring that matched my own.

A look of steely defiance crossed his face. I had seen that look before on boys in the street. Twice I'd met it with defiance of my own and been beaten senseless for my attitude.

147

I was finished with that. Instead, I smiled. "Merry Christmas!" I said to the kid.

"I don't believe in Christmas."

"I don't either, really," I confessed. I needed this kid's help. If Harpur allowed him to wear her ring, it was her business. There was also a possibility that the boy was in love with Harpur. "You're just the person I'm looking for," I told him.

"Why?"

"I need help with a clue from a cryptic puzzle," I said. "I was hoping you and Harpur could assist me. I know you're both whizzes at this sort of thing."

To my amazement, the kid blushed.

"But," I went on, "Harpur's not well today."

At these words, however, she turned, looked me straight in the eye, her green gaze startling me. "Shut up," she said. "The guests have arrived." She reached out and pushed me. Stung, even though I knew she wasn't really responsible, I got up and crossed the room.

"Don't take it personally, sir," the boy commented. "You can ask me what you need to know."

I told him about the St. Agnes clue. I didn't mention anything about a possible connection between the cryptics and the deaths of three women, but I thought Gelo might have read the *Toronto Daily World* article because he said,"If a puzzle is connected to something like a crime, then all the clues are in the puzzle itself. That's how a puzzler's mind would work. In order to figure out the puzzle, you have to figure out the puzzler."

"But what would be the connection between St. Agnes and a computer?"

"That's easy. Think about it. It's partly simple Latin. *Agnus* is Latin for *lamb*."

"You know Latin?" I asked in astonishment. Then I remembered what Stow had said about the boy losing out on a scholarship when he fell under the tutelage of the Ministry of Correctional Services.

I went on. "It doesn't take much imagination to see that 'fall' is another word for 'cascade'. But what I don't understand is the reference to 'computer' and the answer itself."

"Well," the boy said, "usually cryptics are straight word games — you figure out parts of words, like that 'step' and 'hen' thing. But once in a while, the answer depends on general knowledge. It could be geography or history or the movies or TV. This clue is for people who know a little bit about computer games. You know anything about them?"

Aside from being smart enough to keep well away from the young thugs in the video arcades, I knew nothing. "No," I admitted simply.

"Well, 'Lambert's Cascade' is one of the best computer games ever invented and some guy from around here — Toronto, I mean — thought it up. It's not this dumb thing where you shoot virtual enemies with virtual machine guns to get virtual military honors. It's real science for people with real minds."

"Ellis has a real mind," Harpur said. But she was talking to the air. My heart contracted with pity.

"How does it work?" I asked the boy.

"It starts as an algebraic equation with three unknowns. To make a long story short, you keep making choices. If you make a wrong one, the equation freezes and you lose. But you can also choose a combination of variables that flips the equation into infinity. It becomes self-solving."

"What's this got to do with 'Lambert's Cascade'?"

"I don't know who this Lambert guy was," Gelo

149

answered. "Probably the guy that invented the game, but the reason they call it a cascade is that once you get infinity, the computer just keeps spitting up numbers until the whole screen looks like Niagara Falls, numbers scrolling down fast as water. Super, super cool!"

"How hard is it to achieve Lambert's Cascade?" I asked.

"Almost impossible," Gelo responded, "and I've done it twice!"

I wanted to ask him more but there was a knock on the door. Being closest to it, I rose to open it. At first, I didn't see a person standing there. All I saw was a fan of reeds. I kept my hand on the doorknob and heard a chipper voice announce, "I'm here to help Mrs. Stoughton-Melville learn to weave."

Innocent as the statement seemed, it had a remarkable effect on Harpur. She jumped from her chair by the window, flew across the room to the door. "You get out!" she screamed at the woman with the reeds, whom I now saw was a Native and who wore a volunteer badge from the agency where Queenie and I had attended the feast. "You just get out of here right now. Out! Out!"

The startled woman backed away. Harpur slammed the door with so much force that a painting on the wall swung and stopped at a rakish angle. "I hate them!" Harpur yelled. "I hate them. I hate every one of them. I . . . "

She was shaking and flailing her arms. The boy was at her side almost immediately. "Chill out, Harpur," he said gently. He looked up at me and I saw a plea in his young eyes. I knew what he was asking. Without another word, I left the two of them alone.

I worked my way back toward the lobby and the street. Just before I exited the building, I saw two volunteers who looked familiar. "The Nice Lady" and the handsome minister that Queenie and I had identifed among the court groupies. At the sight of them, I hastened my steps. To tell the truth, I didn't like volunteers any more than Harpur did.

The next day I met Queenie in church. I took a chance at finding her at St. James, the great inner city Anglican cathedral, not far from where she lived. Though the church was filled with hundreds of worshippers, I easily found Queenie just where I thought I'd find her, humbly kneeling in the last row.

"What are you doin' near a church and on Sunday to boot!" she teased when I met her coming out of the service.

"I'm taking a lady to breakfast," I answered.

Our breakfast consisted of muffins and coffee across the street from the cathedral but it was good enough for us and the location aroused in Queenie a pleasant memory. "Once I seen Princess Di from this very corner," she said. "They was still together, her and Charles, and they brought their boys here to Toronto, too. The royal family always has to go to a Anglican church when they visit places, I guess, and this is the main one. So thousands of people came that day. They was lined up all along King Street here. I was there at 5 A.M. and it was already crowded even though the service don't start till eleven o'clock. Anyway, a little before eleven, a big car come and the door gets opened and out steps Princess Diana."

For no particular reason, a phrase I had heard in court all week popped into my mind, "A Queen's Justice of the Ontario Court of Justice." That was what I had once been.

"Queenie," I said, "how would you like to help me out on a research project? I want to go to the library, the reference library near Yonge and Bloor. It's open Sunday afternoon and I need to look up a few things."

"Like a book on poison?"

"Yes. And a few other things." I told her about Lambert's Cascade. "I want to see if I can find out who Lambert was."

"Or is," Queenie suggested. "Computers ain't been around for long. So most of the people that invented stuff for them are probably still alive."

"Good point, Queenie! You make a valuable Dr. Watson." I thought to ask, "Once you told me you use the Internet. How is that?"

"Easy. They have a computer at the shelter. You can get on the Internet by clicking just pictures. If I need to find out about something I get somebody at the shelter, like the secretary, to write down the words. Then on the Internet, I match the written-down letters to the typing keys. I can copy words real good and find somebody to tell me what they say. But I ain't gonna be much good in a libary."

I almost corrected her pronunciation but stopped myself just in time.

"It won't be a problem. I'll find some things for you to look at while I'm working. I'd like your company."

Queenie was in such awe of the mammoth reference library that it occurred to me she might never have been in a library before. I didn't want to embarrass her by asking whether this was true but I did offer to find her some magazines with lots of colored pictures. She declined. "I'll be fine, Your Honor," she said, but she did

152

add, "All them books and I ain't likely to ever read a single one."

When I'd worked my last "case", I'd figured out how to use the library's computer terminals. Now I spent an hour on one of them before I found any mention of Lambert's Cascade. It took another half an hour for a librarian to locate three thick volumes of bound science journals in the library's closed stacks. When he presented them to me, I carried them over to one of the tables and sat down. I had just begun to read when Queenie came up. "I got a really good idea, Your Honor. Are we gonna be here a little while longer?"

I assured her that that was the case. I couldn't imagine what she was up to but she seemed to be enjoying the task.

In another hour-and-a-half, I had learned all I needed to know about Lambert's Cascade. It functioned exactly as Gelo had described it. It had never been intended as a computer game. The discoverer of the equation was not Lambert. Lambert had been the discoverer's mentor when he was a student at the University of Toronto. The discoverer had been a genius who was looking for a way to allow computers to operate independently of human intervention by teaching them how to "assume" information they had not actually been fed. Lambert's student discovered other equations besides the cascade, but he did not seem to have profited from any of them financially. And he had not benefitted at all when a commercial video producer had turned the cascade into an arcade game.

Queenie had been right. The originator of Lambert's Cascade was someone who was still living, even if he *was* hanging by a thread. I let out a gasp that disturbed the other readers around me. The discoverer of Lambert's

Cascade was Carl Madison, the "professor" found in the stairwell.

"This is like them 'plot thickens' things, ain't it?" Queenie said when I told her. We sat at a table in the most isolated corner of the library.

"I can't read none of these books," she said, indicating a pile she was holding, "but you can. Every one of them is about saints. I thought about that puzzle again and I remembered something I heard our priest say about December being a good month for saints. I only remember a couple of famous ones. There's St. Nicholas on December 6 and St. Francis Xavier on December 3. And there's St. Stephen, too. The Feast of Stephen is the day after Christmas. When Good King Wenceslas done his good deeds and all. Our pastor told us he got killed by a murderer. What if our murderer plans to kill a certain amount of people by that day?"

I read as much as I could about saints in the following hour or so. I studied descriptions of all the saints of December. But I also needed information about poison. I was less successful there than in my other research. I soon saw that my search was much too broad. Without knowing what kind of poison we might be dealing with, there was little I could do to narrow it. But I did read an article about the effects of poison in general. Gruesome as they were, Carl Madison's symptoms were almost minor compared to the effects of some toxins, such as rendering the victim permanently capable of seeing nothing but flashing blue spots or completely dissolving his bladder. I was glad when the bell rang to announce the library was about to close.

It was 7 P.M. when I got back to my room at Tootie's. I

felt the day had been well spent. But it wasn't over yet. The message light was flashing.

In a voice obviously disguised, a person intoned, *"The wicked shall be a ransom for the righteous, and the transgressor for the upright."*

CHAPTER THIRTEEN

With the same impulsive desire to rid myself of an odious thing, I wiped the phone message away just as I had torn up the postal card informing me of the registered letter. But a desperate desire to tell somebody about the threats plagued me, and after an hour I called the only person I could think of — Ellen.

"Daddy! I'm so glad you phoned. I hope this means we're going to be getting back into touch on a regular basis."

"Ellen, I need to talk to you. Can we meet?"

"Sure. I'll come and pick you up. What's the address?"

I couldn't let her know I was living in our old house. "Let's go for a walk. I'll meet you at the corner of Yonge and Queen. We'll look in the store windows at the Christmas decorations."

There was a silence at the other end of the line. Once Ellen and I had made a ritual of looking at the Christmas windows. But it was part of a lost life and we both knew it.

"Forget the windows, Daddy. Let's just walk and talk."

Before she saw me, I saw her coming, her black curls bounding, her cheeks rosy with the cold. I didn't want to touch her because the rash on my hands had flared up again. She gave me a little peck on the cheek. I grabbed her and hugged her and she hugged me back.

"I'm glad you called, Dad. There's something I've got to tell you, too."

"You've managed to find out more about the dead women?" I asked with a jolt of fear that surprised me.

"No. It's something else. What's the matter, Daddy? You're so nervous . . ." She put her arm through mine as we walked up the street. We had the wide snowy sidewalk to ourselves. Downtown was deserted on Sunday night.

"You first, honey," I said to her. "What's going on?"

She shook her head. "I need to talk to you about Mom."

"Something's wrong with Anne?" I didn't try to hide my alarm.

"No. Nothing's wrong. She's been getting along fine." She had the good grace not to add, *No thanks to you.*

"It's just that things change, Dad."

"What things?"

She disentangled herself from me and pretended to gaze into the window of a dress shop, but I knew she was stalling.

"It's been seven years, Dad. People have to move on with their lives."

"What are you saying?"

She turned back toward me but she didn't touch me. She kept her eyes straight ahead. "I told Mom that she should speak to you in person about all this but she said it's just too late."

"Too late for what, Ellen?"

She drew a breath. "Daddy, without discussing it with you, she hired a lawyer to look into an equitable division of your property. I know it's cruel to file for a divorce without talking to you in person, but under the circumstances . . ."

"A divorce?"

"You sound surprised. Why? Didn't you send word that you wanted her to begin divorce proceedings years ago, right after you got in trouble?"

"Yes. But why now?"

Of course I guessed the answer before she gave it. But I couldn't have guessed that it would hurt me to hear it.

"Because," she said, resolutely avoiding my eyes, "somebody has asked her to marry him."

"Who?"

She didn't answer the question. "Mom sent her lawyer to your house twice to discuss this with you and both times he was chased away by a weird kid who claims to own the house."

"Tootie Beets."

"What?"

"Tootie — Tootie Beets, my landlady. She said a man with a briefcase came to see me. I . . ."

"Mom wanted your signed permission to check into your financial affairs."

I laughed. "What financial affairs? I have $5000 in a savings account. I saved it from that consultation I did on the revegetation of the river valley."

A look of shock came over Ellen's face. For a second, I thought it might have occurred to her that she would have no inheritance from me, except of course for all the treasures in my room, courtesy of Wal-Mart and the thrift shop.

"Daddy," she started to say, "there's some mistake here."

She opened her mouth as if to elaborate but then clearly had second thoughts. She was, after all, a lawyer. She'd probably decided that she might have said too much. As if to get back on track she said, "Did you get a registered letter from Mom?"

"I received notice of one, but I discarded it."

"The letter was sent to inform you that since his efforts to reach you in person failed, Mom's lawyer secured a court order to have access to your financial records."

"Fine, Ellen. That's just fine. You two just send that lawyer or whoever he is back to my place and I'll sign whatever you want. But who the hell is she going to marry?"

"I won't answer that question until you answer one for me."

"What?" I said irritably.

"Why can't you eat? Are you ill?"

"No," I answered, looking right at her. But that's all I could say. Any feeling of confiding in her had fled. If she was her mother's advocate, she couldn't be mine. "I'm just nervous. I've got a lot on my mind."

"Nervous about seeing me? I hope not." She kissed my cheek again. "Daddy, she wants to marry James Pike Richardson. Do you know who that is?"

"No, should I?"

"He's the chief consular official of the United States delegation to Toronto."

"You mean she's about to marry the U.S. Consul himself?"

"Yes," she said, "a man who has the same posting grandfather had."

She put her arm through mine and steered me toward a particularly colorful window. The bright decorations swam in front of my eyes. "Now tell me why you wanted to see me."

"It's not important, Ellen."

"Of course it is. You called me."

"Some other time," I growled. I pulled my arm out of hers and stomped away, leaving her watching a toy monkey swinging from a red satin trapeze. I turned back after only a few steps but she was already gone.

I didn't get back to Tootie's until past eleven. Even though it was late, I went down to the laundry room beside the kitchen. This was a modern addition to the house and had certainly not been there when Anne and I had owned the place.

I threw my two white workshirts into the washer and sat there waiting. I had learned never to leave laundry untended if I had any hope of ever seeing it again.

I had to wait for the shirts to dry, too, but as it was after midnight, I stopped the dryer in fifteen minutes and took the shirts out, intending to iron them a little while they were still damp. Tootie had set up an iron and a board for her roomers but there were strict rules attached to their use. The rules were posted on the wall directly above the only electric plug and read, "Anyone who walks away from this iron without unplugging it will be evicted. Anyone who walks away *with* the iron will be evicted, too." Tootie obviously had little fear of the Landlord and Tenant Act when it came to grounds for eviction. On a sudden impulse, I decided to commit the transgression of carrying the iron away in the middle of the night.

I ran up to my room, hastily hung the damp shirts on the edge of the open door to my closet. Then I reached into the far corner of the closet. On the floor, under a little tent of newspapers and plastic bags that I'd made to disguise something valuable in the closet, I found the shopping bag I'd brought with me when Queenie had lured me out of the valley back to the city.

I opened the bag and took out a wrinkled mass of black silk, a remnant of the badge of my former life, a treasure I never left behind. It had survived jail and the mental hospital. I had slept with it beneath my head so that it would not be stolen in flophouses and shelters, on doorsteps and park benches. It had once been secreted for years in a hole in a tree when I lived in the Don River Valley. It had survived winter's snow and summer's humidity. I had almost but not quite lost it in the great valley flood. It was the only possession I could not bear to lose. But treasured as it was, the once rich and flowing folds of my judge's robe were now shamefully creased.

For no reason I could name, I had to fix it, smooth it, press it.

It took me half the night. I had ironed little in my life but I knew that you needed a wet towel so that the iron never touched the silk directly. This necessitated my risking eviction again by removing a dishtowel from the kitchen.

Since there was no water in my room, I had to trek down to the washroom at the end of the hall every time the towel dried out, which was often.

And, of course, I had no ironing board, so I had to use the bed.

But I did it. I removed every crease, every wrinkle. I smoothed the silk yoke at the neck, the long sleeves with their deep cuffs graced by a wide row of silk-covered buttons.

And when I was done, I reached into the bag and extracted a part of the robe that I had lost but that had been replaced by Ellen — the red wool sash that crossed diagonally from one shoulder to the waist.

I hung the robe on a hanger and arranged the brilliant sash across it. Then I unplugged the iron, took off my clothes, climbed into bed and fell asleep.

Two hours later, it was almost daylight and somebody was banging on my door. I jumped out of bed and yanked the door open. An incensed Tootie Beets in full leather and chrome was fuming on the threshold.

"You're *out*," she yelled. "Just give me back the iron and get out!"

I didn't do it on purpose but I happened to open the door wider, just enough for Tootie to be able to see my robe hanging on the edge of the closet door.

I could tell by the look on her face that she knew what the robe meant. She was no stranger to the courts.

"Who *are* you?" she demanded of me.

"Who are *you*?"

Her eyes narrowed. Her white face was incapable of becoming any paler but her blood-red lips quivered. "Who am I?" she asked. "Maybe I'm some dead rich guy's kid who got all his money when he bought it. Maybe I'm a paperhanger and counterfeited the money to buy this house. Or maybe I'm an ex-coke dealer who made three quarters of a million dollars on one sale and used the money to set myself up in business. Maybe I'm a crook. Maybe I'm a hooker. Maybe I'm going to throw you out of my house," Tootie seethed.

But she glanced again at the robe. "Or maybe," she said more softly, "maybe I'm not . . ."

CHAPTER FOURTEEN

Sleep and the dream of sleep, the wish for sleep, the sweet memory of deep sleep, the anticipation even of that sleep from which there is no waking, spread its dark sleeve over the dozing court. Sleep tipped the head of the judge as, elbow on the bench, he pretended to take notes though his hand did not move across the page. Sleep curved the neck of the registrar so that his chin hid his little white bowtie. Sleepiness made the deputy slouch in his seat beside the judge, made the defense counsel draw idle circles on his long legal pad, circles that ceased before they were closed. Even the Crown seemed half in slumber as he moved for the judge to rule admissible 10,017 wire-tapped telephone calls. The police officer in charge of the investigation who sat beside the Crown had long succumbed to the arms of Morpheus. It seemed to me that I alone was truly awake, but that was only because I had suddenly realized that all the groupies that Queenie and I suspected were in my court right now, except, of course, for Carl Madison, of whom there had been no news.

It might have been mere coincidence for the angelic-looking minister, "The Nice Lady" and the woman they called Brenda to be listening to the same proceedings. But I wondered why several other groupies were present, and why they all sat together straight across the second row behind the prisoner's dock. The blueshirts were quickly on anyone who strayed too near to the accused but none of the groupies would have made such an error. They all knew more about court procedures than some of the judges.

Brenda, the woman who pretended to be a reporter, wore a thin woolen jacket with threadbare elbows. Observed closely, the jacket looked little better than a rag. She wasn't carrying an overcoat and I wondered how she managed to stay warm. Down-on-their luckers had any number of strategies for dealing with the problem of carting around a winter coat. Some wore it always, winter and summer alike. Some were especially good at hiding their coats when the weather was warm or at trading favors with someone trustworthy who had a room with a lock on the door and could stow garments not in use. Of course, if you had a few dollars, you could always buy a new one at the end-of-summer sales at the thrift shops.

The best way to deal with the problem of a winter coat was to force yourself not to be cold no matter what you were wearing. This psychology worked down to a remarkably low point on the thermometer. There was, however, a temperature low enough that even the most malodorous and claustrophobic sought warmth until the weather broke. I had always thought it a miracle that only a few froze to death in the streets of Toronto during the average winter. Queenie was certainly right in being suspicious about Melia, Paulina and Anmarie freezing.

"The Nice Lady", whom I heard the minister address as

Jeannette, was the best dressed of the spectators. She wore a tidy tartan skirt of moderate length, a buttoned sweater in a shade of green that complemented the skirt's colors, a thin chain around her neck with a plain gold cross on it. I saw her carefully fold her brown wool coat and place it on the seat beside her with a precision that marked a perfectionist.

The other groupies who had joined the regulars today were strangers, but I had seen so many of their kind. They were people who shopped not at the thrift shop on St. Clair where I shopped, where I mingled with middle-class bargain hunters from the neighborhood and chose from among items carefully categorized, sized and hung on racks. No, these groupies shopped at the dollar-a-pound thrift store, carrying huge plastic garbage bags from wooden table to wooden table heaped with twisted piles of clothes of all sizes, seasons and conditions. The first time I dug through a pile like that, I had been ashamed of myself for being so clearly in my worst days. Before long, though, I became proud of how I figured out the most warmth for the least weight. I could fill one of those garbage bags for less than three dollars.

I covertly studied the regular groupies. The one sitting nearest the aisle and therefore the one easiest for me to see was the minister. Looking at him, a memory from long ago bubbled its way to the surface. When I was a boy, I had been sent to Catholic school so nuns and priests could pound my young mind into sturdy Catholic shape while saving my immortal soul. Part of both processes, it seemed, was instilling a healthy contempt for Protestants, especially of the evangelical sort, whom we called "Bible thumpers".

It was easy to pick out a Bible thumper even from a distance. They were blonder and fairer than we Italian Catholics. They wore their hair, even in the days when everybody's hair was cut, too short. They wore suits that were pale, narrow and thin as though there had not been enough cloth. The Bible thumpers' voices were as thin as their suits. And they were, most distressingly of all, relentlessly cheerful, as if this mortal vale, with all the evil they were supposedly attacking, were a mere Sunday-school picnic. We knew about the Sunday-school picnics of Protestants. We often sat on the slopes of the Christie Pits and watched them. Only the certainty of landing in Hell prevented us from sabotaging their Bible games, only a little less absurd than our own devout competitions. One of the silliest was to keep our Ash Wednesday cross of ashes on our foreheads as long as possible. Sometimes we went a whole week without washing our faces.

The minister in the courtroom simply looked like a man who was at ease with the groupies as social service workers are at ease with their clients. Closer scrutiny revealed that his manner, even when he sat perfectly still, appeared gentle, cheerful, helpful. His skin was pale, his hair efficiently clipped. He was a thumper all right and maybe a social service worker too. Just one more do-gooder in a city that couldn't produce enough, just as it couldn't stop producing evil-doers for the do-gooders to pull out of the fire.

At exactly 11 A.M., although the lawyer had not paused in his address to the judge, the entire row of groupies simultaneously rose. At first I thought nothing of this, since people were free to come and go as they pleased. But the groupies did not file out. They remained upright and silent in the second row center of the area behind the bar.

An old, almost forgotten sensation filled me, a mingled

wave of anger and panic. I was back on the bench, realizing I had a courtroom disruption on my hands. It took me a few seconds to realize that it was now my job to prevent escalation of the disruption, to get these people out of the courtroom before anyone even noticed. But I was not fast enough or quiet enough. "Constable!" I heard the judge bellow from the bench, "What is the meaning of this? Who are these people and why are they standing in my court?"

"I apologize, Your Honor," was all I could think of to say as I gestured emphatically for the row of people to follow me to the door. I expected them to balk, to defy the judge, to utter some manifesto, but they remained totally silent.

It wasn't until I came around to the empty front row, into which one of the blueshirts had vaulted to assist me, that I saw that on their shabby coats and sweaters, the groupies had pinned paper signs. In black marker were written Amelia Margaret Campbell, Paulina del Mario, Anmarie Susan Marsh. In red was written Carl Madison. Apparently the computer expert I'd found in the stairwell was still alive.

That distinction, however, was lost on Mr. Justice Manus Wellington Wells. Apoplectic, he yelled at me, "Constable, remove these miscreants from my court!"

At his outburst, the groupies squared their shoulders and planted their feet more firmly. I had no idea what they expected to accomplish by their protest, but if I hoped to avoid violence, I had to move them out and fast. The blueshirt had been joined by a second man in guard uniform and both of them were reaching for their mini-batons, which I knew could easily fell a strong man.

"Please!" I uttered softly to the pathetic specimens. "Please follow me out of the court at once."

Feeble as it was, my instruction seemed to galvanize them, primarily because the so-called "nice lady", Jeannette, looked up and smiled at me. The same smile she'd given Harpur at Riverside when she soothed her, read to her and insisted she knew what was best for my ill old friend.

As soon as the others saw that smile, they turned and followed me out the door. Jeannette smiled at me again. There was, I noted, a look of compassion on her face, not unlike the compassion she'd extended toward Harpur. For some reason, her glance filled me with a sense of shame.

I resumed my seat, frozen there by the glacial eye of the judge who kept checking to make sure no more undesirables entered his court. During the long-winded speeches of the lawyers, I had plenty of time to reflect on the passive demonstration I'd witnessed. Was there some connection between the judge, the court, or the case at bar and the groupies? Was there some special significance to the day or the date?

I felt trapped in the courtroom. I wished I could talk to Queenie. But even more, I wished I could sleep. I was becoming so drowsy that I could hardly keep my head up.

I was still mulling over the sad demonstration I'd witnessed, when I was pulled out of the courtroom and herded into a pack of twenty other CSOs for a tour of the courthouse. The intense, dark-haired Marnie Alliston trooped us in and out of such a maze of corridors, cul de sacs, offices, cells, stairways, closets and courtrooms that I ended up completely disoriented.

"Never let a juror catch sight of an accused person in handcuffs, shackles or belly chains," she intoned as she carefully unlocked an empty holding cell near a large courtroom. These cells, secreted in the halls and normally never seen by anyone except the blueshirts, temporarily housed both sexes removed from the large segregated cells in the sub-basement. "If a juror does see an accused in custody, that juror is tainted and grounds for a mistrial automatically come into being. Some trials last more than a year. A moment's carelessness on the part of the jury constable can cost the taxpayer — and the accused or legal aid — hundreds of thousands of dollars and waste years of work on the part of lawyers, judges and the police. You have to be extremely careful here."

In the end, I managed to memorize only the most basic configuration of the building. There were courtrooms on the east and west sides of each floor, separated by the escalator. Along the south side, accessible only by plastic card, was the secure area where a row of small locked jury rooms ranged. Along the north side was a public hallway consisting of offices and witness rooms.

I had a moment's discomfort when, through doors momentarily ajar, I glanced into one of the judge's chambers on a segregated floor. I saw deep, soft couches and rich paintings, books, sculpture. The sight of this cozy den filled me not with envy or regret. It filled me with guilt. Had I not spent so many endless hours in my own chamber poring over cases, studying the law, writing and rewriting my decisions, I might not have lost home, family, chamber and judgeship all in one quick and undignified swoop.

Queenie was pretty sure Justice Wells of the poignant little demonstration was the same judge who'd tried Anmarie Marsh but she wasn't certain. She also felt her idea about the feast of St. Stephen was a dead end after all.

"I thought about it and thought about it, Your Honor," she said, "but I can't think of no way them saints had nothing to do with Melia. She didn't go to church like me, even though I asked her lots of times. I know she heard of St. Patrick because once she told me the best begging was at Osgoode Hall at morning rush hour and St. Patrick subway at afternoon rush hour. Her husband used to say Melia only needed to know two things — how to hold out her hand and how to bring home the money."

We were sitting in the law students' cafeteria in the basement of Osgoode Hall just beyond the main block of prisoners' cells. Marnie Alliston's little tour had ended at twelve-thirty and I wasn't due back into court until two. Queenie had been hanging around the courthouse waiting to talk.

"It's real lucky I found you, ain't it?"

I found myself reluctant to say yes. Queenie was dressed in her usual fashion. She wore a long denim skirt that nearly reached her worn leather boots. I could only imagine how many pairs of tights she had on under the skirt. She wore a bright blue sweater puffed out by the layers beneath it. By the standards of the street, Queenie was one of the best dressers. She was always clean. There were no rips in her clothes and no stains or patches, either. Her hair was sleek, her skin remarkably smooth for a middle-aged woman once addicted to alcohol, who had sometimes slept outdoors month after month, who had suffered the loss of an only child.

But Queenie was unmistakably a street person, unmistakably uneducated, unmistakably not a person one would be seen with beyond the doughnut shops, diners and hidden basement cafeterias of the world.

"Something wrong, today, Your Honor? You're awful quiet."

"I was up late last night, Queenie."

"You mean after we finished at the libary?"

"*Library*. The word is library, with two r's in it!"

The minute the words left my tongue, I regretted them. Of course I did. But the regret could do nothing to alter the look of shock on Queenie's face.

Neither of us said anything for an embarrassed moment. Queenie stared at her cup of tea. I stared at her bent head.

"Forgive me, Queenie. Last night after I left you, I got some bad news, at least it seemed bad at the time. And I couldn't sleep because of it. It's made me testy today. I apologize."

Queenie didn't answer. She stood up, took her coat from the chair beside her, folded it over her arm and walked away. As she moved toward the door, I couldn't help but be struck by her dignity. She had told me long before that Queenie was the street name she had taken because she lived on Queen Street, but I wondered whether her regal bearing had been part of the reason why the nickname had stuck.

I went back to court and saw neither groupies, Queenie nor Marnie Alliston again that day. I was restless and I also couldn't forget the sight of the names of the dead women pinned to the chests of the groupies. As with so many protests, the message they were trying to convey was not clear. Maybe their bizarre action in court had simply been their idea of a suitable memorial to lost comrades. Or maybe Queenie was right and there was some connection between that particular judge and one of the people who had died. There was another possibility, too. Maybe the protest was against the lack of strict security measures at the court. If Melia, who had begged outside, and Paulina and Anmarie, who had frequented trials, had been killed by someone who had followed them, then that killer had been lurking in and around the courthouse without being apprehended, probably without even being noticed. The protesters had themselves come into court with the signs under their clothes. It seemed logical to view their demonstration as a protest against lax security procedures. It also seemed logical to conclude that the groupies might well share Queenie's view that the dead women were indeed the victims of homicide and that a fourth potential victim lay near death.

It wasn't much of a leap from that thought to thoughts about Lambert's Cascade. And then I remembered Gelo had said that if the puzzle had anything to do with the groupie deaths, then all the clues were in the puzzle, and therefore in the mind of the puzzler.

It didn't take me long to get the puzzler's name and address. I used a technique I'd used before. I went to the *Toronto Daily World*, bluffed my way through security, took the private elevator to the newsroom and presented myself as a stringer for the reporter who'd written the piece on the puzzle's connection to the deaths. I was pretty convincing when I told the reporter's secretary that I'd lost the address of the man the reporter wanted me to talk to. She turned over the information without even asking for my I.D. "Good luck with your interview," she cheerily bid me.

The puzzler lived about four blocks from Tootie Beets. His building was a three-story walkup on Dupont Street, and his apartment was third floor front, directly over a Jamaican grocery store from which the odor of frying fish and the pulsating beat of reggae rose.

"I'm one of your fans," I said as greeting, when he answered my knock.

"A fan. Yes. A man needs a fan. Even in Canada. A winter fan. Come in. I'll clear a path, a chair."

He was a large slovenly man in a larger black sweatshirt that purported to be a souvenir from a convention of Friends of Lost Aztecs. His brown hair was pulled back in a ponytail that flapped like a dying codfish as he leaned down to dump a pile of *National Geographic* magazines onto the floor from a rusted metal folding chair. "Sit. Sit."

The place reeked of cigarette smoke subtly combined with mold and was lit by only one bulb near the door. Every inch of the floor of the apartment, which consisted only of a kitchen facing Dupont and a large sitting room, was covered with magazines, newspapers, folders, flyers, maps, letters and puzzles raggedly torn from the publications. The litter was at least a foot deep and the dates went back fifteen years. Towering over this mess were a dozen ceiling-high bookcases with bowed shelves and contents leaning dangerously toward the chaos on the floor.

The miniscule kitchen was full of papers and books, too, on the floor and in the sink. The single window was plastered over with pages from the *Toronto Daily World*. Some pages had holes where articles appeared to have been torn out and other items were circled and underlined as if the puzzler had been reading the papers while standing at the window.

"Research. Lots of research. All the time. Never have to

leave. Winter." This was in response to my glances at his appalling collection of information.

"I've been a fan of your puzzles for a long time," I lied. "And I just wanted to meet and ask you how you come up with your ideas."

"Here," he said, "meet me. Tyler Morton." And he mechanically thrust out his hand. I noticed his fingers were long and slender and stained with tobacco. I forced myself to take them in my own.

"I particularly enjoyed the puzzle with the Wenceslas theme," I ventured.

He nodded. "Victim of homicide. Brother caused it. Feast of Stephen. Boxing Day — after Christmas. No? December 26. Distribution of the proceeds of the poor box from the church. Deserving poor. Yes. Just deserts."

Morton was so bizarre that I could not imagine how he created such intricate, clever puzzles. I also could not imagine him killing a person. He probably didn't even *know* any people.

"When exactly do you write the puzzles?" I asked. If I could discover when the Wenceslas puzzle had been submitted to the *World*, maybe I could decide whether its contents could possibly be considered clues to the groupie murders.

"Here — look —" The puzzler waded through the mass of paper and motioned me to follow. For the first time, I saw a pristine filing cabinet sitting in a far corner. Its drawers were impeccably labelled and each label bore a date. The puzzler leaned down and pulled out the middle drawer. It was filled with dozens of crisp new file folders, each one tidily labelled and dated.

Cautiously, with the care of a dealer in fine drawings,

Morton lifted one of the files from the drawer and opened the folder. Nestled inside was a clean white sheet on which was printed the original copy of the Wenceslas puzzle.

I could see the date on the file folder clearly. It was a date in summer. Two-and-a-half years ago.

"You submit them well in advance, then?" I asked.

Morton's pasty face glowed with pride.

"Two years, four months. I send them two years four months ahead. The redbreasted European thrush-family warbler obtains the groveling, soft-bodied, legless invertebrate!"

By the time I got back to Tootie Beets's I was so hungry I heated three cans of tomato soup that I drank right out of the pot. It was 8:30 P.M., too late for a nap. I closed my eyes anyway when I was blasted awake by the phone.

"Ellis, it's Stow," the smooth voice said. "I'm calling from Ottawa and I need your assistance once again."

"Look, Stow, I'm a little tired. I was up . . ."

He acted as though I hadn't even spoken. "I've just taken a call from Riverside. Harpur tells me she is feeling especially fragile tonight. I think that young man is with her again. I'm beginning to think he's spending too much time there. But she's become quite attached to him. I wish I could be there myself but I have a judgment to render in the morning. I simply can't fly to Toronto and get back in time. I want you to go over there right now. Visiting hours are over but the chief administrator has my instructions for you to spend as much time there as she needs, all night if necessary. You *will* do this for me, Ellis, won't you?"

"Why me, Stow?"

"Because Harpur wants it. Goodbye."

I wished I knew how Stow could figure out what Harpur wanted.

She seemed serene when I knocked on her door at nine o'clock. But after she said goodnight to her private nurse, she lost control completely. Her body began to shake. She pulled at my sleeve like a child. Her eyes shone with tears and terror. "Ellis, you have to help. My horse is in the stable."

"Harpur," I said, as calmly as I could, "you haven't had any horses for a long time now, but if you did, it's fine for them to be in the stable. That's where they belong. It's —"

"My horse is in the stable!" she cried more loudly. "My horse is in the stable!"

"Harpur, please. Calm down. Come lie on your bed."

I couldn't imagine why I had agreed to help someone who had the services of a private nurse and a whole hospital. Why expect an amateur like me to be able to calm her?

"Please, Ellis. Please. Please. My horse is in the stable."

She began to pull hard on my arm and I realized she wanted to show me something. She seemed to be drawing me toward her closet where, I supposed, must hang the expensive robes she always wore.

"My horse is in this stable," she said firmly, and yanked open the door.

He was lying there like a child asleep. His long dark eyelashes curved on his olive cheek. His tousled black curls fell over his smooth brow. His lively mouth was still. His young hands were folded and lay on his leather-covered thigh. His heavy boots seemed to anchor an angel not yet ready to ascend. He might indeed have been taken for asleep were there not a hypodermic syringe protruding from his neck.

"My horse is dead. My Gelo."

Harpur was weeping openly now. She held the silk poinsettia I'd seen her wear in her hair. She was shredding its petals with her fingernails.

I realized with a start that it was December 6. Happy St. Nicholas Day.

CHAPTER FIFTEEN

I stayed until they removed Harpur to another room. She went placidly, her hysteria spent, her mind again in that far country from which, someday soon, it would not make the journey back.

I stayed while the yellow bands of police tape were affixed in a St. Andrew's cross over the closet doorway, trapping the cooling cadaver of the beautiful boy and holding it for the police photographers and the meticulous members of the forensic investigations unit.

I stayed to answer the probing questions of the homicide detectives. They didn't seem to be talking about a drug overdose or a suicide. Harpur could not be questioned but hospital officials were called to the scene. They swore there was no way Harpur could have had access to syringes. They also pointed out that the syringe found in the body was not from their approved supplier. It wasn't until they began grilling me that I realized Gelo was the second victim of violence I'd discovered in four days. Was it my imagination or was their tone with me not investigative but accusatory?

By the time the detectives finished with me, it was 6 A.M. Another night's sleep lost. Between loss of sleep and lack of food, I was beginning to feel as though I were floating, a not entirely unpleasant sensation but not one conducive to clear thought. Nevertheless, I did notice that the golden ring I'd seen on Gelo's finger was not on his corpse. Nor was Harpur wearing any jewelry when she had been led away.

I did not mention the ring to the police. Once I had heard witnesses daily in my court say that they had neglected to report important evidence because no one had asked them about it. At the time, I had thought that their omissions were a species of lie. But my years on the wrong side of the bench and the law had taught me that a person is a fool to volunteer information of any sort and a double fool to volunteer it to someone in authority. Whatever you say can and will be used against you in the street as well as in the court. When I had been able to keep nearly nothing else, I had learned, nonetheless, to keep my own counsel.

Just as I had not told the police about the ring, I had also not told them about my tormenting Biblical quotes. I still didn't know whether a note had been found on Anmarie Marsh, the Forest Hill matron, like the notes that had been found on Melia and Paulina and the highlighting in the Bible in Carl Madison's briefcase. Had a note of some sort been secreted on Gelo? Even in those few moments in which Harpur and I had been alone with his body, I did not touch it. My fingerprints on the victim would have sealed my fate as a suspect.

I phoned a message into Marnie Alliston's voice mail, informing her I was sick and would not be coming into work that day.

The house seemed possessed of an unearthly stillness at that early hour. No arguments, no blaring disc players or whatever it was that even the poorest roomer seemed able to afford. No phones ringing. It wasn't until I had nearly lost consciousness that I began to hear an old familiar sound: the hum of a distant vacuum cleaner. I dreamed of Tootie Beets doing her housecleaning in her leather vest and heavy boots. Then I dreamed of my deceased Italian mother doing the same thing in the same outfit. Then I dreamed of nothing at all.

I slept for ten hours without opening my eyes. It was nearly dark when I awoke to the heavy tread of a man on the hall stairs. It was not a sound I'd heard in the house before. I soon realized that it masked a quieter sound, the fall of another pair of feet, lighter, feminine.

I listened to this in a state of semisleep, idly, but I awoke fully when the steps stopped at my own door and the peremptory hand of a police officer rattled the door on its frame.

The massive body of Detective Sergeant Matt West filled the door frame. He was not only broader than me but considerably taller. My eyes were about even with his stout neck. He wore a clean white shirt. Either he had just come on duty or else he had recently changed his clothes. I was about to ask him into the room when he stepped aside to reveal who accompanied him. My fear turned to shame.

Ellen was clearly not as fresh as Matt West. She looked tired after what had probably been a long day in court. And her day was by no means done; she had a husband and a little boy at home. Her dark hair framed a face pale with fatigue and also with an emotion compounded of memory, regret, disgust and pity. Whatever one might call it, the emotion had brought tears she fought to keep out of her eyes.

Maybe she remembered this room of her girlhood. Maybe she simply felt some vague connection to it. Whichever, she never so much as hinted that she realized her father now made his home in the small room that had once been hers.

"Dad," she said, clearing her throat. "I believe you've met Matt West?"

"Yes, I have."

Matt West extended his left hand. Unlike the day I'd talked to him in his office at headquarters, he was wearing his jewelry, one of the five rings of our lawyerly promises. He wore the ring of Gleason, one of our group who had died the day the rings were bestowed. There was another of the group who was dead: William Sterling. Wearing his own ring, he had presumably drowned in the flood two years earlier. His body had never been recovered. Just before Gleason died, he gave his ring to William. Long before William disappeared, he gave Gleason's ring to Matt. I shook Matt's hand and felt the slight impress of the ring's heavy embossing.

"Mr. Portal," Matt West said in his deep, smooth voice. "Ordinarily, the Crown's office wouldn't be involved in a homicide this early in the game, but your daughter Ellen has asked me to allow her to be present during portions of the investigation."

"What investigation?" I asked.

Matt took the chair. I gestured for Ellen to sit on the bed. She seemed to be making a deliberate effort not to look at my meager belongings.

"What investigation?" I repeated.

"Let's not be coy," Matt West said. "We've got four

homicides and an attempted homicide. Two of the victims were discovered by you, besides which it's now known that you and one of the victims share a mutual friend, Queenie Johnson."

"Are you saying I'm a suspect?" I demanded testily.

"Daddy, calm down," Ellen interjected. "That's not what this visit is about. Not at all."

"Look, Mr. Portal," Matt West said, "I'm well aware of the role you played in cracking the Second Chance halfway house case. Also, William Sterling spoke often of you."

"So you're aware I'm known to the police, is that what you're getting at?"

"I think it's pretty obvious," the detective said, "that you've come to the same conclusion we have. For whatever reason, you find yourself personally involved in this case and it's a mystery to you why and how that might be so. Am I right?"

"About my involvement or about my figuring out *why* I'm involved?" I countered.

Both Matt and Ellen laughed. "Now you sound like an evasive witness in a court case," Ellen said. "Be straight with us, Daddy. Is somebody threatening you? Is somebody after you, too?"

"For heaven's sake, Ellen," I said, beginning to lose my temper again. "I'm an ex-judge. I've put people in jail, fined them, ruined their reputations, brought them into conflict with their families, their employers, even sometimes their churches, their clubs. And as if that weren't enough, I'm a vagrant, a thief and the consort of vagrants and thieves. How could I even keep track of all the people who have reason to harm me?"

"You're being dramatic, irrelevant and evasive,

Daddy," Ellen accused, "and besides that, you're lying. You're hiding something."

"I'm not hiding anything and I'm not lying," I lied. "Why are you tormenting me, Ellen? Why are you here?"

"To get your help in finding a serial killer," Matt West suddenly asserted.

"But you don't even know how they died!" I insisted.

Matt and Ellen exchanged a swift, knowing glance of a type I'd seen pass between the Crown and the police in court countless times.

"Daddy," Ellen said, "get your coat or whatever you're wearing these days. The three of us are going for a ride."

Matt smiled at the gangster allusion but Ellen shot me such a look of aroused impatience that I had my razor in my hand and was halfway to the bathroom before the front door banged shut behind them.

Most departments of the world-renowned Ontario Forensic Sciences Centre, one of the largest and most complete crime labs in existence, keep regular business hours. Yet I think there is never a time of day or night when one dedicated criminalist or another isn't at work in some nook or cranny of the building, which sits right in the middle of the downtown core. The Centre is connected by a special passage to the morgue, which is always open for business.

I followed Matt and Ellen down hallways, up staircases, past labs — some extremely modern and well equipped, others looking like they'd been used for decades — until we reached the small, tidy office of the chief toxicologist, Max Rabinovitch, a dapper man at least seventy. No time was lost in preliminaries of any sort. He got right to the point.

"The culprit here," he said, lightly tapping a closed folder on his desk with a finger of the hand in which he held his reading glasses, "is curare, also known as moonseed, among other things. Like most drugs, it has several derivatives and a number of methods of administration. It's scientific name is *Strychnos toxifera* if its source is the Loganiaceae family of plants or *Chondodendron tomentosum* if it comes from Menispermaceae."

There was — whether in my imagination or in reality — an odd smell in that section of the lab, a scent halfway between sweet and medicinal that was making my empty stomach threaten to heave. I swallowed hard as he went on.

"Every part of the plant is fatally poisonous to humans, but it is the sap that provides the drug. Administered by injection or intravenously, it works swiftly. It causes paralysis, beginning with the eyelids, the face, the neck and throat, ultimately the diaphragm and the lungs. The victim is finally asphyxiated by the total relaxation of the respiratory system. This can occur within ten minutes of an injection of the form of the drug we are talking about, the form found in samples provided to the lab from the victims in this case."

He put on his reading glasses and opened the file. "Victim number one tested positive for a curare derivative called pavulon. Our spectographic analysis picked up fatal levels of this drug in her system. It can tinge the victim's skin blue, an effect that might conceivably be taken for the effect of fatal hypothermia — freezing to death. The victim also had an inflamed liver, though she wasn't a drinker. This finding is also consistent with an overdose of pavulon."

"Overdose?" I interrupted. "Are you implying that there is some standard acceptable dose?"

"Absolutely," the toxicologist replied. "Curare is common in hospitals. One of its derivatives, succinylcholine, is used as an anesthetic. Pavulon is used medicinally as a muscle relaxant."

"Victim number one was the woman called Melia," Ellen said. "What about the others?"

Rabinovitch returned to his file. "Our findings indicate that the two other women and also the boy, Vincent Genovi, died from pavulon administered by injection. Carl Madison, the man presently hospitalized, showed traces of curare in the blood evacuated from his bowel."

My stomach heaved hard and I fought nausea desperately. The sight of the half-dead professor propped against the wall returned with force. However, there was more sickening information to come.

"Some hold that curare is harmless if ingested, eaten or drunk. Personally, I think it's always extremely harmful however administered. And it can be absorbed through cuts or abrasions in the skin. If the drug comes into contact with broken tissue, enough can enter the system to kill. Carl Madison was lucky. Apparently, he has bleeding ulcers. He appears to have swallowed the drug and absorbed a minute amount, enough to paralyze his lungs long enough to make him pass out, but not enough to kill him. His system attempted to eliminate the drug violently as soon as it hit his digestive tract."

"You mean someone put this curare substance into something they knew he was about to eat or drink?"

"Possibly," the toxicologist answered me.

Matt West said, "Assuming the same person killed all

the victims, we're dealing with a serial killer who made a mistake about the effectiveness of taking curare orally?"

"I can't answer that," the toxicologist said, "but I can say that such a hypothesis is consistent with my findings."

"But if it's the same killer each time, why would he or she change methods of administration?" I asked.

"Because of convenience, for one thing," Matt answered. "But also for reasons we may never be able to figure out. Serial killers aren't known for the clarity of their logic."

I wasn't exactly sure why Ellen and Matt West had decided I needed so much information about the poison that had killed Gelo and the others. Maybe it was Ellen's way of answering my request for assistance. Probably she sensed I was afraid and wanted to warn me that my fear was not unfounded. I still wasn't ready to admit to myself or anybody else that I also had been threatened.

We left Matt off back at Police Headquarters, not far from the morgue, and Ellen drove me home. "Why does Matt West think I can help him?" I asked Ellen when we turned on to my street and pulled to a stop in front of Tootie's house.

"Maybe he respects you, Daddy. Maybe he even considers you an equal. Did that ever occur to you?"

"You sound angry, Ellen."

"Why shouldn't I be angry? You're up to something. Something's going on that you're not telling me, Dad."

"Oh, you think so, do you?" I was beginning to feel angry and manipulated, too. "What do you want from me, anyway?"

"I want you to tell me everything you know about this case. I want you to pull yourself together and stop playing games. If you are going to be in court, be in court the way you were meant to be — as a lawyer, as a judge. Stop this ridiculous charade. The time has come for you to . . ."

"Forget the speech, Ellen, and forget about my stellar career. As for helping Matt West on his case, there's nothing but the merest coincidence that ties me to the victims."

"Not so!"

"Don't argue. Let me talk. I *have* done some work on this. Despite their denials, the police must have thought there was some connection between the killings and the puzzle that appeared in the *Toronto Daily World* or they wouldn't have bothered denying the claim. I checked that out. I actually spoke to the man who devised that puzzle. It was written more than two years before being published."

"So what, Daddy? You know as well as I do that people can use the work of others to their own purposes. Maybe the killer is somebody who just *saw* the puzzle and not the person who wrote it!"

"The puzzle was published after the first murder, not before," I told her. "The puzzle was about saints. Queenie pointed out there might be some connection between saints' feasts and our killer but that's a dead end too, Ellen. It doesn't take a genius to understand that *every day* is a saint's day."

"I don't know about that," Ellen said.

"What do you know about the court groupies?" I ventured to ask.

"Those pathetic old souls that hang around the courtroom all day listening to trials because they've got nothing better to do?"

"Yes."

"I know they hang around that minister," Ellen said.

"He was never around until Melia was found dead. I've heard he was hired by the Ministry of the Attorney General to do grief counselling with them because of her death."

"How would the Ministry ever have the budget for something like that?" I asked in amazement.

"I don't know. Maybe he's a volunteer. All I know is that he's a sort of ringleader. Where he goes, they go — in their own roundabout way, of course," she added with a small smile.

"Do you know whether he might have been hired to do that sort of counselling anywhere else?" I asked Ellen.

"No," she answered, "Why?"

"Just wondering." I didn't want to tell her I'd seen the man at Harpur's hospital. In fact, as much as I loved my daughter, I didn't want to tell her anything else. I didn't trust Matt West, even if he did wear one of the five gold rings of friendship.

The next day, Queenie was waiting by the door of the courthouse that I usually entered. I was surprised to see her but more than that, I was surprised to be so glad to see her.

Without even saying good morning, she reached out and handed me a brown paper bag. When I accepted it, she smiled and said, "I brought you lunch so you don't have to be afraid to eat."

"Come in and let's have a coffee before we get started," I invited. I owed her a big apology but Queenie was the most subtle woman — person — I'd ever met. She knew and I knew that my apology was in the word "we".

I told her about Gelo. "I heard that," she said. "Somebody at my house read it to me from the newspaper. Your name was in the paper, too. They said about how you used to be a judge. They said you also found somebody else last week. I don't think that looks so good. Maybe they're gonna think it's you that done it."

I told her about Matt West then, and about the little trip I'd taken to the lab.

"I don't know why the police would want you to help them," Queenie said, echoing my own thoughts. "Maybe they think you know somethin' they don't."

"That could be."

Queenie glanced around the courthouse cafeteria. A dozen or so Court Services workers in their blue blazers were gathered around a long table chatting and laughing, sharing a coffee before they set off for their assigned courts. "There's nothin' we can do in this here courthouse, Your Honor. You're like stuck in here."

"Yes, but it's still the only way we can keep our eye on the groupies."

Queenie shook her head almost imperceptably. "I ain't saying you should quit or nothin'. I'm just sayin it ain't enough."

"What are you suggesting?"

Without meeting my eyes, Queenie said softly but emphatically, "After they did that protest thing, them groupies is sort of in trouble. They ain't exactly been thrown out or nothin', but they gotta watch theirselves. If anything is gonna happen with them, it ain't gonna happen here. We gotta follow them. We gotta see where they go and what they do when they ain't here."

I gave it only a brief moment's thought. "Queenie, I said, "you're right. And we have to start today." I didn't add *before anybody else gets killed*.

She caught my eye and nodded again. "We," she said.

I didn't see her again before lunch. I took the bag she had given me out of my locker and I ate what was inside without worry: a sandwich, a cookie and an apple. Just as I finished the last bite, I realized she'd also put a paper napkin in the bag. I used it to wipe the last crumbs from my face.

I was eating in the locker room where a few of the male Court Services Officers were gathered. "Time to get back," one of them announced. I stood, gathered the napkin, the paper bag the lunch had come in, and the plastic wrap Queenie had used and balled them in my fist.

There was a trash can just outside the locker-room door, and I planned to deposit the garbage on my way out. But when I opened the door, I saw that one of the cleaners was emptying the trash into a big mobile bin that he pushed around the halls of the building.

Seeing this, I started to toss the paper ball in an arc over the large trash receptacle. As I did so, I saw something I had not noticed about the paper napkin, even when I'd held it up to my face. On the outside of the ball I'd made of my refuse, I could clearly see that written on the napkin was a message in a dark, strong but not too steady hand.

Instinctively, I grabbed. But it was too late. My aim was excellent. The ball of paper landed effortlessly right smack in the middle of the bin and sank into a mixture of pounds and pounds of other paper.

"Come on, Portal, we're late," someone urged me.

I watched helplessly as the cleaner moved on, pushing the full cart down toward the end of the hall where the incinerator lay.

CHAPTER SIXTEEN

My stomach hurt all afternoon, but the first faint twinge of real pain didn't come until the last annoying twang of heavy metal relinquished my half-asleep ears. I glanced at the clock radio I'd brought home from the thrift shop a few days before. It was nearly midnight. I wondered where Tootie was and why she wasn't reprimanding the roomer who'd broken the eleven o'clock rule.

The next time I glanced at the digits on the bedside clock there were too many of them. They seemed to swim in a small crooked circle, a red blur of dashes and dots. I was studying them in amazement when suddenly my torso rippled in an excruciating contraction from my solar plexus to my groin.

Instinctively, I curled into the fetal position, but another spasm even more intense than the first grabbed me and I straightened my legs in a futile attempt to relieve the pressure. It radiated from deep inside me and built until my skin felt as though it could not stretch enough to accommodate whatever it was that was exploding in my gut.

It hurt so much that I had to fight the urge to cry out. The last thing I needed was for my fellow rooming-house inmates to start yelling at me to shut up. Even the effort of pressing my lips together seemed to increase the intensity of my pain as well as adding a tremor of impending nausea to my problems.

Before too many more agonizing moments had passed, I began to sweat — a cold, clammy film that coated my whole body and sent shivers across my shoulders and down my legs to the back of my bent knees.

I don't know how long it took me to realize I had to get to the bathroom, but the realization of just how far away it was hit me at the same time as the conviction that if I didn't get there at once, I would die in a disgraceful puddle just like Carl Madison's.

I could not stand upright. Crouching along the hall, supporting myself by one hand pressed to the wall, I somehow managed to negotiate the long dark corridor.

I suffered greatly once I reached that room, but I did not exactly suffer in solitude. Four times people pounded on the door, wanting to use the bathroom. Each time I managed to get them to go away without incurring their complete wrath. I remembered once having boasted that nobody in my house ever had to knock on a closed bathroom door. We had enough for everyone. Tootie Beets, unfortunately, could not make the same claim.

It was past 3 A.M. when I crawled spent and shaking back into my bed and pulled the still-wet covers over me. I had just dozed off when I sensed someone hovering over me. I started out of my fitful sleep to feel a cool hand against my bare chest pushing me back against the bed.

"Don't be scared, Mr. Portal. It's just me, your landlady.

I heard you in the bathroom. I brought you a glass of water."

"No." Even the thought of water made me feel sick again.

"Come on. Just drink some. You'll feel better." She slipped her hand behind my neck, lifted my head and held the glass to my lips. I decided I was too tired to fight any more. I took a long draught. And then I closed my eyes again, prepared to sleep the sleep from which one does not awake.

Despite my ordeal, however, I did wake up — and in plenty of time to get to work. I sat up in my bed expecting the room to spin but it didn't. I swung my legs over the edge of the mattress and tested my feet on the floor. They seemed willing to support my weight. True, I felt somewhat lightheaded. In fact, I thought, considering all that had passed out of me one way or another, I wasn't just lightheaded, I was actually lighter!

This grim joke did nothing to lessen the mixed anger and fear that infused me. I had eaten nothing the day before except the lunch Queenie had given me. And I had taken it directly from her and put it in my locker, which had a padlock to which there were only two keys. I had bought the padlock myself. One key had been in my pocket the whole day. The other had never left my room.

I got up, opened the door and peered down the hall. The door to the bathroom was open. A towel lay twisted on the floor, my towel. I hastened to throw on my trousers and shirt. I wanted to make sure I hadn't left any other reminders of my awful night and to take advantage of the early hour. Nobody else was up at 6:30 A.M.

As I splashed water on my face, I saw that the rash on

the back of my hands had returned with a vengeance. I had been putting antiseptic cream on them every day but nothing had ever soothed like the Cree remedy Queenie had applied. I remembered how strong her hands were as she ground the rotted wood dust to a fine powder. I remembered how cool and soft they were as she had rubbed her medicine into my skin.

As I brushed my teeth, I thought about the lunch again. In criminal cases, one of the main ways of determining what has happened is to examine the physical objects that played a role in the crime. These are commonly referred to as exhibits. An exhibit is virtually useless unless it has continuity. Quite simply, continuity means the uninterrupted account of the whereabouts of an object. If an exhibit has continuity — a bullet from a murder weapon, for example — one can say exactly where that bullet has been from the time it was recovered at the scene to the time it appears in a courtroom.

Did Queenie's bagged lunch have continuity? I had not lost track of it from the time Queenie had given it to me to the time I ate it, but could Queenie vouch for its continuity from the time she had made it to the moment she had placed it in my hands?

I thought of how many cases there had been where a few lost seconds had an enormous impact. A stolen vehicle pursued by police speeds around a corner. Two seconds later the police car turns the same corner. A man runs away from the scene. Is he the driver of the stolen car or is he just an innocent man who was on the scene?

A woman turns to say goodbye to her friend. When she turns back, her child is missing.

How many times do we lose track of our world for only

a second or two? How many times do we turn back to find that world has changed forever?

I dragged myself to work and got assigned to a trial for breach of trust. The manager of a bank had been arraigned for an alleged staged robbery of a teller. I was so engrossed that I hardly heard the door of the courtroom open. Marnie Alliston's hooked finger summoned me.

"I need you to work with a sequestered jury," she said. "I know you've never done it before but the matron will help you. Can you stay overnight if they can't reach a verdict by 9 P.M.?"

I nodded. It was only 11 A.M. My stomach was still. I didn't know what sort of case it might be but I knew it was fairly unlikely that a jury would deliberate for more than a few hours.

"Courtroom 4-3," Marnie said. "Get there right away."

I took the escalator two flights up, scanning the crowd for Queenie. It puzzled me that Matt and Ellen had shared the information with me about the poisons used on the victims. Again I wondered: did they know, without my ever having told them, about the notes I'd received? Was the visit to the toxicologist their way of warning *me* to be careful? Clearly I had not been careful enough.

Counsel for the Crown was giving the final address to the jury in courtroom 4-3. The case, I figured out from the summary of the evidence, was home invasion and armed robbery. As a judge, I had heard thousands of grisly tales. One of the reasons I had turned away from the courts was my conviction that these bleak fables of weakness and malice would never end, would recycle endlessly through the calendar of the court year like moveable feasts.

So I had to remind myself that the anxiety on the faces

of the jury reflected that all this was new to them. They watched in rapt attention and not a little fear as the Crown held up a semiautomatic for them to consider, its large gray exhibit tag swinging from the grip, from which, I could see, the clip had been removed.

I glanced at the spectators in the court. As though at some bleak wedding, two sets of people were huddled on the wooden benches. Behind the Defense sat the family and friends of the accused, wearing the same anxious faces as the jury. Behind the Crown sat a man, a woman, three young teenagers and an elderly couple. These I took to be the victims and their family. Their expressions were anxious, too, but compounded with their suspense as to the outcome of the trial were two other emotions: righteousness in the seeking of justice and revenge.

The usually somnolent air of the courtroom sparked with anticipation in this case. Everyone sat mesmerized as the Crown concluded and the judge began his charge to the jury.

I slipped into the empty CSO's chair by the door and listened, thinking that it might have been me addressing this court, instructing these jurors, presiding over this case. I thought of my robe hanging ignominiously in a rent-by-the-week room. I heard the judge say, "Swear the constables." With those words the jury was now officially deliberating, now legally sequestered. As required by law, I rose to approach the bench to be sworn in. I was past the bar and halfway to the spot in front of the registrar where I was supposed to stand and take the Bible in my hand. Something compelled me to turn and look toward the back of the courtroom. The handsome groupie minister in his Protestant suit had silently slipped into court and was sitting among the members of the family of the accused.

"Do you swear," the registrar intoned, "that you will keep everyone of this Jury in a private and convenient place, that you shall permit no one to speak to them or any of them, nor shall you speak yourself, unless it be to inquire whether they have agreed upon their verdict, without the leave of the Court, so help you God?"

"I do so swear," I uttered, surprising myself. Without quite noticing the moment of transition, I seemed to have graduated from scoffer to believer.

The registrar handed me a package of exhibits, including the gun and its clip. I took it and followed the single file of jurors out their door.

The empty hours passed at their own erratic pace. I had no watch, but sometimes I managed to catch a glimpse of the matron's. By law, the jury room door could not be opened unless both the matron and I were present. Once in a while, the matron had to leave and I was left alone knowing I couldn't open the door without causing a mistrial, even if a juror summoned me for emergency assistance. But I was kept busy bobbing up and down like a duck on a rough pond as judges passed back and forth. From time to time, prisoners in handcuffs and shackles clanked down the hall escorted by blueshirts.

"If the jury can't decide in the first hour," the matron said finally, "then it's usually a long one." She reached over to the cart we'd used to pile up all the books, newspapers and magazines we'd taken from our jury, which was not allowed reading material during its deliberations. Their cell phones, pagers, radios and notebook computers were also on the cart. The matron took a magazine and idly thumbed through it, studying the pictures.

I studied the hallway that stretched the whole length of the south side of the building, several hundred feet. The entire area was secure, able to be entered only by plastic card, though it could be exited via a complex system of doors leading to every part of the courthouse except for the judges' chambers. Some of the doors were always locked. Some never. A person who didn't know what he was doing could end up trapped in this maze, while one who *did* know could use that knowledge to great advantage.

The jury was out for twenty-six hours. At 6 P.M. we took them across the street to the Maple Leaf Cafe for dinner. At 9 P.M. we took them all to the Diplomat-Dundas hotel, where they slept, and the matron, deputy and I stayed awake all night guarding their rooms.

The foreman delivered the verdict at 2 P.M. the next afternoon. As he rose and uttered the word "Guilty," one of the jurors began to silently weep, the tears coursing down her exhausted face. The matron hurried to offer her a tissue.

The family of the accused was also distraught. And they, too, had their comforter. The minister wordlessly opened his Bible. All those among whom he sat put their hands on its pages. What had empowered him to offer solace to the troubled souls of the court? I renewed my determination to find out.

CHAPTER SEVENTEEN

It was 3 P.M. when we escorted the last of the jurors from the courthouse, the matron and I doing our best to keep them from coming into contact with the weeping family of the accused and the gloating family of the victims.

I stowed my uniform blazer in my locker and headed back upstairs to the Armory Street door of the courthouse on the north side of the building. After being on duty for thirty hours, I felt not exhaustion but an odd sense of exhilaration. I circled through the revolving door of the courthouse.

"Your Honor, I been real sick."

I jumped at the sound of Queenie's voice as thin and disembodied as if it had come from inside my head.

I swept my eyes across the complicated set of glass doors that formed the exit. The revolving door was centered between two other doors and the whole area was inset beneath a broad concrete lintel. I finally made out Queenie nearby, cowering in the gloom. She seemed to be wearing even more layers of clothing than usual and her head was covered with a thick black shawl. I had never seen Queenie wear a headcovering of any sort.

"Queenie?" I questioned, joining her in the shadows and reaching out toward her shoulder.

With a nearly imperceptible gesture, she moved her shoulder so that my hand could not quite meet it.

"I been sick since two days ago. As soon as I ate lunch the other day, I knew something was wrong."

Beyond the doorway in which we sheltered, the snow was falling in the fat, creamy flakes that indicate it's not really cold. Yet Queenie was quaking so, she could hardly speak.

"I'm starved but I ain't been able to keep nothing down."

"When's the last time you tried?"

"Breakfast."

"Let's try again."

She shook her head but I took a chance in holding out my hand. She hung on to it as we negotiated our way across Armory Street and north up Center Street to Dundas and our Chinese restaurant. I thought being somewhere familiar would make it easier for her to attempt to eat a little. I managed to convince her to have some chicken soup with wontons.

"Queenie," I ventured to ask after she'd sipped a bit, "did you bring a lunch for yourself the other day?"

"Yes, but I made the lunch real careful, Your Honor. From the time I bought the stuff to make the sandwiches and also the fruit and that, nobody touched nothing except me."

"Did you ever lose sight of the lunches?"

Queenie gave the matter a moment's consideration.

Then, she said, "You know how they have that stand by the door to City Hall?"

She was referring to a coffee-and-tea concession at the east end of the courthouse. It opened onto a secured lounge where prospective jurors were given orientation. On the other side was a counter open to the public. It was one of the busiest spots in the courthouse.

"Yes, Queenie, I know what you mean."

"Well, I had enough money for a tea the other morning when I come in. I bought the tea and went to put some sugar and milk in it. They're on a little table at the side. The milk run out, though, so I went back to the counter and asked the girl if she had more. It took her a while on account of there was a lot of people bein' served. When I left both the lunches on the little table, I wasn't lookin' right at 'em." She pushed away her soup bowl as if she'd suddenly lost her appetite again. "But I don't see how nobody could add poison to our lunches without unwrapping the sandwiches. Mine didn't look like nobody tampered with it."

I suppressed a smile. Queenie's time in court was beginning to teach her the jargon.

"Queenie, there is a way somebody could have poisoned those sandwiches."

"How?"

"The other day I got a call from Matt West. He knows how Melia and Paulina and the others died. They were injected."

"Injected?" Queenie's eyes widened. She was no stranger to needles.

"Yes. Think about it, Queenie. A victim could easily be caught unawares. It only takes a fraction of a second to stick a needle into somebody or something. It's certainly easier than shooting or stabbing, isn't it? The poison was something called pavulon. It's used in hospitals."

"But hospitals guard everything. You don't just go into a hospital and grab a drug."

"Unless you are somebody who is a regular in the halls or the rooms. Or unless it's part of your job to administer drugs. Or unless you have swift fingers."

"What do you mean?"

"If somebody was especially quick with his hands, he could swipe things, drugs or needles. And he would also be quick enough to do something like injecting the contents of a paper bag quickly."

"You don't have to swipe needles."

"Do you mean that you can easily get them from the anti-HIV free needle exchange?"

"No, Your Honor, that's not what I mean at all. What I mean is, that's one of them things you can get free if you have a drug card."

"A drug card?"

"Yeah. All the seniors have them. If you're over sixty-five, you don't need to pay for no needles. The government pays for them, of course. Paulina could also get free needles, too. Remember she had the deal with the insurance company to get free medical stuff? That was one of the things she used to get free for Melia's husband. He's a diabetic."

"Matt West is treating these deaths as though they were the work of a serial killer."

"We gotta try to talk to Matt West about them Bible notes again," Queenie said. "Maybe he can figure out why the killer is after certain people."

I had forgotten about the notes for a moment. "Queenie, was there a note in your lunch?"

203

"No. You know I couldn't of read it, anyhow. Was there a note in yours?"

"I think so. I saw some writing on a paper napkin."

"I didn't put no napkin in the lunch."

We were united in fear. After a pause she went on. "Them serial killers always seem to be after something, sex or insurance money."

"Regrettably, there have been enough serial killers that quite a lot is known about them," I answered. "They are almost always white males between the age of thirty and forty. They tend to kill people in a different social class from themselves. They *might* get money or sex as a result of their killing. And sometimes they take trophies, almost like souvenirs, things belonging to their victims. But the killing is usually about something else. It's usually about the killer's own inability to be accepted by society, to be accorded the respect and recognition he thinks he deserves. Sometimes the killer has a vision of society that he thinks can be achieved if he eliminates certain people. He sees himself as an angel or a visionary. He wants to rid the world of riffraff."

"You mean riffraff like us?" Queenie asked. And despite the fact that we had both just escaped death, the two of us burst into laughter.

I left Queenie at the southeast corner of Nathan Phillips Square near Bay Street and doubled back toward University Avenue. Tired as I was, I felt a desire to walk through the softly falling snow. Walking past the ornate wrought iron fence of Osgoode Hall, I saw the cadre of groupies obviously finished with their week in court. The minister was herding them along like the shepherd he was.

Without giving the matter a moment's further thought, I decided to follow them. Still together, six entered the subway. There the group separated, the minister and the woman named Jeannette heading for the southbound train. There were only one or two other passengers on the platform. The minister and Jeannette were so engrossed in conversation that it was unlikely they would notice me standing behind one of the thick supporting pillars.

Jeannette spoke in an animated manner. Her face seemed to light up every time her gaze met the minister's. She also seemed to have minimum control over her hands. They fluttered as she spoke, flew up as if to pick some small speck off the sedate brown suit of her companion, who flinched as her fingers met the cloth of his jacket, though his expression did not otherwise change from its calm, benign stillness, nor did his own long fingers stray from where his hands were modestly crossed in front of him.

When the train arrived, I managed to slip into the next car, keeping my eye on them through the window in the door between the cars. The train swung "around the loop", the bottom part of the huge U it makes underneath the city, changing from southbound to northbound. Jeannette got off at Bloor station. When she got off, the minister pulled a small black book from his pocket. Had he been a different sort of man, I would have wondered whether he were choosing a date for the weekend. I decided that what he was really doing was reading the Bible. I was surprised when only four stops later, he stood abruptly as the train pulled into Davisville station.

Davisville and Yonge is a lively downtown section of the city where high-rise tenants mingle with single-family house dwellers and enjoy busy coffee shops, fruit and vegetable marts, English-style pubs, trendy dress shops. It wasn't hard to follow the minister along Davisville half a block east to a large apartment building. He did not "buzz up", use the intercom to get someone in an apartment to let him in. He used his key.

I had come a long way but all I'd learned was that he lived in a nondescript apartment building, just like 25,000 other people in his immediate neighborhood.

The next day was Saturday, and I slept all day and most of the night. I heard the phone ring. I heard a knock on the door. I heard Tootie Beets calling my name. I ignored them all.

By Sunday morning, I was all slept out and I awoke in the pitch dark at 5 A.M. I lay in bed for awhile, thinking about how pale and fragile Queenie had been on Friday. Then I realized the minister would be going to Sunday morning services. He had taken the subway home the night I'd followed him. That might mean that he didn't have a car, which would mean that he would take public transit to church, or even walk. Either way, I could easily follow him again. And since the subway wouldn't open until 9 A.M. because of Sunday hours, I decided to walk the couple of miles to Davisville and Yonge. It would take about an hour.

When I opened the door of my room, I saw a thick envelope with my name on it lying at my feet. The writing was Tootie's. She often stuck things between the door and the frame. This was probably yet another edition of the house rules. I tossed it on the bed, locked the door and took off.

At 9:45 A.M., two hours after my arrival at the minister's building, my target stepped out of his elevator.

I had to follow him at a good distance because the

snowy streets were nearly deserted. He did not head in the direction of the subway but instead took a winding path south across Balliol Street, across Merton Street and through the gates of Mount Pleasant Cemetery.

Against the pristine snow, the Christmas green-and-red wreaths on the graves were startling. But the minister did not seem to be sightseeing. He strode purposefully and I stalked him stealthily. Before long, we were on the grounds of a gray stone church with a medieval-style bell tower and massive stained-glass windows. I suddenly remembered the hours I had spent as a child studying the windows of our church. We were poor people but our church was huge and grand. Not far from Tootie Beets's rooming house, my old house of worship still stood. It would not be decorated for Christmas until the last waning hours of Advent. I remembered my mother trudging through the snow to help with the decorations. I brushed those old thoughts from my mind.

Before I knew it, the minister opened a small door at the rear of the church complex that I now saw comprised several additions and levels. I was too close to him to hide or to flee. He paused, turned and to my amazement, politely held the door open before me. As he did so, I thought a flicker of recognition passed across his face, but he smiled and said, "Good morning. If you're here for Bible class, please follow me. You can wait in my study for the others."

I hesitated. *Who* was I about to follow and *where*? If he did recognize me, he didn't let on. I stamped the snow off my boots and proceeded behind him down a labyrinthine hall, then up a short flight of stairs. "I don't believe I've told you my name," the minister said.

"No."

"Mark. You can call me Mark."

"Angelo Portalese."

Either my fear was working on my imagination or else a look of puzzlement came into the minister's eyes. But he just shook my hand and ushered me into a study of glass-fronted bookcases, a mahogany desk, two wing chairs upholstered in a pale gray felt. A small leaded window caught the morning sun and gently filled the little room with soft light.

"I'll be back shortly," Minister Mark told me. He turned toward the door, but then, as if as an afterthought, he turned back, walked to one of the bookcases and removed a well-worn leather-bound volume. Then he disappeared into the carpeted hallway, leaving me with the Bible in my hand. But I forgot the word of God because I had spotted a smooth leather briefcase on the floor, leaning against the desk. I got down on my haunches and ran my fingers along its metal clasp. Without resistance, it sprang open.

I peered inside. There were a number of financial statements and I slid them partway up without removing them from the case. As I pushed them back down, I heard voices far off down the hall, a run of piano notes and a few singers warming up. I pushed the papers down harder. I met resistance. There was something else in the case. I reached in and at the bottom, I felt a hard object that seemed to be wrapped in soft cloth.

The cloth was white linen — a fine, sheer Irish linen handkerchief. I could make out the curved stitching of a hand-monogram. Four letters were ornately intertwined but clearly discernible: HBSM. Harpur Blane Stoughton-Melville. My fingers began to tremble as I worked open the little bundle. A single thick band of gold, heavily embossed with two related but different designs — the blindfold of the goddess of justice and the scales of justice — lay on the handkerchief. Justice is blind. Justice is balanced.

I knew that Harpur's ring bore an inscription that pertained to her alone. I had never seen that inscription. Before I could get my glasses out of my pocket, I heard Mark's voice join the others in the hall. Hastily, I rewrapped the ring in the handkerchief, dropped it back in the case, propped the case back against the desk, rose and ran off. Was being in church the obstacle that prevented me from stealing the ring?

There was a phone message waiting when I got back to Tootie's — from Carl Madison, who claimed to have gotten my number from the police. The poisoned professor had recovered sufficiently to have been sent home from the hospital, and he wanted to thank me in person for "saving" his life. I called him back and we spoke only long enough to arrange a meeting at his home on Tuesday when I finished work.

When I'd completed these arrangements, I turned to the envelope from Tootie, who, I had learned from a fellow inmate, was spending the afternoon singing Christmas carols door to door with some of her friends. The thought of a choir of chrome and leather-clad, blood-lipped street urchins was enough to get me interested in Christmas again.

As I tore open the white envelope, I saw that it contained a smaller envelope of thick, creamy-colored paper. I turned it over. On the back on the point of the flap was a seal embossed in gold. The seal of the Supreme Court of Canada.

I was suddenly so sure that something dreadful had

happened to Harpur that I was almost unable to open this note, which of course was from Stow.

But I did open it. Inside the envelope was a folded card the front of which was embossed with the same golden seal. The card bore the previous day's date. I realized Stow must have sent a driver with the note. Beneath the date was a single sentence in Stow's surprisingly delicate handwriting. It said, "Harpur has asked you not to abandon her and to prove that you have not by coming to see her at home on the evening of Wednesday, December 15 at 7 P.M. for a private conversation."

There was no request to R.S.V.P. Stow just assumed that I would come as summoned.

Carl Madison lived in a condominium on Gloucester Street south of Bloor. It was an unpretentious street in an unpretentious neighborhood. Still, a condominium in the downtown core couldn't be had for less than $100,000. How would a man with no apparent job acquire so much?

There must once have been a time when Madison's apartment was a showplace but it appeared to have suffered a decline. Black-and-white drawings, some in charcoal, others in ink and in pencil, shared the gray walls with artfully framed photographs. But for every artwork that *was* there, two weren't. The wall was dotted with patches of darker gray where works had been removed.

Cheap, prefabricated bookshelves bowed under the weight of fine old leather-bound volumes, but there were spaces here, too, showing that items had been taken off the shelves and never replaced. Atop a rosewood console sat a tiny portable TV. Beside a brocade Victorian settee, a cardboard box with a plastic tablecloth served as an end table. It was a standing joke on the street that you weren't really poor until you had to sell the furniture to pay the rent. It seemed Carl Madison was working his way into poverty one possession at a time.

"Thanks for coming tonight," Madison said. He seemed remarkably at ease for a sick man who had just survived an attempt on his life. "I credit you with saving me. If you hadn't come upon me in the stairwell, I'd be dead today."

He seemed so congenial. "How did you come to be in the stairwell, anyway?" I ventured.

"I'm a bit foggy," the professor said, "but I recall that just before lunch on that day, I started to feel dizzy. The last thought I remember having was that I didn't want to disturb the court by walking out in the middle of a witness's testimony. The next thing I remember was waking up in the hospital and being told that one of the Court Services Officers had rescued me."

I took the opportunity to push him a little more. "Do you think it was something you ate? I mean something unusual?"

"It could have been anything. I have breakfast with friends at the court every day. None of us are what you'd call well-off, so we share. One or two people bring for everybody. We take turns." He hesitated, glanced at me, seemed to make up his mind about something and after a little pause, went on. "The truth is, we take turns going over to Extra Gleanings — that's a food bank. There's a quota. You can only get so much during a week. So we worked out a system where if we take turns, we end up with enough for breakfast for everybody all week."

"That's good planning," I said. "It takes a lot of thinking to keep from being hungry when you're not pulling in a regular salary anymore."

"Yeah," Carl Madison said with a rueful little laugh. "I was not always as you see me today."

"What happened?" I dared to ask.

I didn't think he'd answer, but after a long pause, he did. "I think the best way to put it is to say that one day I woke up and discovered that for a long time my life had been running without me. I'd been a whiz kid in grade school, a genius in university, a great white hope in my research, a tenured professor at the impossible age of twenty-eight. But *I* wasn't anywhere in the picture. No interests. No leisure. No friends. And I'd been having worse and worse stomach pains. One day while I was lecturing, I passed out. I ended up spending months in the hospital. I never saw the inside of a university classroom again and you know what? I couldn't care less."

I couldn't detect any bitterness in his voice. Which made me think he probably still had the same habit of hiding his emotions that had most likely led to an ulcer.

"I burned out, too," I admitted.

"So I hear."

"What?"

Madison locked eyes with me for a moment. Then he looked away. "You're Ellis Portal. Former judge. Former criminal. Now court worker. It looks good on you."

"Are you trying to insult me?"

"Far from it. I know who you are. You know who I am. I invented the concept of Lambert's Cascade. I didn't make a penny on it. Never will. But I'm a happy man. So I eat leftover baked goods? So I wear somebody else's old clothes? Do I have to worry about recessions and tax brackets and rising costs of living? I don't have a cost of living. My understanding is that you have the same economics."

"How do you know so much about me?"

"It's around the courthouse."

I was stunned at this bit of news. "People know who I am?"

"Look, Ellis, don't get upset about all this. A lot of the CSOs used to be executives. One was even a lawyer. Now they all earn only enough to make ends meet. But they live peaceful lives. You can, too. All you've got to do is to accept that the past is dead and gone."

I changed the subject quickly. "What do you know about the Wenceslas puzzle in the newspaper? The one in which your invention was a clue? And what do you know about the quotation in the courtroom Bible found in your briefcase?"

Carl Madison stood up. He was unsteady on his feet, either from physical weakness or sudden emotional intensity. "I don't know anything about either. I don't know why the puzzle seems to have referred to me and I don't at all know what kind of demented crank would use a sacred text to threaten someone's life. What I do know is that I was saved by you. I hope I'm not called upon to return the favor because I can't."

A veiled warning about my own safety? Maybe Carl Madison knew more about the killer than he was willing to tell.

CHAPTER EIGHTEEN

The next evening, I was in the heart of Rosedale, the mansioned center of Toronto's old, big money, a section of the city too expensive for me even when I'd been a judge.

I had sometimes been a guest in John Stoughton-Melville's Rosedale home, a simple stone two-story on a cul-de-sac treed with evergreen and the now-bare branches of ornamental apple, pear and cherry.

But its simplicity was deceiving. Twenty years earlier when Anne and I finally moved out of my immigrant neighborhood, Stow was razing a house on this lot on Highland Avenue and replacing it, stone by stone, with a so-called "cottage" removed from the grounds of one of the manor houses of England.

While Anne and I were buying our first dishwasher, Stow was emptying the chapel library of one of the medieval universities of Belgium to provide books for his own library. At about the same time that we had one of my father's associates dig out our basement, lower the floor and put in what was referred to as a "rec room" in those days, Stow was installing in his hallway a curved wooden staircase that had once known the footsteps of a Scottish king.

Don't mistake my meaning. Stow was not a scavenger. He was a savior. What he paid for the contents from that old Belgian library built a new one for the modern university's students.

All of this, however, was totally irrelevant to me as I stood beneath his stone portico in my thrift-store coat and rang his doorbell.

It was not a maid who answered the door. It was a nurse. "Justice Portal?"

That name was as little my own as "Angelo", but I nodded in assent.

"My patient is waiting for you," the woman said. "We've had a number of quiet days and the time at home has done her some good. She's been somewhat more lucid and attentive. But of course, we still have to be careful. Mr. Justice Stoughton-Melville would like his wife to be able to stay home until after Christmas." She gestured for me to step into the foyer, a panelled enclosure of mahogany, brass and etched glass. There was a coat tree there. As I removed my coat and hung it, she continued. "You understand that any conversation that would upset Mrs. Stoughton-Melville might ruin the Justice's Christmas plans."

I followed her across an expanse of burgundy carpet. At the center of two sweeping curves of staircase, appearing to be embraced by them, was a Christmas tree nearly as tall as the room.

I stared at the fourteen-foot spruce in amazement.

"It's for me," a voice said, the voice of a woman who, long ago, had often read my mind. "It's the last Christmas

215

tree I'll ever see, so my husband has indulged me. What do you think of it?"

Gold gauze garlands. Gold beads. Golden globes of shining glass that mirrored the room's expensive antiques. Loops of golden ribbon holding little golden horns and violins. Angels of gold, gold stars. "It's pretty."

Poised on the bottom step of the great staircase was Harpur herself in a sheer gold robe beneath which she wore a pale cream-colored gown that hinted not of the holiday but of the sickroom. Her hair was caught in a large bow at the nape of her slender neck. There was a flush on her cheeks and her lips were flushed, too.

She held one more golden ornament, and the sight of it almost distracted me from seeing that Harpur was wearing her ring again. How had it gotten from Mark's study back to her finger?

As though we were still childhood companions, she took my hand and led me away from the glittering tree and its oppressive gleam. In a dark corner of the huge room, two chairs were set beside a small table. She lowered herself into one and I sat, too.

"Harpur, how did you get your ring back?"

She looked surprised at the question. But then her expression changed and a teasing contemptuous grin flicked across her face. "What makes you think I ever lost it? Maybe you make mistakes now and again, Ellis. Do you think so?"

It was the old game. The object was to make me look like a fool. I used to fight so hard not to let Harpur make me feel inadequate. But Harpur was dying now and I no longer cared about others' opinions. "I'm sure I've made a great number of very serious mistakes in my life, Harpur."

"Including loving me?"

"What?"

"Years ago, Gelo, I promised you that you could ride my horse. Do you remember that?"

"We were children . . ."

"I was rich and you were poor."

"You're still rich and I'm still poor."

For an instant, she got that startled look again. "No. No," she swore with such sudden vehemence that I feared her lucidity was slipping away again. She quieted at once, though, and for awhile, we both stared at the golden apparition of the tree.

"I never lost my ring," she said. "Sometimes Stow makes me take it off but I never lost it."

She stood, moved closer to the fire. She opened her golden robe, and for a moment, she held it out like the sheer wings of a moth, her slender body silhouetted against the flames. Then she turned and as she did, she reached into the pocket of the plain gown she wore under the rich robe.

"Hold out your hand, Ellis," she said with a teasing laugh, "and close your big Italian eyes."

I did what she said. I held out my hand. I kept my eyes closed. I could hear the soft crackle of the fire. In the distance I could also hear the faint strains of Christmas music, Handel or Bach. It seemed like a long time before I felt anything in my palm.

And even then, it took me a minute to realize what I held. First, a slight stiffness, then softness, fabric, thread, then something hard at the center.

My eyes flew open. Harpur still wore her ring, yet in my hand I held the ring wrapped in her handkerchief, the little bundle I'd last seen in Mark's study. Each ring was inscribed with a version of the words, "I promise". I fumbled to find my glasses. I lifted the golden circle so that the room's soft light fell on the inscription inside it.

Ma parole est mon honneur. William Sterling's ancestors were Norman. In his lifetime he was fluently bilingual. This ring had to be his alone — the one I presumed he had taken to his death. Without asking what it might mean about William's fate in the flood two years before, I considered what the appearance of this ring in this place meant to Harpur. The minister had to have brought it. He must have been here in Rosedale during the past three days.

"How did you get this, Harpur?"

I saw Harpur struggle as if trying with all her might to understand my question and to answer it. The effort might well be useless. Alzheimer's is not affected by determination. Yet somehow she managed. "At the hospital. The night Gelo was killed. I saw it on Gelo's hand. He was such a good boy. He didn't steal it. I was so afraid everybody would think he stole it, only he didn't. He found it by the river. He was in the stable and Mark came and I gave him the ring. Mark said he would take care of it for me."

"You saw Mark at the hospital the night Gelo was killed before I came?"

"Yes. That's when I gave him the ring."

"Why did he give it back and when? Did he come here?"

"He visited me. He said it was wrong to keep the ring because he couldn't figure out whose it was. He told me to give it to my husband."

"But how did Mark know where you live?"

Her hands shook and Harpur steadied herself by gripping the back of the velvet-upholstered chair beside me. "I can't remember anymore. And you'll be upset with me. Everybody is always upset with me."

"No. No, Harpur. You were right to call me to tell me about the ring. I'll take it. I'll make sure the right person ends up with it." I slipped it onto the middle finger of my right hand.

Harpur shook her head violently. "No. No. My ring. My ring."

I thought she wanted the ring back but that was not what she was trying to tell me. Instead, she took off her own ring and held it toward me, pleading. "No. My ring. My promise. My ring still has your promise, doesn't it?"

"Yes. You never asked me for anything."

She sat across from me, leaned toward me. Her pale face strained with an intensity that carved her eyes and lips into a rigid mask.

"All right, Harpur. Whatever it is, I'll do it." She bent her head and kissed the ring on my left hand. When she raised her face, her eyes were glazed but she did not weep.

Her lips parted. She spoke only two words. Yet they seemed to echo for a long time in the vast expanse of the wonderful room. I heard them once in my ears, but I knew I would hear them in my heart for the rest of my life.

What she said was, "Kill me."

The temperature had risen suddenly, then rapidly dropped. The snow turned to sleet. The streets were slick with ice but I ran anyway.

At the eastern end of the Bloor viaduct, I cut down behind the Adult Learning Center at Broadview Avenue. I needed to get to the wild. I pulled my coat closer around me as I ran through the park parallel to Broadview Avenue. Above me loomed Riverside Institute.

I fled over the river on the Broadview footbridge and slithered my way down the ice-covered metal staircase that was the only way to get to the lower river at this point.

I missed the last four steps and fell flat on my face at the bottom, but I didn't even feel the paved path scrape my chin, didn't taste the blood where my teeth met my tongue. I just kept running until the city around me seemed to disappear and the wilderness of the valley reached up and cupped me in its empty hand.

On such a night, even some of those who swore they would never sleep under a roof again changed their minds and knocked on the doors of hostels and shelters and begged for one more chance to prove they could keep the peace for the length of a night.

Mercy. That was what one sought when there was absolutely nothing else to seek. I remembered how the people used to stand before my bench and beg for mercy. And I remembered how I used to tell them that justice alone was what I dispensed. "There is no room for mercy in a court of law," I used to say. I was wrong. There is room for mercy even in the wild night, even among those who have spat in the face of mercy.

"Kill me." It was the ultimate plea for mercy. The strongest plea there is. I had not answered Harpur. If mercy is beyond justice, I asked myself, what is beyond mercy?

"Nothing," the sleet seemed to say as I curled up beneath a thick bush and prepared to sleep for the night. The first time I slept in a sleet storm, I caught pneumonia and ended up trapped in a hospital for six weeks. Then I learned the secret of sleeping under sleet. But nobody needs to know what that is except me.

I awoke at 7 A.M. I walked back up into the city streets. As the sun rose, it cast its pink light on a forest of ice, turning the whole city into a palace of rose-colored crystal.

"After mercy," some inner angel said to me, "comes grace."

And suddenly, I saw the sense of it all. The puzzle, the Bible quotes, the victims, the courthouse. I saw what tied all these together. It was, as such things always are, remarkably simple. I saw what the killer was trying to accomplish and why I merited a place on the list. Every day I showed up in court dressed in my CSO uniform was one more proof to the killer that I deserved his attention, indeed, his devotion.

I had put off admitting my real involvement in the case of the dead groupies as long as I could. Now it was time to lay my cards on the table, to do something I have always hated to do: to ask for help. So I decided to contact Matt West.

Not surprisingly, Matt agreed to see me as soon after work as I could get to Police Headquarters, a walk of less than ten minutes from the courthouse. I had not come alone. Queenie was with me, confident she knew Matt better than I. He also didn't seem surprised to see that I was carrying a plastic bag from my local convenience store. Such battered receptacles were as de rigueur in my present world as Gucci briefcases had once been.

"Melia, Paulina, Anmarie, Carl, the boy Harpur called Gelo . . . ," Matt West intoned. "Good King Wenceslas, St. Nicholas, the Bible . . . What do all these things have in common?"

"Melia was once an athlete but was reduced to begging," I answered. "Paulina was a disfigured former beauty. Anmarie a disgraced Forest Hill matron. Carl was a promising scientist who ended up selling off his possessions to pay the rent."

"So?" Matt asked. He shifted in his chair. Like everything else in his office, it creaked.

"Every one of those groupies had been a victim," I said. "It doesn't take much imagination to figure out that anybody who hangs around a courthouse day in and day out has been in some kind of trouble. Everybody knew Paulina had some crazy scheme to right the wrongs of her insurance case and Anmarie Marsh had a conviction for credit-card fraud. Maybe she . . ."

"The record doesn't show she appealed that conviction," Matt West interrupted.

"That may be irrelevant," I argued. "Carl Madison claims not to care that he was robbed of his profits from developing Lambert's Cascade, but maybe he's hiding his desire for a payback. Court is a place where people bide their time." *If it doesn't run out first,* I could have added. "I don't know if any of the other groupies have been disgraced in some way. But if they have, they may be vulnerable to a person who's convinced he can help out."

Matt West opened one of his carefully labelled folders. "The woman they call Brenda," he said, "once really *was* a reporter. She lost her career when she was sued for libel."

"And Jeannette?" I asked. "She's the one they call 'The Nice Lady'?"

Matt flicked through the papers in the file. "Shoplifting," he said. "But that's a very minor offense. Surely you don't think that somebody is killing these unfortunates in order to extract justice? I don't get it."

"Not justice," I answered. "I think the murderer sees these people as beyond justice. I think what he is trying to give them is not justice, but mercy. I think we are dealing with an angel of death."

"A serial killer who murders people because he thinks they're better off dead," Queenie added.

"Like the Guardian Angels Hospital baby case," Matt West said speculatively.

"Yeah," Queenie answered. "Just like all them sick babies somebody killed so they didn't have to be sick no more."

Matt didn't need theories. He needed proof. "What leads you to this conclusion?" he finally asked. He looked at me expectantly. So did Queenie. I hoisted my bag onto my lap.

"I'm convinced the killer knows about my own past," I said to Matt. "That I was once a respectable man but became a street person. I think he figures I fit into the same class as the people he's killed. He knows I'm someone who's fallen from grace dramatically. Maybe he thinks I got a raw deal having to do time in a mental hospital to stay out of jail. Not to mention living in a box in the Don Valley."

Every note I'd received was in my bag. I began to sort and place the notes on Matt's desk. Even upside down, I could read that the note closest to him said, *The Lord raised up judges, which delivered them out of the hand of those that spoiled them.*

"We found a note on the body of Gelo," Matt said. "The handwriting is similar to this." He picked up a note, studied it, then abruptly put it down as if he'd suddenly realized the note was evidence. "These all seem to be similar in content to those we found on the women, too.

They're about delivering people and ransoming captives and . . ."

"These are about saving someone in particular, Detective. Me."

"Where did you get them?" Matt leaned forward. Finally I was telling him something he didn't know.

"The first ones came when I lived up in the abandoned fish hatchery that used to belong to the Ministry of Natural Resources. When the hatchery closed a couple of years ago, somebody forgot to tell the provincial inter-ministry courier. He still goes up there. He's the one who brought the notes. I didn't take the notes seriously at first. When I was a judge, I was often threatened. Generally I ignored it. I would have ignored these, too, had they not begun to show up on the poisoned victims."

Matt shook his head. "There's more to your hesitation. You discovered the stricken professor. You were alone, except for the incompetent Mrs. Stoughton-Melville, with Vincent Genovi when the police arrived at the scene of his murder. You were afraid of being considered a suspect. Maybe you're still afraid of that possibility?"

I knew better than to respond to that comment. When I'd been a judge, I'd considered every police officer honest, reliable and helpful. My life on the skids had given me a slightly different perspective. If I admitted to fear of being taken for a suspect, the detective would demand to know *why* I was afraid, implying I must have reason to be. If I denied fear, he'd take the denial as defiance. I was used to the police. I kept my mouth shut.

"Look, Portal, you're *not* a suspect in this case. The likelihood *is* that you're a victim. You've got a lot of evidence here. Help me out. Talk about it. Don't leave me holding a bagful of papers. I'm on your side. Open up."

Queenie said she knew Matt West better than I, but I knew about his dead lover William Sterling, and that Matt wasn't just a cop; he was a man, a man with his own problems.

So I told him about the note that had come to Tootie Beets's house. About the highlighting in the court Bible found beside Professor Madison. I explained how Queenie and I had eaten a poisoned lunch. The more I talked, the more he leaned forward across the old kitchen table that served as his desk. When I was finished, all the notes were still arranged in neat rows. I picked up the one written on the bottom of the cryptic puzzle torn out of the newspaper.

"The newspapers seem to think this puzzle was somehow connected to the killings," I said. "There was a suggestion that the police might think so, too."

Matt West shook his head. "You wouldn't believe the phone calls we got from the public on that! People all over the city thought they saw connections once they read reports of the deaths. But that puzzle was written a long time ago." I didn't need to tell him that my own investigation had led to the same conclusion.

"It's possible, though," I said, "that the killer was aware of this puzzle, that the King Wenceslas theme fits in with mercy killing. The song says, 'Ye who now will bless the poor, shall yourselves find blessing'. The solution to the puzzle depended on saints' names. Vincent Genovi was found dead ten days ago. December 6th. The feast of St. Nicholas."

"He's another one of them saints famous for helping poor people," Queenie offered.

"There's no mistaking the fact that the victims were down on their luck, down enough to arouse the sympathy of somebody who identified with St. Nicholas and St. Wenceslas, too," I finished.

"But this teenaged boy who liked puzzles," Matt said, "surely he can't be seen as somebody whose luck had run out. He was just a kid."

"Justice Stoughton-Melville had him investigated when he befriended Harpur. The boy blew his chances to go to Oxford when he was convicted of a crime."

"What we need to do is to catch the killer in the act," Queenie contributed. "Trick him into thinking he can kill somebody that's weak and then grab him."

Matt looked from one to the other of us. He didn't say anything but his green eyes were interested. "I guess you consider yourself a bit of a sitting duck, do you, Portal?"

"He's already attacked us once."

"And you guarantee you won't take matters into your own hands and do something foolish like acting as a decoy?"

"The thought hadn't occurred to me," I said. Actually, it *hadn't* occurred to me but it had occurred to Queenie.

"I'll do it!" she said.

"We've assisted the police before," I offered.

He ignored that. "I'll contact you," he said, glancing at his watch. "If my supervisor agrees, we can set something up at the courthouse first thing tomorrow morning. Until you hear from me, do nothing. Understand? If I find out you've tried anything on your own, I'm going to slap both of you with 'Obstruct Justice'. Is that clear?"

It was. What wasn't clear was how in thirty minutes I'd progressed from seeking police protection to luring the killer without even considering any intermediate position. Nonetheless, I felt exhilarated. Once I'd dispensed justice daily. Now, it seemed, I was again an accomplice of the blindfolded goddess.

We were halfway out the door when I remembered the other part of my mission.

"Detective," I said, "last night something was given to me that I think rightfully belongs to you." I turned over my bag and slid the handkerchief-wrapped bundle into my palm. I unwrapped the ring and held it out to Matt West.

His face immediately locked into unreadable stillness. He took the ring, held it so that the fluorescent light of his office fell on the inside of it. When he read the inscription, the only thing that changed was that the set of his jaw became more rigid.

"I have long known about your relationship with William Sterling," I said. I was the last man to see William alive and I was also one of the original five who owned similar rings. I owed it to William to make sure this ring — his ring — ended up where it belonged. I have no idea how it got from William's hand to the silt in the marsh but floodwater is a mysterious thing."

So, of course, is human love.

CHAPTER NINETEEN

"All I got to do is tell him I need to talk to him about something real private." Queenie's whisper was so low next to me I could hardly hear her, which was good. It was 10:05 on a Friday morning and I was in position guarding the courtroom door. Whispering audibly was against the rules. Normally, I would signal a questioner to step out into the hallway but Minister Mark sat in the second row behind the accused's box. I'd had to do some sleight of hand on the magnetized assignment board to get my name into this court, so I didn't want to lose sight of him.

"As soon as Detective West is ready in the witness room," Queenie advised, "I'll come in and tap the minister on the shoulder. I sure hope he believes me when I tell him I'm in trouble."

She was, she said, "undercover". Her eyes looked as blurred as if she'd not slept in a week and her usually shining hair was matted, her too-large coat wrinkled, her heavy boots grimy and rimmed with salt. I didn't have time to ask about the authentic-looking details, but I suspected the police had helped. Whenever I entered a court-room and noticed one set of people impeccably dressed and clean-shaven and a second set dirty and dishevelled, I always knew the well-dressed ones were the criminals and the grungy ones the cops. I hoped Minister Mark wasn't as perceptive about that as I.

"It's best if I stick to my post, Queenie. Matt will be watching. But this may take awhile, so don't worry if all you manage with Minister Mark today is a conversation."

I was trying to keep up her spirits. I was amazed at her courage. While neither Queenie, Matt nor I were expect-ing to accomplish more than a few self-incriminating statements from our suspect, Matt had obtained a warrant to allow Queenie to be "wired up", as she put it.

"Be careful," I told her. I suppressed the urge to take her hand.

I resumed my seat by the door and listened patiently as the Crown began closing submissions to the jury. There was a small possibility that the jury would be deliberat-ing that afternoon, which would mean that I would be sequestered with them. Most judges, however, hesitated to charge a jury after noon on Friday, not wanting to run the risk of having to be on call for a verdict brought in on Saturday. On Friday afternoons I usually had to force myself to stay awake, except that today I was keeping my eye on someone who would soon need the eloquence of a determined Defense counsel.

That thought was running through my mind when I heard the knob of the door behind me turn, my ordinary cue to stand, open the door, allow whoever it was to enter, and silently close the door behind them.

On entering, Jeannette, "The Nice Lady", looked every bit as distraught as Queenie was planning to be. Her usual saccharine smile was nowhere in evidence. Instead, a look of barely-controlled fear pulled her features into an immobile mask.

Nonetheless, I smiled at her. And, in return, I was pleased to see her features soften with a look that I could have called fondness.

With the quiet quickness characteristic of having spent a great deal of time in court, she slipped into the room, slid onto the bench on which the minister was sitting and sidled up beside him. He turned, and, though he tried to hide it, a look of annoyance crossed his handsome features. The woman reached out and touched his shoulder. It was hard to read her expression because I was behind her and could see only her profile. Yet her posture seemed tense, even desperate.

I felt desperate myself because I saw that her touch was a wordless plea for him to leave the courtroom and follow her.

The knob turned again. I pushed the heavy wooden door open without a sound. There stood Queenie and behind her Matt West, who gave me the signal that all was in place for Queenie to lead Mark into a witness room in the public hallway north of the central area. Once Queenie had Mark alone, she could begin to convince him that her problems were without a solution achievable in this world.

The Crown counsel droned on. The matron sat at the ready near her jug of reviving water. The deputy kept a wary sidewise eye on his exalted charge. But the jury was attentive and the judge was awake.

Moving with inaudible steps and a smoothness that belied her cumbersome disguise and arthritic legs, Queenie made her way up the aisle and slipped into the seat directly behind the minister. If she was surprised to see Jeannette sitting close beside him, she had the wisdom and the skill not to let on.

But I could see that she was going to have a hard time getting Mark's attention. An experienced court observer, he knew that any breach of etiquette, such as carrying on a conversation, would result in ejection. So would any deviation from strict posture. One must sit facing the front with eyes ahead and hands, feet and legs in a respectful knees-together, feet-on-the-floor position. No leaning permitted. No slouching. No reclining. And absolutely no bending forward to speak to the row ahead.

But even had the minister, like the other groupies, not been so consistently conscientious about his court behavior, there were other reasons why he might be expected to ignore Queenie's attempts to get his attention from behind. The first was that he seemed enthralled by what the Crown was saying. The case was a simple matter of sexual assault, a regrettably common type of trial in this courthouse, but I marvelled at the intensity of the minister's attention.

Even more disturbing for our plan, however, was Jeannette's behavior. She seemed to be growing more distraught by the minute, fidgeting, folding and refolding her coat. Maybe Queenie needn't act as a decoy at all.

When the minister gave up trying to listen to the proceedings, whispered something in Jeannette's ear and rose to leave, I saw that clever, street-smart Queenie understood that Jeannette was as good a decoy as she could have been. All Queenie needed to do was follow and see where the minister took Jeannette. I watched as Queenie waited a few seconds, then rose and followed Jeannette and the minister toward me and the door.

I rose, too, and opened the door for the three of them. Good court groupies that they were, each bowed in the direction of the bench before slipping out the door and into the public hallway. I kept the door ajar for a few seconds to see where they were headed. I could not be sure they would head for the witness room and Matt West now. Queenie was in danger, on her own as a "tail" to a murderer. But we'd agreed that I should stay on duty in the courtroom.

I offered a silent prayer to the God I'd long ago convinced myself I didn't believe in that the three would head toward the witness room, but they didn't.

Instead, Jeannette, now in tears, stopped by the escalator. Queenie, still tagging behind, pretended to use a nearby pay-phone. She was sticking tight.

But just before my door closed completely, I saw Jeannette pull away from the minister and head toward the door to the secure area that could only be opened with plastic security cards. A group of jurors had just marched in behind their matron. Behind the last juror was Jeannette. Behind her was Mark. Queenie took up the rear.

I had just seen three unauthorized people enter the out-of-bounds secure hallway. I didn't wait. I bolted. I didn't even try to keep the courtroom door from slamming. If any jurors *had* fallen asleep, they were wide-awake now.

Within seconds I was standing in the secure area. The hall that stretched south along the entire length of the building was deserted. For a moment I just stood there looking up and down the wide empty corridor. The hall was lined with more than a dozen jury rooms, and with doors to the prisoners' holding cells and to the internal staircase that ran the height of the building.

Any one of the jury-room doors might be locked from

either side. I had no idea whether the minister and the two women had entered one or had left the floor altogether. Mathematically, my chances of finding Queenie were not good.

I debated whether I should try all the doors to the jury rooms. I would have to be very quiet so as not to frighten my quarry. I had just decided that one-by-one was my only choice, even though I was not sure what I would do when I faced the minister, when I heard a scuffle behind one of the doors only a few feet away. But before I could move, I also heard one of the doors to the stairwell click open at the far end of the hall. Two of the building's biggest blueshirts strode toward me. A third person walked between them.

Relief filled me. The blueshirts had radios. With a free hand, one of them could easily get assistance.

I took a step toward the advancing guards.

Then I realized they were not escorting a prisoner. This third person was not wearing shackles, was not even wearing handcuffs. The small woman whose hands swung freely at her sides, balled into fists of anger, seemed familiar. It took me a minute to realize that the woman stomping toward me was Marnie Alliston, my supervisor. And my years on the skids had given me the fugitive's sense of impending capture.

"Ellis Portal," I heard Marnie intone, "you are unauthorized to be in this area. You are here under false pretenses. You falsified your papers. You are *not* an employee of the Ministry of the Attorney General of Ontario."

Another thing I'd learned from the street was that if someone is standing in front of you, the only way to gain an advantage is to run right at them, not away. So I bolted past officious little Marnie and her flunkies.

But the long corridor full of doors confounded me. I struggled to figure out which one was the exit into the central area. The blueshirts were close enough to reach out and touch me.

I figured I was done for.

Then suddenly, another door sprang open and two more blueshirts spilled into the hall.

There was no way I could foil four of them. I stood still, ready to surrender. Visions of another jail term swam into my head.

But these new blueshirts *were* escorting prisoners, three men chained together by handcuffs. One of the three caught my eye. As if some understanding had passed between us, the men moved quickly as one and stood like a barrier between me and the four blueshirts and Marnie.

There is no honor among thieves, let me tell you, but there is cooperation in thwarting "the man". The three prisoners stood as far apart as they could, their hand-cuffed arms making a fence on one side of which was the fuming Marnie and the blueshirts and on the other side of which was me and the still-open door to the stairwell.

"God bless you, guys," I said to my fellow captives.

I shot down the stairs, blasting into a gaggle of matrons at the bottom, near the basement cafeteria. My hip caught the edge of one of their wheeled tea carts, ripping my blazer and sending danishes, muffins, coffee and juice crashing to the floor.

I could hear the matrons screaming as I veered toward a long narrow corridor and metal steps down into the underground parking garage.

The footfalls of my pursuers clanged a metallic warning, then echoed behind me in the concrete vastness of the garage.

The blueshirts knew the intricacies of the building better than I did but I was running on the instinct of the man who wishes above all to remain free. I just kept going in whatever direction lay open before me.

At the far end of the garage, white cube-vans with barred windows — Court Services Vehicles — blocked my way, but I zipped around them and through the narrow tunnel past the main holding cells for prisoners from across the city. Through the barred window of the cell-block office, I could see a half-dozen more blueshirts.

But my pursuers did not shout for help as they ran after me to where the tunnel abruptly ended into a wide loading dock that stretched across the way in front of me.

Only ten or twelve feet behind me, I heard the blueshirts slow their steps, as if they, too, saw that I was cornered now.

I spun wildly. Ahead of me I saw nothing but a platform loaded with boxes. But there had to be a way for trucks to get into this space. Before I could figure it out, I saw two law students exit a small door I hadn't even noticed. Beside it, an awkwardly lettered sign read, "Law students' cafeteria — rear entrance".

Without thinking about how I would get out of the cafeteria, I dove into it.

It was a small, bare utilitarian room filled with plain metal tables at which sat twenty or thirty young people reading, chatting and drinking coffee and tea. At the far end of the room was a wheelchair ramp. I headed for it. Behind me I heard the scrape of metal chairs against the concrete floor as students got out of the way of the pursuing blueshirts.

The ramp led up into a carpeted hallway, through a white wooden arch, across a mosaic floor and directly into the lobby of Osgoode Hall where a few lawyers in their crisp black robes and white linen collars were gathered.

I skidded to a stop in front of them, winded, scared, tired and whipped.

One of the lawyers, all of whom stared at my ripped blazer and dishevelled appearance in disgust, was my daughter Ellen. Standing beside her, no doubt soon planning to have lunch as Ellen's guest in the Barristers' Dining Room, was her mother Anne. In front of these two women I was unceremoniously grabbed by the puffing blueshirts, cuffed and dragged to the front door of Osgoode, where they uncuffed and dumped me as if I were beneath their contempt.

I could have let humiliation overtake me but I didn't have time for that. I had to get back to Queenie. Despite her courage, I was not going to leave her unassisted in the hands of a killer.

I tossed my ripped blazer behind one of the carefully trimmed evergreen shrubs at about the same instant a cab pulled up. I guess the cabbie associated my impatience with a big tip. I prayed I'd have enough money at home to pay the fare. I certainly didn't have it in my pocket.

"Wait for me," I told him when we got to Tootie Beets's.

The house was deserted. Though I didn't exactly have a lot of time to think about it, I found that amazing. I had assumed that my rooming-house neighbors had nothing to do with their days but watch television.

I rushed up the stairs, went into my room, knelt beside my bed and reached beneath the mattress for my little cache of twenty-dollar bills. I found three. Then I grabbed a plastic bag from the top drawer of my dresser. Into it, I stuffed the only thing that would get me into court and back to Queenie. I rolled my judicial gown carefully but I moved quickly.

Ten minutes later, we were back near Osgoode Hall. It took me a minute to figure out how I was going to change into the gown without attracting undue attention. In the end, I decided the simplest thing would be to hide behind the stonework of the portico nearest the main door of Osgoode Hall. This I did, slipping the black silk robe over my white shirt and hoping nobody saw that I was not wearing the regulation barrister's jacket underneath. I wasn't wearing tabs — the white linen collar — either, but I wasn't about to ascend the bench. All I needed was to gain leverage to move freely in the courthouse without being thrown out again. I reached into the bag and removed my crimson sash.

Just as I fastened the sash, I heard a stirring in the shadows beneath the portico, and I realized I'd performed my transformation from CSO to justice right before the astonished eyes of one of the homeless who slept there.

Although it is frowned upon for a judge to wander around in the public area of the courthouse dressed in his robes, it is certainly not unheard of. I cared not a bit about marring the decorum of the court by mingling with the common crowd.

It was not uncommon for a member of the court staff to see one of the ninety justices one day and not see him or her again for months. An unfamiliar justice would not be questioned. I could not run, of course, but I walked as briskly as I could. Yet I could not help but notice how people stepped aside for me, how almost everyone greeted me with the utmost respect. Whenever I saw a CSO, I tried to keep my head down, but one or two looked me directly in the eye without showing any sign of recognition.

I still had my plastic card on a chain around my neck and I used it to enter the secured area.

Matt West stood among a small crowd of police officers at the jury-room door. His intelligent green eyes narrowed when he caught sight of me in my robe. "We've got ourselves a hostage situation," he said calmly.

My heart jumped. "Queenie's been taken hostage?" I asked him.

"No. She's standing by. She's describing what she can. Jeannette appears to be the hostage. Jeannette and the minister are holed up in the restroom in there."

"Is that locked?" I asked, indicating the jury-room door.

"From the inside. We don't have a key and even if we did, it wouldn't do any good. Once that door's locked from the inside, it can only be opened from the inside."

"Does Queenie know you're out here?"

"I'm sure she does. With the wire she's got, we can hear her but she can't hear us. She would have figured out that we'd find her if she just kept talking, which she did. She's a clever woman."

We were interrupted by static. Then Queenie's voice. "I'm in between the restroom and the door to the hall," Queenie whispered. "They're only a little ways away, by the door to the restroom. They're talking to each other, and that's how come I can talk to you right now."

As abruptly as it had begun, the voice stopped. If only we could talk to Queenie, give her some guidance or at least some encouragement.

"If you get in," I said to Matt, "will you be able to get Queenie out of the way without harm?"

"We'll do all we can," Matt replied. "In situations like this, we have to make sure the hostage-taker doesn't get a glimpse of any police paraphernalia. The mere sight of a

238

badge or — God forbid — a gun, is enough to drive some of them over the edge. We've got two innocent bystanders in there."

"Matt," I said, suddenly struck with an idea. "This hostage-taker is a court groupie, a person who spends every hour of every weekday willingly under the control of a judge."

"What are you getting at?"

"I want to go in there. I want to talk to him."

"You'd be risking your neck."

"Only for a few minutes. Once I'm in and Queenie's out, I'll ease out, too. This killer is a poisoner; he's not a shooter or a slasher."

"We don't know that," Matt warned. "He's escalated to hostage-taking. Besides, how are you going to get in? You'd have to find a way to get Queenie near the door without putting her in any more danger."

"I can do that, Matt. I've got an idea. Will you let me give it a try?"

He studied me for a minute. "You've got the lives of at least four people in your hands if you go into that room."

"Yes."

He eyed me critically, his gaze scanning my robes. "Okay, Justice Portal, if you've got an idea, then let's go with it."

To call out in any way would scare everybody: Queenie, the hostage-taker and the captive. But there was another way not only of getting Queenie's attention, but also of letting her know who exactly was on the other side of the wall. I put my ear to the door. I could hear the faint, regular sound of weeping. I waited a second. Then I raised my hand and scratched the wood of the door.

Behind me, all fell silent, waiting.

But the weeping in the room went on.

I scratched again, and within seconds, I heard the answering sound of fingernails on wood. It was so close that I knew Queenie had to be up against the other side of the door. "Queenie," I whispered, "unlock the door and let me in. I'm here to help."

My voice was soft, only a breath, really. But by some miracle, she heard. The key turned in the jury-room door, and I reached in, grabbed Queenie's wrist and swung her into the waiting arms of Matt West. Then, I closed the door behind me and locked myself in.

As I did so, I realized the weeping had stopped. The room was silent and empty. A long bare table flanked by twelve chairs sat under a plain, round government-issue clock high on the windowless wall. That was it.

But at the far end of the room a door led to the men's room, which I knew held a single toilet and a pedestal sink. The other door led to a ladies' room that I assumed was exactly the same.

Cautiously, I crept toward the door of the men's room and pushed it open an inch. The little room was dark but a ray of light from the main room penetrated the ink. The washroom was empty.

I let the door close silently behind me and crossed to the other door.

Again I opened the metal door an inch. Enough to see that the light was on. Enough to smell the scent of human perspiration. Enough to hear frightened, labored breathing. Enough even to see that, small and cramped as it was, the tiny restroom held two people kneeling on the floor, face to face. Each had one arm outstretched as though engaged in a powerful but equal struggle, like a well-matched pair of arm wrestlers. Mark's outstretched hand held neither Bible, nor cross, nor knife, nor gun. It held a syringe.

"Stop," I said. "Stop at once."

It was the tone of Justice Ellis Portal of the Ontario Court of Justice.

Frozen by my authoritative voice, the combatants just stared at me.

The expression on Mark's face was of shock.

Jeannette's face, however, held something I could not read. It was not shock, not even surprise. It was a look similar to those fond glances and smiles of recognition she had sent my way in Harpur's hospital room and in the courtroom. But something else was mingled with the expressions of goodwill, some emotion that might almost be labelled triumph.

"*The Lord,*" Jeannette said, as if reading a text, "*raised up judges, which delivered them out of the hand of those that spoiled them.*"

Then she snatched the syringe from the minister and plunged it deeply into her own neck.

CHAPTER TWENTY

"Mark Mailland suspected all along that Jeannette was unbalanced enough to harm herself, but he only began to realize that she had harmed others when she begged him to hear her confession."

"But he's not a priest," I protested. Matt West sat back in the old armchair behind the battered kitchen table that served as his desk.

"No," he said. "Mailland is an ordained Baptist minister whose pastoral work has been among accused and prisoners since he was sixteen years old. Jeannette is not his first murderer."

"He was trying to help her, trying to keep her from acting out her craziness, and you knew it all along?"

Matt looked genuinely surprised. "Not at all," he said. Then he laughed, tentatively, as though he distrusted humor. "Cops aren't the only people who work undercover," he said, meaningfully.

"Jeannette committed herself to justice as she saw it," I commented. "As a judge, I always used to feel outraged when people took the law into their hands, but now I know that the world has its own justice. I no longer believe that justice is confined to the courts or even to the law."

"That's a dangerous idea," Matt said simply. "I'm sure your daughter would disagree."

Ellen had filled me in on Jeannette's history, which included several bouts of hospitalization for psychotic behavior. Ellen had done a bit of research on "angel of mercy" serial killers. They were often women. They often poisoned. They often were volunteers working with the helpless and the hopeless. They even often used pavulon and similar drugs. "We should have figured it out sooner, Daddy. We could have saved people."

Matt gave me a brief but penetrating glance. "Seems to me you were next on the killer's list; all those notes she wrote to you."

"Yes."

"So, like a cat you find yourself with yet another life."

"I suppose I do, Detective."

Before he got the notion that he had the right to ask me what I planned to do with that life, I wished Matt a happy holiday and left Police Headquarters.

Case closed.

It was a week before Christmas Day and no matter how I might wish to ignore the season, there was no avoiding its brash and persistent presence on Yonge Street.

There had once been a time when I loved Christmas. In those days, I had spared no expense in its name. My parents, good Catholics, had always insisted that the spiritual aspects of the holiday were the most important and always seemed embarrassed by the gifts I gave them: a new car, a diamond ring, trips to Italy and the Holy Land. I was always trying to prove something to them, prove that my success made me worthy of the love and forgiveness they had always given me with no price attached.

Which brought me to the question of whether I should perhaps purchase a few small gifts for two people on my so-called Christmas list: my landlady, Tootie, and my good friend, Queenie. I told myself that I would worry about the rest of my life just as soon as the holiday was over. Then I withdrew a healthy hunk of the dwindling cash in my savings account and went shopping.

At 6 P.M. on Christmas Eve, the eight roomers of a teenaged, streetwise landlady sat down to a dinner she had prepared.

In the weeks I'd lived at Tootie's, I'd never once ventured into the depressing dining room at the front of the house. A long, narrow, highly-polished wooden table nearly filled the room. An ill-matched assortment of chairs, most often littered with newspapers and magazines, gave this room the appearance of doing double duty as a library. Tonight the room was transformed with sweet-smelling garlands of spruce, white lace doilies, slow-burning candles, holly wreaths and dishes that actually matched.

As I glanced up and down the Christmas Eve table at those whom Tootie referred to as "brother neighbors", I felt as though I'd never seen any of these people before. Like me, they had taken special care for the festivities. Tootie wore a dark red velvet dress with a low, square-cut neckline that revealed an expanse of skin so smooth and white that I wondered if the startling paleness of her face

244

might not be her own. Her usually spiky black hair was now softly curled. Her lips were still the darkest of reds, but her mouth seemed softened and warm.

Flanking Tootie were two young men whom I'd never actually seen for longer than a few seconds at a time. I knew them to be the worst offenders in playing rock-and-roll at megavolume, but they were quiet tonight. It seemed they were students living in inexpensive quarters to save money. I did learn, however, how they managed to study with the stereo going full blast. "It's good preparation," one of them cheerfully told me.

"I've lived here five months," our only female resident said, "since I left my abusive husband. I used to live near Rosedale but I like this rooming house much better."

I began to feel absolutely provident. In some bizarre way, I had moved aside so that these young people might live in the house that once was mine. One even owned it. "Tootie," I said, inviting a tale, "tell us how you got this house."

A look of steely determination crossed the pale face now flushed pink with wine and the heat of the crowded room.

"My grandmother bought this house," she began. "All the time I was little, I used to come here. Sometimes I slept here for days. Then my mother or father would come after me and drag me home.

"My grandmother was the only friend I had. She died when I was fourteen and I ran away. I lived on the street for three years. If my parents ever looked for me, they didn't find me.

"But one day, when I was sleeping in a squat — an abandoned grain elevator down by the harbor — this suit came after me. He had some good news about my grandmother. He said she left me her house in her will. I wasn't quite eighteen and I was scared my parents could take this house and sell it and it would be gone forever. So I asked that lawyer if I could go to court to get to run the house even though I wasn't twenty-one. At court the judge said it takes a lot of money to run a house and he asked me how I was going to get the money. I told him I'd rent rooms to people who knew how to follow all the rules so the house could be a kind of community place, like a shelter only way nicer and better. I told him how I learned which people are responsible from all the different kinds I met when I lived on the street and in the squat. He listened really careful. Then he said I could keep this house."

I gave her the present I'd chosen, a carefully wrought little silver angel, a brooch with filigree wings and a benign expression. "Way cool," Tootie said. "It'll look great on my black leather vest."

In Canada, December 26, the Feast of Stephen, is a legal holiday called "Boxing Day". Nobody seems to know why, but everybody thinks it has something to do with providing gifts to the poor and those otherwise unblessed. I had heard that Queen Victoria had packed boxes of food for the poor on that day each year, and also that that was the day the poor box in churches and on ships was opened for distribution to the worthy. Of course I had also heard that Boxing Day was so called because it was the day on which people put gifts they did not like back in the box and returned them to the store. That had nothing to do with my Boxing Day intention, which was to visit Harpur and to somehow let her know that her life was not and never would be in my hands.

She and Stow, I learned, did not have their lovely Christmas at home. Harpur was back at Riverside Institute, this time to stay.

Though it was only the day after Christmas, the elegant decorations that graced the lobby of Riverside already seemed stale, the live holly dull, the overblown poinsettias limp, the piped-in carols tinny and cloying.

All who could possibly manage had been sent home for the holidays, so only the most seriously ill or thoroughly deserted remained.

"She's not well today," her nurse told me as she ushered me in.

Harpur looked like an alabaster statue but not a sculpture representing the classic beauty she herself had once possessed. No. She was lifeless, cold, immobile and pale. She sat beside the window outside of which the bright flashes of tobogganers in the park yet again livened the snowy whiteness of the hill that sloped toward the Don River.

But all that bounding motion struck no responding chord in her. Nor did my voice. "Hello, Harpur," I said softly, but she did not turn her head or even blink.

"Is it all right if I just sit here for a while?" I asked the nurse.

She nodded. "I'm glad you came," she said. "When you left after your visit to her last time, she kept crying out for you. I promised her that she'd see you again."

"Of course," I said, stunned at the suggestion that the time would ever come when I'd not see Harpur again.

"I also wanted to give you this. The volunteer committee left it here for you."

She stepped over to a bureau on top of which was a

small wicker basket tied with a red bow. Attached to the bow with a gold string was a white tag. Someone had carefully printed my name on the tag in plain roundish letters in black ink.

"Why would the volunteer committee give me a gift?" I asked. The basket held an assortment of travel-size toiletries — aftershave, shampoo, soap. I recognized them as donations from corporations, the sort of donations I had once helped others to solicit in the long ago past when I'd sat on the boards of charitable organizations.

"The volunteers worked on these baskets for months," the nurse said with a smile. "They had a team to fill them and a separate team to write all the nametags and distribute the baskets. They wanted to give one to every family member who visits here to thank them for all their help. I know you're not a family member, but Mrs. Stoughton-Melville has had only you and that poor boy as visitors these past weeks and the committee thought . . ."

"No."

The word seemed to come not from Harpur but from somewhere in the white air outside the window beside which she sat.

"She seems always to be thinking of the past now," the nurse commented. "I don't think she's really here at all."

Since Harpur had not acknowledged my presence in any way, I was inclined to agree with the nurse's assessment of her mental state. I cast a quick glance her way. She seemed to be gazing into the unknown.

"Please tell the volunteer committee that I appreciate the thought," I said. "And I appreciate the gift, too."

"I'm not sure they're really things people can use," the nurse said wryly.

Though I had long been one who felt that Christmas

gifts were famous for being useless, I felt an unexplained urge to be polite. Maybe it was a hangover from the festive spirit that had imbued my Christmas Day spent wandering the city alone but strangely happy. "On the contrary," I commented. "Here's something I can use right now."

"No, no, Gelo, no. No." Harpur's voice was growing insistent. I feared she might be thinking of the murder of her young friend. The idea that such disturbing thoughts might now obsess her was so upsetting that I felt I wanted to touch her, to calm her as I had never had the courage, or the right, to do before.

I crossed the room. In my hand, I still held the item from the gift basket that I knew I could use. It was a tube of cream, the exact brand that I had been using on my hands for the past month to quell the rash still visible there.

I thought it remarkably observant and considerate of the volunteers to have included a small plastic tube of this cream among the components of my gift. Someone had to have seen me use the cream and realized that I would welcome an additional supply.

I neared Harpur's chair. I reached out my hand to touch her hair. The gray strands seemed more numerous. They lay on her shoulder loose and wild, the way they had the day I'd come upon her and Vincent Genovi below the hospital in the Chester Springs Marsh. Harpur was slipping back into the chaos of nature where human will, no matter how strong, eventually relinquishes its power. She already seemed powerless.

But she was not quite without will.

She rose from her chair. "No! No! No, Ellis, no!" she shouted. And she struck my hand with such violence that tears sprang to my eyes.

I was so stunned by the quick fury of the gesture that at first I did not realize that the hand Harpur had struck was not the one I'd used to touch her. It was the other one. The hand that had held the small plastic tube of cream before it had gone flying from her blow.

And then I understood it all. I understood that somewhere in her muddled brain, Harpur had figured out how to save my life.

I remembered all I knew about pavulon. That it could be absorbed by broken skin with fatal results. That a skin rash like mine would have rendered me vulnerable to just such poisoning. Our murderer was dead, but behind, she had left one victim as yet unharmed. She would have known I'd visit Harpur at Christmas. She probably even guessed that Boxing Day, the Feast of Stephen, was the most logical day for me to come.

But that was incidental, really. The Wenceslas puzzle and the carol and the saints — all those had been incidental. It might have given The Nice Lady a certain perverse pleasure to see what others were reading into her actions. But all that was really germane was the immense arrogance of a killer who tried to play God even after she'd taken her own life.

The plastic tube lay on the floor of Harpur's room. Later, I would retrieve it and give it to Matt West who would have the toxicologist confirm what I now knew.

But for the moment, I let the little tube lie where it had fallen. For the second and last time in my life, I took Harpur in my arms. "Thank you," I whispered.

She laughed — a faint, weak shadow of her former rich, tormenting laugh — but her laugh all the same. "I love you," she said. I wondered who she thought she was talking to.

She died during the night. No one was with her. In the morning Stow called me. He accused me coldly and baldly of homicide. He said the excitement of whatever had happened between her and me on Boxing Day had been more than she could take. He said I killed her.

Part of me hoped it was true.

CHAPTER TWENTY-ONE

December 28, the Feast of the Holy Innocents, was the first business day after Christmas, the day I had promised myself to decide what to do with the rest of my life.

This decision was complicated by the fact that it was also the day the man with the briefcase finally caught up with me.

I'll make this short. He said he represented Anne in the matter of our divorce. He said he had been retained, in part, to determine the exact share each of us was entitled to with respect to what he insisted on calling "the marital holdings". He seemed to think I was going to give him some sort of argument about all this, and he was beyond even conceiving that I had long ago cheerfully abandoned any claim on what Anne and I had once owned. I didn't even bother to try to tell him that I had felt Anne was entitled to everything.

"Any refusal to claim your share," he said gratuitously, "will be construed as an aggressive attempt to lay the grounds for future frivolous litigation."

"Okay," I told him. "Tell me what Anne wants to give me."

"It's not what Mrs. Portal wants to *give* you," he answered testily. "The fiduciary rights in question arise out of the legislation of the Province of Ontario."

"Okay, then. Tell me what the Province of Ontario wants to give me." Obviously it did *not* want to give me the salary I'd sort of earned working for the Ministry of the Attorney General during the previous several weeks!

"Well . . ." the lawyer began.

It took him two hours to explain it all. The house. The contents. The stocks, bonds, coupons, funds. And even my judge's salary, which had not stopped but had been held in escrow because, according to the record, I was on sick leave and had not yet claimed my benefits.

"3.1 million dollars," he announced.

"I own half of 3.1 million dollars?" I asked in astonishment. "That's absolutely ludicrous!"

"No, no, of course not," the lawyer said, laughing. "Not half — you own *all* of the 3.1 million. The marital holdings are worth $6.2 million. $3.1 million is your share."

What does a man who sleeps under bushes in a sleet storm do with 3.1 million dollars?

"What's the matter with you, anyway?" Queenie asked as I stood on the doorstep of her rooming house with two dozen long-stem yellow roses. "You gonna sell flowers on the street corner, now that you're out of work again?"

"No. These are for you and you know it."

"I don't know nothing. Are you coming in or are you plannin' on freezing your feet in the snow all day?"

I followed her in. Her room was decorated for the season by a tiny tree laden with ornaments, though it was only two feet high. She reached beneath it. "Here's a present," she said with touching awkwardness.

I opened her gift to find a small oval box completely constructed of the quills of a porcupine. "Queenie, it's beautiful."

She smiled. "They don't kill no porcupines to make them," she said shyly. "They gotta wait till the porcupine gives them quills. Like he gives a gift so other people can give a gift."

"It's lovely and I'll treasure it. Thank you." I leaned across the small space that separated us and gave Queenie a kiss on her smooth cheek. She smelled of smoke, snow and soap.

"You know, Your Honor, on Christmas when I went to church, I said a prayer for Melia and for the others."

"Yes."

"And for the killer, too."

"I think that's appropriate, Queenie."

"Matt West says she was a good person almost all her life. She was a nurse and did real well until she lost her job and fell on hard times, just like the people she killed. I guess she just wasn't as strong as you and me."

"She felt sorry for us. She couldn't understand that we *are* strong, that we can survive without many things other people think are absolutely necessary."

"Some things are real necessary, Your Honor, even to people like us."

"What?"

"A person needs to know that they can help other people," Queenie said simply.

"Let's go for a little walk," I said abruptly, still uncomfortable with moral instructions.

She eyed me warily. "Just anyplace or you got something up your sleeve?"

"I have something up my sleeve," I laughed. "I have something to give you, but before I start, I want you to make a promise."

"Like them ring promises?"

I hesitated for a second. "Yes, Queenie, a new promise as important as the old promises with the rings."

"That still go with some of the rings."

"Yes."

"What's the promise?"

"I want you to promise that in the future no matter what I offer you and no matter what you choose to accept, you will stay my friend, because all I offer, I offer out of my feelings for you."

She looked at me for a full minute. I have no idea what went through her head, but in the end, what she said was, "Okay."

We walked northwest, crossed busy Queen's Park Crescent and found ourselves on the campus of the University of Toronto, its gray stone a subtle contrast to the green of fir trees, the white of fallen snow and the muted colors of the students winter jackets. "Let's get inside, I want to give you your Christmas present."

We entered a common room in Hart House, the alumni building, and chose a seat beneath one of the graceful leaded windows. Queenie whispered in awe, "This here is just like a rich person's living room." Her eyes scanned the room's polished floors, the Oriental rugs, the leather couches, the Canadian masters' paintings, the roaring blaze in a stone fireplace at the far end.

"How do you know what a rich person's living room looks like?" I teased.

"I seen it in the movies," she said. Then she smiled. "I didn't read it in no libary."

I reached into my pocket for the small, flat package I carried there. I handed it to Queenie.

Her careful fingers undid the tape, lifted the paper. As she saw what the package contained, her puzzlement grew deeper.

"A book, Your Honor? she asked skeptically, opening it. Then more politely, "It's got awful big words, don't it?"

"Yes. But not as big as in the original. This is a simplified version of *The Hound of the Baskervilles*. It's about the famous detective, Sherlock Holmes. The story is so good that the words become easy to read."

She turned a few pages but didn't seem convinced.

"Queenie," I said, "I want you to let me educate you."

"Educate me? Like you mean send me to school?"

"Yes."

"Because you think I can't talk to you right?"

"No, because I think you *can*."

"But you know I can't read!"

"I can teach you. We can start here. Today."

"Now?"

"Yes."

"You'll teach me?"

"Yes."

For just an instant, her face blazed with hope. "Okay, Your Honor. Let's do it."

And so we began. Outside, night came and the weather worsened, but we didn't particularly care. We talked and we pointed and we puzzled and slowly, we began to read. We sat within the warm glow of our friendship and let winter have its way.

I didn't pause to consider how slow the streetcars

would be, how long it would take me to get home, or even how everything in the world would seem different in the morning, new and clean and somehow made miraculously pure and fresh yet again.

We just let the thick snow fall. Deep and crisp and even.